THE THERAPY ROOM

SAM BARON

Storm
PUBLISHING

To request permissions, contact the publisher at rights@stormpublishing.co

Ebook ISBN: 978-1-80508-416-7
Paperback ISBN: 978-1-80508-418-1

Cover design: Henry Steadman
Cover images: Getty Images

Published by Storm Publishing.
For further information, visit:
www.stormpublishing.co

for
May
&
Sheila,

my
alpha
&
my
omega

and

for
Leia

my
tau

"The very emphasis of the commandment: 'Thou shalt not kill', makes it certain that we are descended from an endlessly long chain of generations of murderers, whose love of murder was in their blood as it is perhaps also in ours."
—Sigmund Freud

ONE

There is a knife on his threshold and the door is ajar.

The knife is a wicked-looking thing, curved and serrated with razor-sharp teeth that form a jaguar smile.

A sliver of light slips in through the door, making the blade gleam in the darkness of his room.

Why is it here?

He pushes tentatively at the door, not actually expecting it to yield. When it swings wide open, he is astonished.

This has never happened before.

He looks around, trying to make sense of it.

All the other doors are still locked.

Why has only he been let out?

He moves through the basement. After weeks—or is it months?—down here, he has never seen any other part of the house.

Another surprise: the door at the top of the basement steps is ajar!

He climbs with a rising sense of dread, expecting at any minute to be challenged, forced back to his room, made to undergo more therapy.

He cringes at the thought.

When he reaches the top of the stairs unchallenged, his confidence grows.

He can hardly believe his luck.

Stepping onto the first floor, he is startled by a familiar sound. Music! The sweet strains of a classic oldie and the savory aroma of food evoke memories. Saliva floods his parched mouth.

Moments flash across his mind's eye. Dancing. Singing. A pretty young woman. Days spent working in an office. Nights at a karaoke bar with friends. The taste of spicy wings and cold beer.

All that was taken from him!

Anger flares white hot, setting his brain ablaze.

He grips the knife tightly and pads through the house on bare, filthy feet, seeking out the source of the melody and the aroma.

He finds it in the kitchen, where a man sits at a table, digging into what looks and smells like a sumptuous feast.

He feels an overwhelming rage at the sight of this tableau.

This monster, who has held them all captive for so long, subjecting them to unspeakable suffering, depriving them of even the most basic human necessities, stripping them of all dignity, reducing them to a state of near-animalistic existence. This bastard *is feasting*!

He approaches from behind, the ugly weapon raised high to strike.

The eating man pauses, mid-mastication. Perhaps he has caught the scent of the other's unwashed stink.

He starts to turn—too late.

The wicked blade rises and falls, rises and falls, until it is little more than a red blur.

TWO

I could kill her now. Before her husband brings their four-year-old home from swimming lessons. She always leaves the back door open. It would be easy to slip in, come up behind her, and slide a knife in without her ever seeing me. All this pain and rage I carry bottled up inside me will finally have a place to go.

My name is Susan Parker. I'm an FBI agent. It is late November, the night before Thanksgiving. I should be home with my family.

Instead, here I sit in my Prius in the leafy shadow cast by a large elm, between streetlamps on a deserted suburban back lane. Watching a house. The brightly lit living room has a picture window. Inside, a woman around the same age as me is setting a table for dinner.

I don't know this woman. I've never met her, and as far as I can tell, we have no friends or social acquaintances in common, even though I live only a few miles from here.

But she is the last person to have seen my husband Amit alive.

The dump from his phone's GPS shows this address as his last stop that night. Camera footage from a neighbor's

3

surveillance camera shows Amit's pickup truck stopping in her driveway, him getting out, walking to the porch, then going in. He comes out again around half an hour later and drives off.

Not long after that, an anonymous call reported gunshots from a house only a couple of miles from here, and when first responders arrived on the scene there, they found Amit lying dead in a pool of blood, a gun in his hand. No suicide note was found.

His phone had no contact matching this woman's name, address, or phone number. I had never heard him mention her. In her statement to the police, the woman claimed she had never seen him before in her life. She couldn't explain Amit's visit to her house that afternoon and denied meeting him. She claimed she was out at the time, running errands, but there's no way to prove or disprove her alibi, except for the fact that her car wasn't visible in the driveway in the neighbor's surveillance footage.

Who is she?

I don't mean that literally. I know she's a preschool teacher at a local daycare center, happily married by all appearances, with a four-year-old son, a husband, and a mortgage. Said husband is a lawyer with a big firm who works in the city and commutes. But that's it. There's no connection to my husband, none that I could find, nor the Santa Carina Valley Police Department and FBI.

But really, who is she?

What was she to my husband?

Were they having an affair?

The question prods my already aching heart. I feel like I'm disrespecting Amit's memory simply by thinking it. While we weren't a perfect couple—who is?—we were certainly close enough for complete, undoubting trust. Guilt pricks at my conscience for questioning his fidelity.

But given his actions on that last day, and as a law enforcement officer myself, it's a question I can't avoid.

Was guilt over his infidelity one of the factors, or maybe even *the* factor, in his subsequent suicide? It would explain some of the things that are driving me crazy.

Amit was a straight-arrow guy with a clear moral compass. If he did stray, which I can't imagine him ever doing, it would have eaten away at his insides, hammered at his conscience, tearing him down. I still can't see him taking the extreme step of shooting himself over it, but maybe that's what infidelity did to him: drove him temporarily, emotionally insane.

And if not infidelity, then why was he here at this strange woman's house on that particular Wednesday afternoon? Twenty-eight minutes is a helluva long time. Why did Amit choose to spend those last precious minutes with this woman? Did she in some way influence him to take his own life? Why? These questions buzz like a swarm of hornets trapped inside my skull. But the lawyers and my own superiors were very clear about the fact that if I am ever caught harassing her, there will be serious consequences.

Just to be clear: I'm not a bad person and thoughts of murdering random women in home invasions are not my usual daydream fare. But I have seen some very bad things in my career as an FBI agent, and experienced trauma in my personal life. Those experiences change you. If I have moments of frustration when I feel tempted to use deadly force to compel this woman to talk, it's only because that's how my obsessive-compulsive mind works: I *must* have answers, one way or another.

In the brightly lit diorama of the picture window, happily unaware of my dark thoughts, the woman finishes setting the table just as my phone buzzes.

I look at the message:

Home for dinner? N's asking.

Damn. I lost track of the time. Have I really been out here that long?

On my way. Home in 5.

I start the Prius and bring it around, remembering to switch on the lights. The beams flash across the picture window of the house across the street. The woman pauses in the act of setting down a bowl of mashed potatoes. Our eyes meet.

With the headlights in her face, she can't actually see me, but I still feel a pang of guilt. What was I thinking, sitting out here? Parked out on this quiet, leafy, suburban street, watching this strange woman and her family? I should be home with Natalie and Lata.

As I drive away, I console myself that my stalking her isn't an obsession. I don't know this woman or what her relationship might have been to my dead husband, but I do know that she's the last person to have seen Amit alive. She must know *something*.

Less than four minutes later, I turn into my lane.

That's one advantage of surveilling someone who lives in Santa Carina Valley. The entire township is spread out over a few dozen miles. You can drive from one part of it to the other in under twelve minutes, even at rush hour. It's also a disadvantage because there's a better than average chance your subject might recognize you from somewhere.

I feel a rush of pleasure as the Prius slows to a halt.

That Schwin bike with the purple handlebar tassels leaning against the garage door—instead of the side wall where it ought to be parked—is my daughter, Natalie. The dust-spattered Jeep Explorer with the four-wheel drive, offroad tires, and the bumper sticker with the USMC logo and the words "The Few,

The Proud" is my sister-in-law, Lata. This dusty, overworked Prius in desperate need of a tune-up and some TLC is me.

And this charming little cottage on its tiny lot, the one with the red roof, the bright blue door, and the avocado tree in the front yard, this is us.

Welcome to the Parkers.

Caution: we are not all we seem.

THREE

Natalie is on the couch, bent over her iPad as she usually is at this hour. She doesn't hear me come in, of course, but Lata pops out of the kitchen, an unlikely figure in an apron. The short-cropped hair with red and blue streaks, kohl eyes, nose stud, toned arms and ridiculously fit physique go surprisingly well with her spatula-wielding sponge *Bakers Gotta Bake* apron.

"Hey, SpongeBob Martha Stewart," I say as I hang up my jacket.

She ignores my quip and asks, "All good?"

I make a circle with my thumb and forefinger. "Copacetic."

She looks skeptical.

I change the topic by gesturing at Natalie's back. "How's munchkin?"

Lata gives me a double thumbs up.

I come up behind the sofa, leaning over and suddenly dropping my upside-down face in front of Natalie's. "Boo!"

Natalie stares at me then signs with mock attitude, "Halloween's over, Mom!"

I indicate the ghoul-infested game on her screen and sign, "Yet here you are, playing that game again."

Her little face breaks into a pretty smile as she gives up the pretense of being upset with me for not being here when she came home from art camp.

"I was just kidding," she signs. "You know I love Halloween!"

I laugh, signing, "And yet you get freaked out every year when we dress up and go trick-or-treating!"

She pouts. "I can't help if some of the costumes are *too* scary!"

I laugh and hug her. "It's fine, sweetheart. To be honest, I get a little freaked out, too."

She looks at me to gauge whether I'm joking.

"Honest," I sign.

She laughs and points at me. "You? Get scared? That's *crazy!*" she signs vigorously, the deaf equivalent of yelling.

"*Ya got me!*" I sign back just as vigorously.

We laugh together.

Then she hugs me unexpectedly. I savor the hug, knowing that these precious years will pass, like all good things in this world.

"I love you, Mom," she signs.

"Love you, too, sweetie," I sign back, feeling a lump in my throat.

Holding her little seven-year-old body to mine, feeling our hearts beatmatching, I feel a great rush of love and joy. These are the moments when the darkness that has taken up residence inside me retreats, kept at bay by the bright light of living, at least for a while.

Over dinner, Natalie pours out all the things she usually shares with me at the end of each day, telling me everything she saw, felt, did, learned, and said today. Her observations about the world, her friends, teachers, anything and everything under the sky.

I ask a few questions, comment a couple of times, but

mostly just sit watching her and take it all in. Basking in her energy. It's an incredible feeling knowing that you sent this new life out into the world who is very much her own person, navigating her own path through the vast wilderness. I live for these moments, content simply to be her parent and a part of her wondrous life.

Lata watches us, her soldier's face a calm mask, only her eyes betraying the pleasure she feels in observing us. I smile at her with my eyes; she smiles back.

We are a family now. I can't say we were the best of friends before Amit's death; in fact, I barely even knew Lata because of her military tours and postings, but less than a year after his passing, we're as close as can be. The truth is, I could never have survived this past year without Lata, and I can't imagine how things would have been for Natalie, who was six when it happened, and has only just turned seven this month, without Lata to take up my slack. Especially during my darker days.

We're halfway through dinner when my phone vibrates in my jacket pocket.

"You going to answer that?" Lata asks after it continues for several seconds.

"It can go to voicemail," I say. Though I can't help wondering.

"It's okay, Mom," Natalie signs. "It might be important."

She says it so sincerely, I give in. For the past several months, I've been focusing on family time, on simply "being present in the moment" as my therapist calls it, and one consequence of not being on active duty is that I can ignore my phone at such times. It's also important because we're trying to set a good example by showing that we can do without our devices.

But something compels me to reach for my phone.

"Susan Parker," I say as I take the call. I dropped the "FBI" part a while back, again, on my therapist's advice. I am suspended, after all.

There's a brief pause, then, "Special Agent Susan Parker?" a man's voice says.

"Speaking," I say.

"This is Detective Naved Seth, Santa Carina Valley Sheriff's Department."

I frown, aware that Lata is watching me without seeming to watch me, while passing Natalie the mashed potatoes.

"How can I help you, detective?" I ask.

"This will sound a little strange," he says.

"Try me."

"I need you to come down to view a crime scene."

"Where?"

"A farm on the north end of the Santa Carina valley. Keep heading north after LARC Ranch. You'll see an old dirt road that winds left up to a ridge and then down again after about a mile, until you see an old, abandoned ranch house—"

"The old Dirty Tricks Ranch?" I ask.

He sounds surprised. "You know it?"

"What is this about, detective?"

I hear a low keening sound in the background, similar to a dog howling but at a different pitch.

"I think I've found Splinter," he says.

My heart thumps like a trap drum in my chest.

"Agent Parker?" he asks as the seconds tick by.

I make eye contact with Lata. She knows that something's up. It's probably written all over my face.

"Be there in ten minutes," I say, and hang up.

Lata raises her eyebrows.

"I have to go," I say to her.

Then to Natalie: "Sweetie, something came up. I might be back really late, okay? Aunty Lata will put you to bed."

I glance at Lata who nods.

"Sure, Mom," Natalie signs.

I give her a hug and kiss her on her forehead. "Bye, sweetie."

"Bye, Mom," she signs as I sling my jacket over my shoulder and start for the door. "Stay safe!"

Her words echo in my mind as I leave the house.

Stay safe.

She says it out of habit, I know, because she's aware, in her own fuzzy, seven-year-old way, that my job involves hunting down dangerous people.

But it has special resonance tonight.

Because tonight, I have a date with a serial killer.

FOUR

A pair of red eyes floats in the darkness.

My foot eases off the gas and taps the brake.

I come to a halt less than ten meters from the coyote.

She stands in the middle of the road, head low, shoulders hunched, staring directly at me. With the headlights in her face, she shouldn't be able to see me through the windshield, but I think she does, somehow. She holds my gaze for a moment, and I feel the same prickle of unnamable emotion I experience every time I encounter a creature in the wild.

After a moment, she turns her head and licks at something on her far side, then resumes trotting across the road, ignoring me completely.

As she reaches the shoulder and turns, I see the little one beside her, small, mangy, unsure. His tiny eyes reflect my head-lights. He was probably fascinated enough by their appearance that he froze in the middle of the road. With almost no traffic out this way, this might be his first human encounter.

The mother coyote turns her head and looks at me once more as if giving me permission to continue.

We're not so different, you and I, I think, *just two mamas protecting our young in a savage, uncertain world.*

I put the Prius into gear again and am about to drive on when I glimpse it on the left. A dirt track winding its way uphill.

If not for the coyote, I would have missed the turn and spent precious minutes backtracking.

When I look back in my rearview, the mother and cub are gone, returned to the wild darkness where they belong.

For the next several minutes, I keep both hands on the steering to navigate the bumps and dips in the dirt road. At one point, the undercarriage of the Prius clanks alarmingly as it hits something, probably a rock, and I wince. I can ill afford a repair bill right now. This year has been hard, financially as well as otherwise. After the incident eleven months ago, my boss Deputy Director Connor Gantry, put me on mental health leave which entitled me to disability unemployment insurance. But disability unemployment only pays out for six months. So as of now, we're basically living off Lata's salary and my almost depleted savings.

As I crest the rise, I see it.

A larger building than most of the ranch houses in the area, too large to house just a single family. Old, too. The missing window shutters and roof tiles, bleached exterior, and general look of decay all testify to absent or neglectful owners. Broken windows stare blindly out at the black night. Even though just a single story, it dominates the flat land, silhouetted darkly against the November sky.

Before it lies a large, neglected field, whatever crops it once carried now buried under decades of overgrowth. Out in the middle of the field, a dark silhouetted figure stands, hands outstretched as if pointing both west and east at once.

There's something unusual about that scarecrow but in the moonless night, I can't tell what it is exactly.

I turn the car left, curious, letting my headlights play over the field.

I peer for a moment before I see it: that isn't just straw stuffed into an old shirt and trousers, those are long chips of wood sharpened to points, bristling.

Splinters.

This is a serial killer with a sense of humor. Hannibal Lecter, move over.

From behind me, a voice calls out, "Agent Parker?"

I turn the Prius around, parking beside the solitary car before the house. Then I do a double take. A solitary car?

There's something very wrong here.

Splinter is one of the most high-profile serial killers in criminal history. The hunt for him has been ongoing for years, and has involved multiple Joint Task Forces, with the Bureau overseeing every time. If he's been caught, there ought to be a riot of law enforcement vehicles parked before me.

Instead, all I see is a late model Camry without any markings. There's a light on the dashboard, flashing red and blue, but any nutcase with a cop fetish could get one of those.

Where are the first responders, the SWAT van, FBI, evidence investigators, LA County sheriff's deputies, California state troopers, and the inevitable reporters and vloggers?

My hand reaches down to my hip holster and unfastens it.

A short, slender man in a jacket, checked shirt, and jeans taps on my window.

"Thanks for coming," he says.

I get out of the Prius, keeping my hand close to my open holster.

The contrast between the warmth of the vehicle and the brisk November night makes me shiver involuntarily. I reach in through the window and pull out the red jacket on the shotgun seat, slipping it on.

"Could I see some ID and a driver's license, please?" I say.

The shield looks brand new. The SCV Sheriff's Department ID is for *Naved Sulaiman Seth. Detective I.* The driver's license has a Brooklyn address and a picture of the man in front of me minus the moustache.

He's a compact man, lean but wiry, with a smattering of gray in his hair and pronounced widow's peaks. An angular face, brown eyes, neatly trimmed moustache, and a general sense of competence but not arrogance. There's something else about him; a sense of sadness baked into the corners and edges of his features. This is a man who's seen suffering and knows that life isn't all roses. Welcome to the club.

"You're a long way from Brooklyn, Detective Seth," I say.

He nods. "My first week on the job, arrived in Santa Carina ten days ago. Haven't had time to go into the DMV and get my license changed yet."

"NYPD?" I ask.

"Eleven years. Detective second grade."

I frown. "Yet here you are on the other side of the country, with one grade knocked off your shield."

He grimaces. "Long story."

He looks at me as if waiting for me to ask him to tell it.

I'm not really in the mood for exchanging personal biographies.

"So what's going on, detective?" I ask, indicating the empty lot. "Where the heck is everyone?"

He nods. "I know. Protocol says to call in the feds if there's any indication it could be Splinter. But my instructions were to call you."

This isn't making any sense. "What instructions? Given by whom?"

He jerks his head at the house. "Them."

Them.

He holds up his hands. "Look, I know this sounds hinky.

Even the 911 despatcher didn't take the call seriously, thought it was another crank. But they got me at the end of my shift, on my way back home, so I said, okay, I'll check it out. The last thing I expected was to find, well, to find *this*."

"And you decided it would be a good idea to call my personal cell?" I ask, even more suspicious now.

"I recognized your name from that article in the *New York Times*. It said you were the special agent in charge of leading the investigation into Splinter."

The article was a million years ago, but I nod. "Okay?"

"So this is a federal matter anyway, right?" he asks.

"It is," I say.

"And I thought, okay, by calling you in, I'm as good as calling the FBI. Since it's your case."

I'm tempted to correct him, to point out that I've been on extended leave and there's probably another special agent in charge handling the Splinter case, but decide against it.

"And you said the people who told you to call me, they're in there?" I ask, jerking my head at the house without taking my eyes off Detective Seth.

He nods, looking at the farmhouse. "Yes, ma'am."

I follow his gaze.

In the flashing light, its bleached walls glow red and blue.

The effect is macabre.

Halloween, not Christmas.

If there were an architectural style named California Creepy, a picture of this house would illustrate it perfectly.

The wind whips at me, slipping icy fingers around my neck and down my spine. Somewhere not far away, it feels like rain. A patch of the night sky seems darker than the rest, something large and brooding gathering on the horizon, biding its time.

"Okay," I say, reaching a decision, "talk to me. What am I going to find when I go in there?"

Detective Seth follows my gaze.

"You need to see for yourself," he says.

I zip up the jacket, unholster my Sig Sauer, check the magazine and action.

"All right then," I say.

We walk toward the house, guns drawn.

FIVE

The house stinks of death.

The rich ferric stench of blood fills my nostrils, creeps up my sinuses, and triggers a forgotten childhood memory of a butcher's shop in Goa I entered as a little girl, clutching my mother's hand, as a pig was being slaughtered for some saint's feast day. It's not a happy memory.

I inhale through my nose and release slowly through my mouth to re-center myself. The Sig Sauer feels comforting in my hands.

"Did you clear the house?" I ask, moving across the dusty vestibule.

When he doesn't answer, I glance back at him.

He shakes his head. "I only got as far as the kitchen," he says. "Then I retreated and went outside to call you."

I stare at him a moment longer, trying to show my exasperation at this display of gross carelessness.

"Let's do it now," I say.

He starts to say something but shuts up when I shoot him another scathing look.

I point left, and I go right.

We move through dusty rooms filled with antique furniture. There's no sign of footprints or human presence. High vaulting ceilings, cobwebs everywhere, murky windows, several seasons' worth of dried leaves in the doorway and beneath the half-opened windows, filthy plush sofas, a grand piano, a grandfather clock that probably hasn't worked in decades. The stench that assaulted my nostrils when I crossed the threshold grows thicker as I clear room after room.

We meet again in the hallway. There are only two doors left at the end, toward the rear of the house.

"Which one's the kitchen?" I ask.

Naved jerks his head.

Of course. The one from which the strongest stench emanates.

I brace my back against the hallway wall, call out, "FBI!" then enter with my gun raised and ready.

It's a fairly typical farm kitchen. Large, roomy. An ancient black oven dominates the row of appliances and sinks against the wall. A dining table with eight chairs occupies the center of the room. At the head of the table is an enormous figure, seated facing the door. My pulse quickens.

I point my gun at the figure as I approach.

When I'm close enough to see him clearly in the light from my flashlight, I lower the gun slowly.

I don't need to check for a pulse.

The body at the head of the table is clearly dead and has been dead for several days, judging from the smell and the congealed blood.

The extent of violent trauma inflicted on it is so extreme that it's barely recognizable as a person. Its advanced state of decay and putrefaction have robbed it of all the usual traces of identity. In the FBI, we use the term *unsub* for any unidentified or unknown subject of a criminal investigation. This cadaver definitely qualifies as an unsub.

My best guess is that it's a white male, possibly middle-aged, dressed in what was probably a red-white-and-blue striped shirt, black jeans, and black cowboy boots. There might be a scarf around his neck but it's hard to tell because of all the wounds and bleeding in that area. From the position, it appears that he was seated at the head of this table, facing the door, when he was attacked, and then slumped sideways, coming to rest with his head and one arm on the corner of the table. His own considerable weight is probably the only thing keeping him from sliding all the way to the floor.

I look at Detective Seth. "Any ID on him?"

He raises his hands. "Didn't touch the body. Didn't want to mess up forensics."

"I'm guessing he's not the guy who told you to call me."

He points. "This way."

I follow, keeping my gun in hand, pointed downwards.

He stops at a door midway down the hall. "Down there."

I frown. "I thought you said you only went into the kitchen."

"Yes. But I heard a sound and opened the door. And—" He points.

I frown. I don't like any of this. The whole situation stinks, and I'm not just talking about the rotting corpse.

Every fiber of my being tells me to get the hell out of here, call Deputy Director Gantry, hand this over right now. For all I know, there could be an armed killer behind this door, waiting to blast me the second I open the door. I don't even have my vest on. I'm already taking a stupid, idiotic risk just by being here right now.

But once I make that call, I'll be shut out.

I might not get any answers for months at the very least, maybe never. And if that decrepit cadaver back there really is Splinter, then there's a possibility, however slim, that I might finally be able to get some answers about Amit's death. Because though it was ruled a self-inflicted wound, I still can't entirely believe that it was suicide.

Someone in this house gave Detective Seth *my* name and number. That must mean *something*. If there's even the slightest chance that I could learn something related to Amit's death, I'm willing to take the risk.

I look at Detective Seth. He nods, stepping back and pointing his weapon, ready to cover me.

I reach for the door handle, turn it with my left hand, then use my foot to kick the door all the way open.

I aim my weapon, calling out, "Federal agent!" as the door swings wide open.

The doorway is empty.

I lower my hand, pointing the flashlight down to reveal wooden stairs descending.

Detective Seth and I exchange another glance and move forward together, each of us showing as little as possible of our bodies as I point my gun and the flashlight down the stairs.

"Down there," he says.

I look at him doubtfully. "Really?"

He stares back at me. "I'll be right behind you."

Like that's supposed to reassure me.

But right now, it's all I have.

I take a moment to reassess. It's still not too late. I've found a body. That's enough to call it in. The deputy director is just one speed-dial call away. There's no need for me to go down into a dark basement and risk my life.

Everything about this is wrong. It stinks of a set-up. A trap.

And yet.

Once I call in the cavalry, I'll be out in the cold again, literally. I may never know why my name and number were given to Detective Seth. Or by whom. It's a myth that the bad guys are always caught, that every case gets a neat, tidy ending with a bow on top. The truth is, there are countless crimes that go unsolved and even those that end in an arrest and prison rarely get full closure. The odds against me learning what really happened to Amit that last day of his life are astronomical.

This could be my one-in-a-million chance to get the answers I need so desperately.

"Okay," I say, "you lead the way."

He nods without protest and starts down the wooden stairs. They creak under our weight, and I feel very exposed. I can't help touching my chest, where I wear my wedding ring on a silver chain. It's been decades since I last stepped into a church, so that's the closest I'm able to get to actual prayer. Not for my sake, but for Natalie's. The thought of leaving her orphaned is too much to bear.

There's a different smell down here. Not the dusty moldy odors of the house upstairs. This is different. I recognize this smell. It's a combination of bodily effluents, medical disinfectant, and that undefinable smell we all recognize from a visit to hospitals and clinics. The pervasive smell of sickness, suffering, and death.

The hallway ends in another door, this one metal-reinforced and requiring a security code to open. This door is ajar. Detective Seth pauses to glance back at me to indicate that he's going to open it. I nod. He goes through the door.

I take a deep breath, then follow.

The stink is stronger here. We're in an open space surrounded by multiple doors. They all appear to have electronic locks on them. All of them are ajar right now. The unmistakable stench of unwashed human bodies is powerfully strong. Whoever maintains this place clearly hasn't been doing their job recently.

We check out the first door, Detective Seth using his foot to push it open the rest of the way, while I hang back. I keep my head on a swivel, trying to watch all the doors around us. It's an impossible task.

Detective Seth looks back at me from the first door, leaning back to allow me a better view of the interior of the cell. That's what it resembles, a prison cell.

There's a single person inside, a man. He looks terrified, haggard, ill-fed, and ill-treated. His eyes swivel from Seth to me and back again. Here then is the source of the stench, or one of them at least.

Detective Seth looks at me. I nod.

He moves on to open the next cell.

Same thing, except this one's a woman, staring eyes under wild, tangled hair, emaciated with very pale skin. Again, she looks from one to the other of us as if trying to guage which of us is the bigger threat. She looks frightened out of her wits.

If not for their eyes and reactions to the intrusion, I'd almost doubt they're alive. They're half-starved, clearly abused and beaten down, barely hanging on, yet they all have that same unsettling look in their eyes.

By the time I reach the fourth door, I'm done.

"We've seen enough," I say. "Time to call in the cavalry."

SIX

I'm sitting sideways on the front seat of my Prius, elbow resting on the steering wheel, door open, boots in the weeds. It's several hours later the same night.

A keening sound comes to me, like a dog howling, but wilder, sadder, mournful. It's the same sound I heard in the background when Detective Seth called. I look up at the dark shapes of the hills; the sound comes from that direction. Is it the mama coyote and her cub I saw earlier, maybe now united with their pack? Wolves, bears, mountain lions, none of them sound like that, though we have plenty of all those species and more here in Santa Carina Valley, being right on the edge of the Angeles National Forest. My money's on the coyotes.

The lot is a whole lot busier. SCVPD, fire department, sheriff's deputies, California state troopers, FBI, an FBI SWAT armored van, an FBI evidence investigators' van, more cars. The whole shebang. Probably three dozen or more vehicles parked haphazardly, lights flashing. Radios crackling. Orders shouted and passed on. A helicopter circling somewhere high above, searchlight slicing the night like a flaming sword held by an invisible god.

I debated texting Lata hours earlier, when I called in the troops, to tell her that I would probably be home in the morning. I held off. Lata's a light sleeper, a habit formed from combat tours in foreign, hostile lands, and the ping of the text notification might rouse her.

Besides, we've done this before; she knows the drill. It's been a while since I've leaned on her this way, and while I can't help feeling a tad guilty, my sense of excitement at being back on the hunt more than balances that out.

The place is crawling with law enforcement and first responders. A lot of big guys, bulky from pushing iron and pulling drafts, but there's more than a few women in the mix, too, holding their own. If there's one overwhelming theme, it's that whiteness dominates. The sheer proportion of big-built white men is overwhelming, as is the buddy-buddy camaraderie between them, conveying a sense of the 'boys club' mentality that seems baked into the history of law enforcement. Detective Seth and I probably stick out in this white male crowd like a couple of sore thumbs—*brown* sore thumbs. But even that's starting to change, thankfully. After all, we are here, and we're the first ones on the scene, a fact all our esteemed colleagues are just going to have to live with. Welcome to the twenty-first century.

From time to time, someone or other will glance over at me. Heads swiveling, eyes flicking, tongues wagging. I should be used to it but I'm not.

"You turn a lot of heads," Detective Seth says. "And I'm not talking about your appearance."

I look over at him.

He's leaning against his Camry, only a few feet away. He takes occasional pulls of his vape device, exhaling a fragrant cloud of mango-scented smoke. He speaks softly, just as he did when he called me right after discovering the butchered corpse of Splinter. I like that about this guy, the fact that he keeps his cool in the face of mortality. It must take a helluva lot to faze Detective Naved Seth.

I shrug at the comment.

"I guess I earned it," I say.

"How?" he says.

"The hard way. By giving them a reason to talk smack about me."

He puffs on his vape for a moment, waiting patiently.

I like that about him, too. That fact that he waits for the other person to tell their story in their own time. It makes me want to confide in him. Why the hell not? Back in that basement, I trusted him enough to go into a potentially lethal situation with possibly multiple armed unsubs waiting in ambush.

"My husband Amit died almost a year ago," I say, then pause as a lump forms in my throat. It just occurred to me that I've not actually talked about this to anyone except my therapist. My sister-in-law Lata, sure, but that's different; she's family.

Naved removes the vape device from his mouth and holds it down by his side, giving me his full attention. I see the gesture for what it is: a form of respect. It's appreciated.

"I went... a little crazy," I say. "Did something that simply isn't done. Especially not when you're a young female agent, one of the youngest to make special agent in charge in LA field office history, and a woman of color."

"I think I might have heard something about that," Naved says. "You got into some kind of fight with an FBI consultant, right?"

I nod. "Dr. Keller. He was consulting for us at the time. As a matter of fact, I was the one who suggested to my boss, Gantry, that we hire Dr. Keller."

"'Doctor' as in...?"

"Therapist," I say. "Psychiatrist, to be exact. You know that Splinter only went after therapists and their families, right?"

"It was all over the news," Naved says.

"So based on that fact and the nature of the brutalities inflicted on the victims, BAU came up with a profile."

"That's the behavioral analysis unit at Quantico?" Naved says.

"Yup. So BAU's profile of the unsub, the unidentified subject, pointed to Splinter likely being a therapist or former therapist himself," I say.

"Because of the way he bound, tortured, and killed the victims and their families," Naved says. "Like it was personal to him."

"Exactly. The BAU's theory was that the unsub was a therapist himself, or at the very least had clinical experience in therapy. This was based on the recordings he made and left at the scene."

Naved nods. "I read about that. Splinter made the family members torture each other, all while confessing stuff about each other. He left the recordings for law enforcement to find along with the bodies. Sick, twisted bastard."

"Oh, you have no idea," I say, grimacing as I try not to remember too many of the worst details from the previous murders. It's like a closet stuffed with awful, unspeakable images, all threatening to come crashing down on me if I open that door. "It wasn't enough that he tortured and killed them all, entire families, while their loved ones watched, leaving the therapist himself or herself for last. Oh no, that wasn't good enough for this sick fuck. Splinter had to push them to the edge of sanity, force them to say all this terrible shit. It was like he wanted to destroy everything sweet, good, and beautiful about each family, reduce them to bleeding, screaming animals that were desperate enough to degrade themselves in the worst possible ways in the pathetic hope that he might spare them."

I take a deep breath and exhale again. "Which he never did, of course. The son of a bitch."

I shudder, unable to suppress the revulsion I always feel when I go over that part, then go on, "Anyway, so BAU felt it had to be a therapist himself because of the way he posed questions while he made them torture each other. There were details, phrases, that all suggested professional training."

"This was all on the recordings he left behind at the scenes?" Naved asks.

I nod. "He used a voice modulator, so we could never be sure what the actual Splinter sounded like. We couldn't even be sure he was a 'he'."

"So how did you end up suspecting this Dr. Keller?" Naved asks.

"We didn't, actually. We drew up a list of potential unsubs, which was also a list of potential victims, of course. Therapists, therapists, therapists, all the way. The only differentiator that we could find between suspects and victims was family."

"The potential victims all had happy families," Naved says.

I gesture. "Happy, unhappy, who really knows. 'Intact families' is what we called them. Couples with kids who weren't divorced, separated, or estranged, all living together under the same roof. That much was pretty consistent."

"And Dr. Keller was a likely suspect?" Naved says.

The wind whipping around me has tugged a few strands of my ponytail loose. I capture them and tuck them behind my ear. "No. Our best suspect, the unsub we thought was the gold star winner, was that corpse in there, except of course he wasn't a corpse a year ago when we looked long and hard at him."

"Magnusson."

"Yup. Magnusson was our numero uno. He had a wife, a kid, an aging father. He lived in Woodland Hills at that time. Nice house, family SUV, backyard trampoline, and barbecue. He fit the profile to a tee except for his physiological issues."

Naved nods. "His weight problem, the resulting health issues, limited mobility?"

"Right. Since Splinter always used blades, never a gun, and was able to overpower and restrain even healthy, fit adult and adolescent victims, it suggested an unsub who was at least reasonably fit, if not athletic, and able to move quickly, up and down stairs, etc."

"Magnusson wasn't capable of all that," Naved says.

"Nope. But Keller was," I say quietly.

Naved frowns at me. "But you'd already ruled out Keller," he says.

"Yes. But then, as I said, Amit died. And he died at the scene of Splinter's most recent mass murder. The house of Dr. Venkatesh Rao, right here in Santa Carina Valley."

"How does that connect to Keller?" he asks.

"It was the same day that Amit had had his longest, first unscheduled session with his own therapist..."

"Dr. Keller," Naved says, suddenly getting it.

"The very same. In my emotionally confused state, it just seemed to suggest *something*. My husband seeing a therapist for the first time, then dying in the house of another therapist, the murder house where Splinter had claimed his most recent victims. It all seemed to add up to some kind of twisted conspiracy, in my confused mind at the time. And then there was the documentary evidence which I misread."

Naved frowns. "Evidence?"

"I had asked my team to pull Dr. Rao's house ownership records. They had pulled the county home ownership records of all the previous victims, and somehow, part of Keller's file got mixed in with those others."

Naved nods slowly, finally getting it. "So you went after Keller?"

I take a deep breath and exhale slowly. "Like gangbusters. I burst into his clinic during a patient therapy session, confronted and accused him. He tried to call security for help, while his patient dialed 911, and I just lost it. Next thing I knew, Keller was on the floor and I was whaling on him. It took four LAPD officers to drag me off him and I still got in a kick to his ribs. I broke one."

Naved looks at the house where FBI Deputy Director Connor Gantry is standing on the porch, having words with Chief McDougall. I can see my team stripping off their forensic suits and looking at me.

"You were still in shock," Naved says. "You were grieving."

I make a sound in my throat. "Don't sugarcoat it, detective. The fact is, I went fucking crazy that day."

We're both silent for a moment as we watch my team walk toward us.

"We all go fucking crazy some days," Naved says at last. "At least you had a damn good reason."

I look at him gratefully. I don't actually say thanks, but I see what he's doing and I'm thankful for it. He gets it.

We sit in companionable silence for a few seconds more before a tall, gangly shape approaches, silhouetted by the bright scene lights that have just been switched on. Naved loses the vape device as I brush off my jeans and start to rise.

The tall shape makes a beeline for me.

SEVEN

I rise, opening my arms. "Briney boy!"

Special Agent Brine Thomas almost has to fold himself in half to give me a hug. "Susan," he says.

His floppy blond hair is a little longer than I remember but his cornflower-blue eyes are as vivid.

"You look taller. Been eating your Wheaties?" I ask, meaning it as a joke.

He rakes a hand through his golden mop, handsome face looking embarrassed. "Three quarters of an inch."

"Whoa. How tall does that make you now?"

"Six five," he says reluctantly. "And a half."

I whistle then indicate Detective Seth.

"Detective Naved Seth, SCVPD. Trainee agent Brine Thomas. Spelled 'ine' but pronounced 'Brian'."

"Susan was my supervisor," Brine says.

"Agent Thomas," Detective Seth says, shaking hands with Brine.

"We're all on a first name basis, our team," I say, then pause. "Or we were. We were tight, weren't we, Brine?"

"Oh yes," Brine says. "Susan's my mentor. But she's also a friend."

I like that he uses the present tense, not the past. I didn't want to assume.

Detective Seth looks over my shoulder.

I turn to see three more familiar faces.

Special agents Ramon Diaz, Kayla Regis, and David Moskovitch.

"Guys!" I say.

They all greet me in their own ways: Ramon with a respectful nod, David with his usual shy grin, and Kayla with a hug even bigger and warmer than Brine.

I know all their families, their lives, and there's so much catching up I'd like to do, as would they I expect, but it's not the time or place. For now, they're happy to see me and that makes me happy. I've forgotten what it feels like to be needed, to be useful, someone that my co-workers look up to and respect. I introduce them to Detective Seth.

"It's a rat king in there," Agent Ramon Diaz says.

I nod. "Multiple suspects, who also happen to be victims, and no way to tell them apart."

Like a swarm of rats with their tails entangled together.

"And no murder weapon," Agent David Moskovitch adds.

Kayla raises her phone to point at a gathering of cops and first responders listening to Chief McDougall. "They're setting up a grid search of the surrounding farmland."

"And the body?" I ask.

All four of them exchange glances.

Kayla huffs out a breath. "Guys! It's Susan."

To me, she says with an apologetic tone, "Our orders are to freeze you out. We're not even supposed to be talking to you right now."

"Figures," I say. "Gantry always was a stickler for protocol.

33

Look, I don't want you guys to get into trouble. You do what you have to."

They all shake their heads, except Agent David Moskovitch who looks hesitant. But then, David is always hesitant. Ramon is not.

"Fuck that," Agent Ramon Diaz says. "Marisol found ID in his rear pants pocket."

Special Agent Marisol Mancini is our chief evidence investigator. That's the real-world equivalent of what TV shows call CSI. She's the one in charge of recovering and processing all evidence from the scene as well as conducting all autopsies. If there's anything to find, she'll find it. Right now, due to the sudden death of SCV's last Medical Examiner, she's also filling in that position.

Diaz goes on: "Corpse is one—"

I interrupt him: "Dr. Viktor Magnusson, psychiatrist."

Diaz makes a flourishing gesture, ending in a tip of an invisible hat. "See? I told ya she'd ID him right off the bat," he says to the other three.

"Fingerprints confirmed by his California license registration," Kayla adds.

I nod. "I was pretty sure it was. His size alone."

"The ranch house and farm, which includes a sizable property," David says, reading from his tablet screen, "is in the name of the Wolfgang Trust LLC, who leased it to Magnusson for an annual fee of one dollar. The trust pays the property taxes which are up to date."

Kayla gestures. "All this for one dollar a year? You could fit a dozen city blocks in this space!"

David shrugs. "Probably some kind of arrangement. The trust is a non-profit so maybe they didn't care."

"Besides, look at this place," Brine says. "Who'd want to rent it in this state?"

"What about the victims down in the basement?" Naved says. "The ones he kept captive? They were all his patients?"

Everyone looks at Naved, uncertain for a moment. Kayla looks at me, as if asking permission. They're all great guys but Kayla's the sweetest.

I nod at her and the others. "I've brought Detective Seth up to speed. He's all clued in."

David nods as if that's good enough for him. "We don't know the identities of the people down in the basement. There's some legal issues involved. The deputy director is having them looked at by the EMTs. They're hands off for the time being."

"Makes sense," I say. "They were victims, after all. God knows how long those poor bastards have been kept prisoner down there. In that dark and squalor."

We're all silent for a moment as we each try to picture being abducted, quite likely after being drugged, then waking to find ourselves in a strange, dark room, held captive by a psychopath who had God-knows-what planned for them. I can't imagine what they might have gone through down there. The very thought of being trapped like that, with no way to reach Natalie and Lata, gives me chills. Even ten years in the Bureau doesn't prepare you for anything like that.

Brine, who is tall enough to see halfway to Vegas, says quietly, "Incoming."

Everyone disperses, pretending to be absorbed in their phones.

A tall, lean man in a black suit comes striding toward me, his jacket flapping, the angular lined face creased in a hard expression. Deputy Director Connor Gantry looks his usual brusque, irritable self.

"Agent Parker," he says, scowling down at me.

"Sir," I say.

"I must admit, you're the last person on earth I expected to see. And yet here you are, first on the scene," he says.

"Technically, sir, Detective Seth here was first on the scene," I say.

The deputy director gives Naved a cursory glance. "Detective. You just happened to be driving by?"

The undertone is loud and clear: he isn't happy about Naved being here either.

Naved says calmly, "I was at the end of my shift, on my way home to Plum Canyon, when the call came in. Dispatch thought it was a crank caller but asked me to check it out."

Gantry looks at him skeptically. "And instead of calling it in at once, you decided to dial Agent Parker here? Who also conveniently just happened to be in the neighborhood?"

"I live right here in Santa Carina Valley, sir. Less than ten minutes away," I say.

"I called Agent Parker because I was instructed to call her," Naved says calmly.

Gantry frowns.

I notice my team reacting as well.

Even I blink at that.

In the rush of adrenalin following our search of the house and after what we found in the kitchen and then in the basement, I haven't had a chance to circle back to the question of why Naved dialed me in the first place. He used the same word "instructed" when I questioned him about it earlier, too. When I asked him by whom, he pointed to the house and said "them". Now, hearing him say it again, knowing what he probably meant, some deeply buried emotion resurfaces, uncurling its taloned wings. The darkness inside me, never out of reach, spreads through my senses, like the inky fog of an octopus in deep waters.

At the far end of the lot, Chief McDougall uses a megaphone to order the search teams to start working the grid.

Several dozen men and women, some using dogs, start walking in a precise pattern designed to cover the maximum area in the shortest time, picking up and bagging anything that might possibly be evidence. I know they're searching for the murder weapon in particular, but sometimes, grid searches turn up the most unexpected treasures.

Gantry, hands on his hips now, frowns in that direction for a second before returning his scrutiny to Naved.

"'Instructed', did you say, Detective Seth?" Gantry asks skeptically.

"Yes, sir."

Gantry shoots a glance at me as if suspecting some kind of conspiracy. Finding no clue in my blank face, he turns his attention back to Naved.

"And how exactly did you get these 'instructions', detective?" Gantry asks.

Naved reaches into his jacket pocket and pulls out a plastic evidence baggie. As he holds it up, I see the simple words printed in block letters on the yellow Post-it note. *SUSAN PARKER*. Followed by my cellphone number. Seeing my name on that small yellow square, written by a stranger's hand under these circumstances, causes goosebumps to erupt along my forearms.

"This was stuck on the door to the basement," Naved says.

He offers it to the deputy director who recoils as if it's a live snake.

"Chain of evidence," Gantry says in his usual cryptic way. He looks at me for a long moment. "Agent Parker, do you have any idea why your name and number were on that note?"

I shake my head slowly, thinking aloud. "Could be any number of reasons. I was named as the SAC leading the Splinter investigation, that's all over the internet. Wouldn't be too hard for someone to track down my cell."

Gantry frowns. "It's also well known that you've been on

susp... on leave for almost a year. In your absence, I've been heading up the investigation. Wouldn't it make more sense for them to ask for me instead?"

I suppress a flash of irritation. Typical of Gantry to waste precious time debating protocol instead of rolling up his sleeves and getting down to the real work. "Sir, instead of us standing around trading theories, why don't we just wait for the victims to be checked out then start taking statements from them? They've been down there for God knows how long, subjected to who knows what. They must be dying to tell us everything they know and then some."

Gantry looks at me for a long moment, then at Naved, then off into the distance. His hands are still on his hips, his coat flaps flickering in the night breezes. His jaw is set in a tight, inscrutable expression.

"That is what one would usually expect," he says.

Right about then, the emergency medical technicians—EMTs—start bringing out the victims from the basement. The law enforcement and first responders around the front entrance of the house move aside, making way. EMTs come out two by two, each carrying a stretcher on which a blanket-shielded figure rests. They carry them to the ambulances that have been backed up and parked before the house.

I count eleven in all. There were twelve rooms down there, as I recall, but then again, I didn't search them all. Apparently, one was empty.

Only one comes out walking. Despite her obviously emaciated appearance and stringy, lean physique, she manages to walk on her own two feet all the way to the ambulance. Her eyes seem too large for her pale, bony face. She turns once, looking around as if searching for something and her gaze finds me, across the several dozen feet and almost as many people that separate us. There's something about her stance, the way she just stands there for a moment and stares at me—directly at me—that makes my skin crawl. She turns away mercifully and climbs into the ambulance, much to the relief of the two EMTs accompanying her. They shut the doors and then the ambulances start to drive away, lights flashing but sirens off.

Gantry and the rest of us have been watching the whole operation with silent interest.

Now, he stares at the departing convoy of ambulances with a faraway look, as if considering something.

When Gantry doesn't speak for the better part of a minute, Naved and I exchange a look.

Gantry's eyes refocus on me, as if seeing me for the first time. He seems to come to a decision.

"They're not talking," he says.

"Who, sir?" I ask.

"None of them, Agent Parker," he says, gesturing at the last departing ambulance. "None of the victims are willing to talk to anyone."

EIGHT

My daughter's face is the first thing I see when I open my eyes the next morning.

Before I can speak, Natalie flings herself at me, presses her face to mine, hugging me as hard as her little arms can squeeze.

Over her head, I see Lata in my bedroom doorway. She hangs back, letting Natalie have her moment. I nod at her and she nods back.

I focus my entirety on Natalie.

It feels wonderful to hold my daughter again, to smell and touch and see the precious life I brought into this world.

She makes happy sounds, heaving against me.

I don't need words to know how glad she is that I'm alive.

She pulls back just enough to look at me. I stare in awe at her pretty, heart-shaped face. She is perfect, so perfect. How did two imperfect people like Amit and me ever make something so perfect?

I push a lock of hair off her face, tuck it behind her ear.

I kiss her forehead, her cheeks, her nose.

She makes a face.

I smile.

"I. Love. You. So. Much," I say, signing and emphasizing each word even though I know she can read lips in three languages. I'm so used to signing to her while speaking that just using spoken words feels incomplete.

"I love you, too," she signs back, then puts her hands on her hips and pouts. "Why did you have to leave during dinner last night?"

"Something important came up," I reply. "A work thing."

She squints at me doubtfully. "On *Thanksgiving*? Nobody works on Thanksgiving, Mom!"

"Honey, you know my job," I sign and say aloud. "It doesn't keep office hours."

Lata cocks her head in the doorway, looking at me curiously. I waggle my eyebrows to convey that I'll explain later.

"Anyway, I'm sorry I didn't make it home yesterday. And I might as well warn you that I'm going to be working all hours from now on," I say to Natalie, my hand on her shoulder. "Is that okay with you?"

My daughter frowns, thinking about it. "Is it important work?" she asks.

"Very," I reply.

"Can't someone else do it?"

I smile and brush a lock of hair off her forehead. "Maybe. But I can do it better."

She grins at that. She likes the idea of her mom doing her job better than other people. Then a change comes over her face as something occurs to her. She grows more thoughtful.

"Will you be catching another bad guy?" she asks seriously.

I know better than to lie. "Yes."

"Will it be dangerous?" she asks.

"It could be."

"You might get hurt? Again?" she asks, looking worried now.

This time, I really want to lie, but this is no ordinary seven-year-old. Natalie lost her dad at the age of six; she's lived with the knowledge that her aunt Lata is a soldier who goes to faraway lands to fight for her country and risks her life, and her mom carries two guns and a bulletproof vest because my job is to hunt and catch dangerous, violent criminals who will do anything to avoid arrest.

"I'll be very, very careful," I say, meaning it with all my heart. The last thing on earth I would want is to leave my beautiful daughter orphaned.

She thinks about it then nods. "But you'll still have to take some risks, right? Because no risk, no reward!"

That was one of her dad's favorite phrases.

"Right," I say, a lump in my throat.

"Okay then," she says, in a perfect imitation of me now, right down to the curt nod. "Okey dokey, artichoke."

"Come here, you little artichoke!" I say, pulling her in for a tight hug.

"Mom, you're squishing me," she pretend-complains.

I kiss her all over her face and her head.

She sighs and rests her cheek on mine.

We breathe together, in synch.

It's our thing.

Just lying together, cheek against cheek, breathing. Feeling our hearts pulsing next to each other.

Beatmatching.

Lata has disappeared from the doorway. From the smells drifting upstairs, she's probably making breakfast.

Suddenly, Natalie sits up and signs: "You'll still come to see me in the school play, right, Mom?"

"I really want to come, sweetie. But I don't want to promise and then have to break my promise. The play's two weeks away. I can't say what might happen between now and then. Let's just take it as it comes, okay?"

She frowns, then signs angrily.

42

I nod. "Yes, I do have a lousy job."

She signs again.

"The worst job in the world, yes," I agree.

More furious signing.

"The worst job in the history of worst jobs, *ever*! Yes, yes, yes!" I say.

She sighs and lets her hands slump down by her sides, done with the scolding.

Natalie's anger never lasts long.

She has the sweetest nature of any kid.

Even as a toddler, when she would throw a tantrum, it usually spent itself out in a couple of minutes, and never went beyond a few yells and foot stomps. Things never escalated. It was like, the moment she lost it, she became aware of it and felt embarrassed to have overreacted.

At times, I feel like my daughter is more emotionally mature than most adults.

Even at preschool, the entire class could be squalling like banshees, rolling about on the floor, while Natalie would be off in one corner, building a house from wooden blocks or rearranging the pieces of a favorite puzzle.

She was born that way. So quiet and calm that it worried me at first, even after the doctors told me that she was born deaf due to neonatal sepsis.

I soon learned that it wasn't something I needed to worry about.

It's just her, Natalie.

I've learned to embrace it, enjoy it.

My quiet, calm little island of a daughter.

In the world yet apart from it.

Her own private bubble.

I get her ready and we go down together. Because I wasn't there for most of the day before, and left midway through dinner, she hasn't had a chance to catch me up on yesterday.

43

Over breakfast, she pours out all the things she usually shares with me at the end of each day, telling me everything she saw, felt, did, learned, and said yesterday.

I ask a few questions, comment a couple of times, but mostly just sit watching her and take it all in. I live for these moments. Content simply to be her parent and a part of her wondrous life.

After she finishes, Natalie signs to ask if I'll drop her off at camp today. Her eyes are almost pleading.

"Sure," I say, checking the time. I still have an hour before I have to get going.

Natalie does her happy dance, wriggling from side to side with her elbows at right angles.

"We need to talk," Lata says as I grab my car keys.

"Sure. Soon as I get back," I say with exaggerated cheerfulness as I leave the house.

I already know what she wants to talk about and despite my cheery tone, I'm not looking forward to it.

NINE

"Splinter," Lata says.

We're in the living room.

I'm sipping a mug of Lata's delicious filter coffee. The chicory aroma makes the whole house smell good. I showered and changed after dropping Natalie off and am feeling a little more awake. The hot water refreshed me, but I still feel like I'm hungover, even though I haven't had so much as a beer in months. It's the downside of the adrenalin rush that kept me going all night. I'm vaguely aware of having fallen into bed sometime around 5.30 this morning, only to be awakened by Natalie about two hours later. But sleep-deprived as I am, I can feel the prospect of being back on the hunt coursing through my veins, invigorating me.

"Splinter," I say, nodding in agreement.

Lata looks at me questioningly.

"Are you sure you're ready for this?" she asks.

She leaves a lot unsaid. This is the case that broke me in a sense, that I still blame for driving a rift between Amit and me. My toxic obsession with Splinter almost destroyed my marriage; to this day, I can't help thinking that if only I hadn't become so caught up in it, he might still be alive. Even months of therapy haven't been able to completely dispel that notion, foolish though it might be.

"I'm not sure what *this* is," I say. "Right now, I'm still on leave, officially. It's not like I've been reinstated and given charge of the case again. Gantry's still heading the investigation."

"He's called you in for a meeting," Lata points out.

"He could just be needing to do a more thorough debriefing. On camera. For the record."

"Your name was on that Post-it note, you said," she says.

When I reached home, she was already awake, and I gave Lata the gist of the whole thing so she knows the basics.

"It was," I admit.

"That means something," she says.

She's right but I'm refusing to let myself believe it. Maybe I don't want to get my hopes up, or... maybe I'm just afraid. Of what it could lead to. Not afraid for my own safety, though I should be, with Natalie depending on me; I'm afraid of what dark path it might lead me down and what I might do when I get to the end of that path. In a way, that's exactly what Lata is afraid of, too, and she's trying to caution me against stepping onto that path.

"Anyone could have gotten my name off the internet," I say. "It may not mean anything."

She doesn't look convinced. "Maybe," she admits, "but if there's something more to it, if it turns out that there's a connection to... you know..."

Lata doesn't want to say Amit's name aloud if she can help it. It's a trigger for both of us. He was her only brother. They were close, much closer than Kajal, their second, older sister. What Lata went through when Amit died was no less traumatic than me; she just handled it far better.

"Lata, we talked about this. I don't think there's a connection," I say.

"You used to think there was," she says. "You were adamant about it at one point. That's why you went after Keller."

I wince.

"Lata, you know what happened back then," I say defensively. "I screwed up. I admit it. I've dealt with it in therapy and worked my way out of that hole. That was then. This is now. I'm not that person anymore."

"Yes," she agrees. "You're not. And I don't want to see you become that person again. That's why I'm asking you to think twice about this."

I frown, confused. "What are you saying? That I should refuse to go into the meeting today?"

"No, Suse. Go into the meeting. Do the debriefing, whatever they need. But when you're done with all that Bureau protocol, step aside. Leave it to the Bureau to take it from here. You've told me yourself, Gantry is a pain-in-the-ass play-it-by-the-rulebook kinda guy, but he's also a very good agent. He taught you everything you know. Isn't that right?"

I bite back an argument. "Sure."

"So let him handle it from here on. Besides," she adds, sitting back, "he's already dead, right?"

I frown. "Who?"

"Splinter," she says. "That's the body you found, right?"

I spread my palms. "I mean—sure. It's Magnusson. He had all these people imprisoned in his house. He was one of our top suspects. The team told me he went off the grid some months ago, just up and vanished. They've been trying to track him down. So now that he's turned up, with a house full of abductees, yeah, Magnusson is almost certainly Splinter. We're just waiting on DNA to confirm that the body is, in fact, Magnusson."

She shrugs. "And once DNA confirms it? Then that's it, right? The case is as good as closed, isn't it?"

"Sure, but—"

She shakes her head. "No buts, Suse. You chased Splinter for years. He's dead now. This isn't your case anymore but even if it was, it's basically over. So go in today, do what you have to, then come back home to us. Don't get sucked in."

I frown at her. I want to argue. The old, stubborn Susan would have argued. My nana used to call that the Irish in me. But I don't want to fight Lata. Besides, she's right. About everything.

Lata looks at me intently. "Okay?"

I sigh.

"Okay," I say.

"Promise," she says, taking my hands.

"I promise," I say, meaning it.

She squeezes my hands and gives me a smile before leaving the table to head off.

I sit for a moment.

I lift the mug to take a sip.

The coffee's gone cold.

Lata pops her head back in. "Oh, and don't forget dinner."

"I'm not sure how long I'll be downtown..." I start to say but she interrupts me with a stern look.

"It's Thanksgiving, Susan," she says.

"Oh," I reply. I'd forgotten. "Of course."

"Kajal and my folks are going to join us," she says. "Remember?"

Inwardly, I cringe.

Outwardly, I put my brave face on and smile. "I'll be here."

TEN

The FBI field office at 11000 Wilshire Boulevard in downtown Los Angeles looks strange. Even though I worked here for years, and the place hasn't changed much, if at all, it still feels different somehow. But I know it's not the place that's changed. I'm the one who's different. The Susan Parker who walked in here a year ago was a different woman from the Susan Parker walking in now. Wife to widow, hotshot agent to suspended, decorated, and hailed, to disgraced and controversial; life turns on a dime.

I recognize several familiar faces as I ride up in the elevator with other agents, most of whom either don't recognize me or don't want to engage. That suits me just fine. And yet, when I get off the elevator and walk through those glass doors, a familiar thrill courses through me. That much hasn't changed at least.

I'm just here to be debriefed, I'm not back on the job, I tell myself, but my stupid heart didn't get the memo. Some part of me is still that wide-eyed idealistic woman who walked through these doors almost a decade ago, fresh out of Quantico, and excited to be part of one of the most elite law enforcement agencies in the world. Hunting killers and criminals.

"Hey," Kayla Regis says, appearing by my side. "Let's head for the conference room."

"Look at you," I say in admiration.

Kayla's somehow found time to shower, change into a fresh suit, and redo her hair into a ponytail which only partly contains her dark curly hair.

She smiles. "Well, you look like shit."

We both laugh as we walk.

"Grab some winks?" she asks.

"A few," I say. "Your hair smells so good. Is that hairspray?"

Her dark eyes twinkle. "Shea butter. Just wanna give you a heads up. Gantry is really PO'd. Diaz heard him yelling at Ochoa an hour ago."

"The US attorney?" I frown. The FBI functions under the authority of the Justice Department and in coordination with the US attorney's office, which is the equivalent of what a district attorney does, but at the state and national level.

Kayla nods. "There's been a hailstorm of calls to-and-fro between Gantry's office, the OGC, the director, and the US attorney. Right now, he's sitting in with a dozen suits from the OGC and PR."

"The Office of General Counsel, I get," I say as we turn down a long corridor lined with doors on both sides, all leading to conference rooms of different sizes. "But why the public relation specialists? For the press conference?"

She stops at a door and pauses, her keycard in hand. "Diaz thinks it's because they're afraid the victims might sue."

"Sue whom?" I say.

Kayla shrugs. "Beats me."

She taps her keycard, and the door-lock light turns green. She pushes open the door for me to step through. "Go on in. I'll be back in a sec."

The first face I see in the empty conference room is Detective Seth. "Good morning, detective," I say as I take a seat opposite him.

We barely have a moment before the door opens and a stream of dark suits pour in, led by Deputy Director Connor Gantry. The conference room seats forty-six and by the time everyone's aboard, every seat is filled. My team ends up standing, taking up the wall behind me. Someone removes a chair to make room at the table for Chief Evidence Investigator Marisol Mancini, who's been in a wheelchair ever since she was shot by an unsub who returned unexpectedly to the scene while she was collecting evidence, six years ago. The crowded room hushes as Gantry stands up, his gray eyes as hard as stone as they sweep the table. They come to rest on me and he locks gazes for a moment before breaking it off. I can't read his expression but he sure as hell isn't happy.

I sense Naved's eyes on me, across the table, and exchange a glance. He glances one way then the other as if impressed by the turnout. If he's surprised, I'm completely gobsmacked. I expected to have a brief, cursory meeting with Gantry, be taken into a room to give my statement for the record, then leave. This looks like an all-hands-on-deck war briefing.

With his customary brusqueness, Gantry jumps right in without any preliminaries.

"DNA confirms the body recovered at the scene to be one Dr. Viktor Magnusson—thank you, Agent Mancini, for the quick turnaround. We've collected multiple other DNA samples and a considerable quantity of other forensic evidence from the scene—I believe the term Agent Mancini employed was 'boatloads'. Collection and searches are ongoing with the cooperation of local PD and volunteers. Due to the size of the farmhouse and the adjoining property, the collection process alone is expected to take at least another thirty-six hours. As for comparing biologicals against samples from the multiple victims rescued from the scene, that is where we have run into some complications. Special Counsel Thomas Matteo is here from our Office of General Counsel along with Deputy US Attorney Masaba Ibrahim to explain further."

The two lawyers address the room in tandem, alternating to explain that as of now we have no way to be certain of anything about the eleven individuals extracted from the scene. They caution us to avoid jumping to conclusions and continue to refer to all individuals as unsubs. Standard procedure so far. What's not standard is the part where they start to explain potential liability issues. Apparently, the lawyers have put their wise heads together and determined that there is a serious risk of some or all of the victims—I mean, unsubs—suing the Bureau.

"Could you elaborate on why we think that's a possibility, Miss Ibrahim?" Gantry asks.

In response, the deputy US attorney holds up a plastic evidence bag containing a laptop hard drive and a leather-bound notebook.

"The laptop found in the bedroom contains extensive video archives. These appear to be some variety of interactive sessions between the primary and the various unsubs. This diary appears to belong to the primary. It contains what seem to be notes on those sessions. Prima facie, the recordings, and these notes match the pattern of psychotherapy sessions. Dr. Magnusson was a practicing psychiatrist licensed to practice in New York, not here in California, but if some or all of these unsubs turn out to be his patients from back east, it raises questions of patient-doctor confidentiality. As such, we have been forced to instruct the task force to cease and desist with all further work on these materials, until the legal issues are sorted out."

"What does that mean exactly?" someone asks.

"It means these materials may be inadmissible in court and

anything we might get off them would be inadmissible, too," Gantry says. "Fruit of the poison tree."

This is followed by a moment of silence as everyone takes it in.

I want to ask a dozen questions but restrain myself. *I'm not really part of this, I'm just going to record my statement and go home,* I tell myself.

The PR team have a bunch of questions, all pertaining to how much of this information is going to be revealed to the media, what potential questions the media is likely to have, and how they're supposed to handle them.

"You already know the answer to that one," Gantry says curtly. "The words 'ongoing investigation' are your best friend."

"Are we identifying Dr. Magnusson as 'Splinter'?" someone in PR asks.

Gantry raises his hands to form invisible quote marks. "'Ongoing investigation.'"

PR doesn't look happy.

"His name's on the county land records," one of them says. "It's only a matter of time before some outlet looks that up and leaks it. We should get out in front of it."

Gantry stares at the person until they look down. "One thing I'm not going to do is make an inaccurate identification of one of the most widely reported serial killers in recent history. Like I've already said..."

He repeats the same two words, this time without the air quotes.

The meeting goes on for another hour, which mostly covers procedural matters. That's typical of Bureau meetings. One thing I don't miss is spending hours every day in meetings that seem to focus on everything but the actual cases I was investigating.

One announcement from Gantry that brings me a huge amount of relief is that all future work on the case will be handled out of the task force's workspace in Santa Carina Valley. The crime scene is based there, and the victims are housed at Silas MacKenna Hospital, which is also in SCV. So it only makes sense to operate out of the workspace set up in the old sheriff's station, only a few miles from both hospital and crime scene.

Naved and I exchange a glance and he catches my nod of approval. I'll spend less time commuting between SCV and LA and have more time to spend on the case.

And with Natalie, I remind myself with a twinge of guilt.

When the meeting breaks up, small groups form as each department and team discusses and debates the decisions of the 'powers that be' and how it impacts their ability to do their job.

I've only just started to converse with my team when the deputy director says, "Agent Parker. My office."

Naved comes up as Gantry strides past him without so much as a glance. He looks at me with raised eyebrows.

"Time for my close-up with Mr. DeMille," I say as I walk away.

I'm pretending to be flippant to undercut the stress I'm feeling. The last time I met with Gantry in his office, he informed me that he was taking me off the case permanently and that I was to go on indefinite mental health leave, effective immediately, as well as undergo mandatory therapy sessions with a Bureau therapist.

The elevator doors are closing as I approach. I can see Gantry's dark gray suit and a glimpse of his face. I call out to hold the car. He ignores me and lets the doors shut.

Not a good sign.

ELEVEN

I'm surprised to see Dr. Alamdar Sharif in Deputy Director Connor Gantry's office when I walk in. He's the Bureau-appointed therapist I've been seeing for the past year: thrice a week to begin with, then biweekly, and now once a week. He's sitting on the couch in the corner, intent on his phone screen. Gantry is seated behind his desk, looking at his computer screen. He offers me no greeting or invitation to sit.

"Dr. Sharif has pronounced you fit to return to active duty," Gantry says without preamble.

My stomach flips.

"Of course, you will still continue your weekly sessions, and you'll be expected to report any mental health issues to Dr. Sharif immediately. Am I clear?"

Before I can finish processing what this means, Dr. Sharif speaks up behind me. "I believe you're ready, Susan. But it's only appropriate that I inquire of you whether *you* believe you are ready."

Dr. Sharif is the softest spoken person I've ever met. His tone makes an odd counterpoint to Gantry's curt staccato.

"Ready?" I turn back to Gantry. "Sir, are you saying I'm cleared to resume?"

"Answer the question," Gantry says.

My head swirls with the implications. This is the exact opposite of what I was expecting. Rather than bring me in for a routine debriefing, Gantry wants me to come back to work! Of course. It all makes sense now. Why else would Gantry have let me sit in on the meeting earlier?

"I'm ready," I say.

Sharif nods slowly as if he expected this answer, but I see his eyes. He has that thoughtful look he gets during our sessions sometimes, like he's calculating the odds and isn't thrilled about the result.

Gantry removes my badge, ID, and Bureau-issued handgun from his drawer and shoves them across the desk. But as I reach for them, he holds up a palm.

My fingertips are literally on my shield. I can feel its molded surface under my fingertips.

"This is your one and only second chance, Parker," he says, staring at me. Even seated and using his indoor voice, he's still extremely intimidating. Being on the receiving end of Connor Gantry's stare is not a happy experience, yet he has every right. I screwed up; I know it, everyone on my team knows it, the whole fucking Bureau knows it. He doesn't need to spell it out: I fuck up again and I'm done for good. My career in law enforcement will be over. Nobody will ever hire me again.

"I understand, sir," I say.

He holds the stare a moment longer, searching for any sign of weakness, for the slightest chink in my armor. As recently as six months ago, I wouldn't have been able to withstand this X-ray scrutiny. But I've had time to seal those chinks and I return his gaze with a steady, unwavering look, brown eyes holding his gray.

He leans back, breaking off the stare, and I scoop up my credentials.

I hook on the badge and slip the ID into my jacket. The Glock Gen 5, I slip into my shoulder holster. I wore the empty holster when I put on the suit this morning, even though I had no expectation of filling it. It was just something I did out of habit, like keeping a wallet in one's back pocket even when it's empty.

Gantry comes out from behind his desk, thanking Dr. Sharif for coming in. The therapist shakes his hand and leaves.

Gantry grabs the door, keeping it from closing, and looks back at me.

"You coming, Parker?" he asks with his trademark edge.

"Where to, sir?" I ask.

"Where do you think?" he answers curtly.

As we come out of his office, his executive assistant stops him with some urgent paperwork that urgently requires his signature. Gantry purses his lips but starts signing. Looking at the yellow tags bristling from the thick document, I guess I have a couple of minutes. I use it to visit the restroom.

Thankfully, it's empty.

I splash cold water on my face and lean on the edge of the washbasin, staring at my dripping face.

"What the fuck did I just do?" I ask my reflection.

TWELVE

My past crashes into me head-on as I step off the elevator at Silas Mackenna Hospital.

In the form of Dr. Keller.

It's a shock to see his face with the crease in his cheek that makes him look like he's perpetually wearing a sardonic smile. As a kid, one of my foster families used to watch old movies on VHS. A lot of them were indie black-and-white movies. Some of those were by the actor-filmmaker John Cassavates, best known for his more mainstream work in movies like *The Dirty Dozen*. Dr. Keller has more than a passing resemblance to Cassavates, in his long, lupine face as well as in his below average height, only a couple inches taller than me. But to me, he looms larger than life, forever associated with my worst day as an FBI agent, and one of the hardest as a woman.

"Dr. Keller," Connor Gantry says smoothly.

"Deputy Director," Keller replies.

The men exchange a few polite words, but I hear none of them. I'm doing my best not to meet Keller's eyes. Even though he's not looking at me directly, I can tell he's still aware of me in his peripheral vision. I can *feel* his gaze, like roaches creeping over my skin.

The brief pleasantries exchanged, Keller enters the elevator, stepping past me.

"Agent Parker," he says, almost as a whisper as he glides past.

"Dr. Keller," I say, almost by rote.

I resist the urge to turn around to give him one last look. Instead, I walk away, resisting, too, the urge to run, and feel his eyes on me long after the elevator door whisks shut.

Gantry says nothing about the brief encounter. We already knew Keller is on call here, since this is where I first came to recruit him as a consultant for the Splinter case. The restraining order expired several months ago, and we both know that if I so much as breathe wrongly in Keller's direction, he could have me tossed out faster than I can catch my breath. There's nothing to be said. We walk the rest of the way to the security room in silence.

The security room at Silas MacKenna Hospital in Santa Carina Valley is a full house.

Apart from the two hospital security guards sitting before the bank of screens, there's the four core members of my team, Detective Naved Seth, Deputy Director Gantry, the head of psychiatry and behavioral health, the dean of the hospital, the deputy US attorney, and FBI special counsel. We look like we're divided into teams with our matching outfits: the security guards in gray and black, the two doctors in white coats over light-colored suits, the three lawyers in their charcoal-gray suits, and the seven of us in our G-man black suits.

Dr. Moshe Singer, the head of psychiatry, has just finished telling us that the eleven are responsive in every way except for oral communication. He also informs us that they're severely dehydrated, under-nourished, and display all the classic signs of sensory deprivation: over-reaction to sounds, sensitivity to light, overall fragility. But, as he points out in his chatty, oversharing way, they are all taking nourishment willingly, some quite enthusiastically. He points out one patient on the monitors, telling us how that lady has been making extravagant demands for gourmet meals even after it was explained to her that she needs to reintroduce rich foods gradually to her system to avoid getting sick.

"Just before your arrival," Dr. Singer says, "she was demanding we serve her steak Diane, medium-rare, with a red Chianti and a side of truffles."

He chuckles, clearly enjoying the moment.

When nobody else responds, he loses the smile, tempering his tone to match the room. "What I am saying here is, despite the ordeal they have all been through, none of them appear to have suffered irreparable physical damage and the prognosis for a full recovery is excellent."

Gantry furrows his brow. "Dr. Singer, I thought you said the patients aren't communicating verbally. So how are they making these demands?"

Dr. Singer shakes his head. "No, no, Director Gantry. I said that they are not communicating *orally*. On the other hand, *verbally* they cannot seem to *stop* communicating! I have not seen patients writing so much since we had that famous author last autumn."

This time, he manages to tamp down his own grin before it starts, which must be difficult for him. I sympathize. His bonhomie is probably an effective bedside manner; it's just not very effective in a room full of government suits all of whom probably take their jobs too seriously.

"Could we see these notes, Dr. Singer?" I ask politely.

Gantry says, "Special Agent in Charge Susan Parker will be handling the investigation."

That's Gantry's version of a formal introduction.

I notice Ibrahim and Matteo, the two lawyers, exchanging a

look when Gantry makes the announcement. They both avoid looking at me directly, but I don't need to be a mind-reader to know they have concerns.

The two doctors and I both acknowledge each other as the dean steps out for a moment, returning with a medical supplies box. David Moskovitch intercepts and takes the box from him, his gloves already on. He's always been our team's expert on evidence collection and analysis, and chain of custody—and he's a whiz at paperwork.

"From here on out, we'll set up a system wherein all notes are to be stored in evidence bags by one of our agents posted here," I say, addressing the instruction to David as well as the doctors. "We'll also need to be copied into all tests you run on these eleven patients and receive real-time updates on their condition."

I entrust that task to Ramon, who will handle the data and make sure it's stored in a secure digital lockbox on a Bureau server. He was hand-picked by me from the FBI cyber crime unit when I was promoted to SAC and given charge of the Splinter investigation.

The doctors catch us up on the tests they've run so far, getting into far more pathological detail than we need.

"I'm sorry to interrupt, doctor," I say, "but if I'm right, then what I'm hearing from you is that apart from the malnutrition, dehydration, and vitamin deficiencies, they're pretty much physically unharmed. Would that be a fair summary?"

"There are a few cuts and bruises, a sprained wrist, similar minor abrasions and contusions, yes," Dr. Singer says, "some of which appear to be accidental. I believe they were all confined to small, dark rooms—is that not the case, Special Agent in Charge, Ms...?"

"Parker. Yes. They were kept locked in small cells, eight feet by ten feet, with no light source inside the cells," I say.

"And you do not know how long they were confined in

these cells. Or, for that matter, how often they were provided nutrition and hydration, that is correct, yes, Agent Parker?" Dr. Singer asks.

"As of now, no," I say. "We were hoping the patients themselves might be able to provide that information."

"Of course, of course," Dr. Singer says, noncommittally. "As I am saying, the patients are physically presenting with minor injuries," he goes on, more careful with his words now that the hospital's lawyer is in the room, "but from what we have been informed of the circumstances in which they were confined, they have all undergone a horrific experience. Mere external examination and pathological testing cannot possibly bring out understanding of what psychological trauma they might have undergone. This serial killer you call 'Splinter', yes, he was a psychiatrist, you say?"

I nod. "Magnusson was licensed in New York State although his license expired two years ago," I say, very aware of the Bureau in-house counsel Matteo watching me to make sure I stick to the official script.

"In which case, mental trauma may be doubly complicated," Dr. Singer says. "If this Magnusson was, in fact, the therapist for these unfortunate individuals, then his exploitation of his position to gain these patients' trust only to forcibly abduct and imprison them would be an unimaginable shock. Who knows what these victims have been subjected to, Agent Parker? As you can see, we have admitted them to the psychiatric ward for this reason, yes? It is much too soon to say how deep and lasting the damage is caused by their experiences."

"What exactly are you saying, Dr. Singer?" I ask.

Singer says, "We will require much more further observation in order to fully evaluate."

That sounds like exactly the kind of thing a lawyer would tell him to say. I look at Gantry, then at Ibrahim and Matteo, hoping one of them will chip in. But they seem more intent on their phones and the monitors at the moment. I can't tell if they're deliberately avoiding participating, or just momentarily distracted.

"Let me ask you a direct question, Dr. Singer," I say. "To save us all time. When would it be possible for us to interview these eleven patients?"

Singer hems and haws before finally coming back with, "Once our evaluation is fully complete." He glances at the hospital's lawyer who nods once. "Yes, yes. Once it is complete, we will be in touch."

I can sense my team's frustration. It's a shared feeling. "Doctor, you do understand that our whole case against Magnusson rests on the testimony of these eleven patients. Without them, we basically don't have a case. Do you see that?"

Singer is about to answer when Melmed, the hospital lawyer, speaks up. "Dr. Singer and the hospital's number one priority is the patients' welfare. As he has already explained, a detailed evaluation of their condition is currently in progress. Once that is complete, someone will be in touch."

I spread my hands, attempting a smile. "How about a little cooperation? All we're asking here is if we could have a few minutes with each of the patients."

Melmed locks eyes with me. "The hospital cannot in good conscience permit you to interrogate patients under our care and risk compounding their trauma."

"Who said anything about 'interrogation'?" I say, trying to keep my tone pleasant and the smile on my face. "Any communication would be consensual, of course. All I'm asking is that you inquire if they would be willing to have a brief introductory conversation with me. You're welcome to be present, of course."

Melmed shakes her head slowly. "I don't think you're getting my point, SAC Parker. That is not possible at this time."

I try one more time. "Look, counselor. This is a very big case

—it's making national headlines, as you probably know. We can't just sit back and wait on it. I'm sure you understand that?"

Melmed looks at me without any change in expression. "SAC Parker, we are well aware of the circumstances and the high-profile nature of the case. That is your purview. Our only concern is the patients' health, both physical and mental. When we are confident that they are ready to speak, we shall be in touch. That's all I have to say."

Melmed says something to Singer and the dean, both of whom move toward the door.

I look at Gantry, who is standing with arms folded, looking not at the monitors but at a point on the wall just above them. He's in his listening mode, which is another way of saying he's watching and judging me. I push aside any anxiety I have about that, and say to him quietly, "Sir, we need a way around this roadblock. The investigation's dead without those patients."

Gantry glances at me briefly, then continues staring at the wall, arms still folded. "That sounds like a 'you' problem, Parker. It's your case now."

Kayla widens her eyes and mouths "WTF?" at me—she's standing behind Gantry so only the rest of the team and I can see her.

Once everyone leaves, and only my team and I are left in the room, the mood changes instantly.

"That was stone cold!" Kayla says. "Like, he *burned* you, girl!"

Ramon shakes his head, agreeing with her while decrying Gantry's attitude.

"He's not going to make it easy for you," Brine says.

David holds up the medical supplies box with the scribbled notes. "We still have these. Want me to run them for prints? I checked and the doctors and staff were all gloved, masked, and suited, but I can get their employee intake files from the hospital's HRD and eliminate their prints. We might get a match."

"We need more than that," I say. "We need DNA. Didn't we swab all eleven when we extracted them from the basement?"

"There's been some lawsuits over that," Brine says. "In LA County in general, I mean, which includes Santa Carina Valley. People objecting to the taking of DNA samples without the subject's permission. But the Supreme Court's pretty clear on that one: DNA collection is legally valid and admissible."

That's good enough for me. "David, let's get hold of that DNA and run it against CODIS, FDIS, FDDU, every national database you can think of. Stat."

David touches his forehead with one finger, his version of a salute.

Kayla steps out and returns after a minute. "No sign of Gantry and the lawyers. Maybe they left?"

I shrug. "We're not getting anywhere here, let's move out."

I take one last look at the monitors. I have a sinking feeling.

My first hour on the case and I'm stymied by a major roadblock.

No, not just a roadblock. A brick wall. Without access to the eleven, the video recordings of their 'sessions' with Magnusson, the psychiatrist's notebooks, we have no case, no hard evidence to go on. We're dead in the water before we even start.

THIRTEEN

Out in the hallway, I look around at the others.

"Where's Ramon?" I ask.

"He's still in there," Brine says.

A moment later, Ramon comes out holding his tablet and with a sly grin on his face. He has one of those folding tablets that looks like a large phone when closed.

"Uh-oh," Kayla says. "Fox up to his old tricks."

"Wile E. Coyote," I say, teasing, "what've you done this time?"

In response, Ramon unfolds the tablet and shows me the screen. It's divided into a dozen thumbnail images, each a live feed off the surveillance cameras covering the eleven patients. The twelfth image looks down on an unoccupied room.

He's hacked into the hospital's surveillance system and mirrored their feeds.

David whistles softly.

I aim a fist at Ramon's shoulder, landing a feather punch. "You golden, golden man."

I look at the thumbnails. They're almost identical except for the postures of the eleven patients. Single rooms, bed, window, nightstand, couch. Some of them are lying down, asleep or awake, some sitting up in bed, on the edge of the bed, looking out the window. Not much to see. A nurse comes into one room as I'm watching, says something to the patient, a woman who points to the water jug on her nightstand. The nurse takes the empty jug and leaves.

Something stirs in my mind. A faint glimmer.

"So, what next, chief?" Brine asks. "Back to base?"

I hold up a finger. I'm thinking.

The nurse comes back into the room, places the jug on the nightstand, leaves. The female patient pours herself a glass with a fairly steady hand and drinks water.

"Okay," I say to myself and start walking.

The others follow me as I walk down the hallway, turn right at the intersection, and approach another intersection where it splits into two hallways. One leads back to a nurse's station, the other to a hallway with six doors on either side. Two SCVPD cops are sitting on chairs at the head of this hallway. That's where the eleven are being kept.

"Brine," I say. "Could you go to the vending machine and bring me two cups of coffee? Gourmet if they have it."

Brine heads down the hallway without asking why.

Kayla looks at me. "What're you up to, boss?"

"We need to talk to those patients," I say.

Ramon clears his throat. "What about the legal issues?"

"They're legal issues, let the lawyers handle them."

"What about the hospital saying they wouldn't allow us to 'interrogate' them?" David says.

"We won't. Interrogate them, I mean. We won't even talk to them."

Kayla looks at me doubtfully.

"Pinky swear," I say, raising my little finger to show her.

Brine returns with two steaming cups of coffee. "Best they have."

I walk up to the cops on duty. They're already aware of us and are on their feet.

"Special Agent in Charge Susan Parker," I say, flashing my ID as I check their name badges. "I'm in charge of the Splinter investigation. Officer Torres, Officer Morgan. You guys have been on duty since early this morning, haven't you?"

They both nod. "Due to be relieved at three," Torres says.

"We were both coming off night shifts," Morgan grumbles. "Got pulled in. On Thanksgiving!"

"This might help a bit," I say, taking the cups from Brine and handing them over.

"Mighty nice of you," Morgan says.

"Appreciate it," Torres says.

"So, you're watching over our eleven victims, right?" I say as they take tentative sips.

"We can't let you through, SAC Parker," Morgan says. "Orders from the chief."

"I'm aware," I say. "I just need you to do a welfare check on the patients."

"We do that every hour on the hour," Torres says.

I make a show of looking at the time. "Close enough. I need you to do one right now. I need to know they're all safe and well before I leave the hospital. It's just routine."

They exchange looks. Torres shrugs. "I guess we can do that." He says to his partner, "Morgan, you stay here. It's my turn anyway."

"Just one moment," I say as Torres puts down his cup. "Officer Torres? When you do your hourly welfare check, do you speak to the patients?"

He shrugs. "Just to ask how they're doing."

"So you say something like, 'How're you doing? Everything okay?' Something like that?"

He nods. "Just like that."

"I need you to ask them one more thing this time."

I tell him what I want him to say.

"So you basically want us to ask each of them if they'd like to speak to someone?" Morgan asks.

"Yup, that's it," I say.

Torres scratches the back of his neck as he looks at his partner. Morgan shrugs. "Sounds okay to me."

"Sure," Torres says. "But you guys have to stay right here, okay?"

"Like my feet are in cement," I say.

Morgan sips his coffee while we wait. Kayla keeps him engaged in small talk.

We don't have long to wait. Torres returns surprisingly quickly. After glancing around to make sure nobody else is watching, he hands me what I need. David intercepts and takes it from him, putting it into evidence bags.

"I owe you one, Officer Torres," I say, taking out one of my old SAC cards and handing it to him. "If you ever think of applying to the FBI, hit me up and I'll give you a few tips."

"Actually—" he starts to say, but we're already turned around.

"Text me," I call out as I walk away.

We turn left this time, heading back to the nurses' station and the elevator banks.

I manage to hold out until we're in the parking lot approaching the FBI mobile investigative unit van which David and Ramon drove here. Then I pump my fist in the air and let out a whoop of joy that startles a pair of young Gen-Z-ers in a parked car.

"Sorry," I tell them, then climb into the van. The rest of the team pile in.

David slides the door shut as I clap my hands together in a Matthew McConaughey imitation. "Awright, awright, awright!"

"Just for the record, I still worry this is going to get us into trouble," Brine says.

"That's good, Brine," I say. "You worry about it now, I'll deal with it when it happens."

I make a grabby hands gesture at David. "Let's see what we have."

David has the medical supplies box on his lap. He takes out the plastic baggies in which he's put the Post-it notes Officer Torres gave him. He looks at it for a long moment.

I make the grabby hands action again. "Come on, David. Give it up."

He looks at me with a distinctive lack of expression that I know from experience is, in fact, an expression. Then he hands me a Post-it note with two words scrawled on it in Magic Marker.

I stare at it for a moment.

"What does it say?" Naved asks, leaning forward on the bench seat.

"Give me the rest," I say to David.

He hands me another one, then another, then he gives me all the rest in a pile of baggies.

"What?" Kayla asks. "Give it up, girl. You're killing us here!"

I hold up one of the eleven Post-it notes at random.

"They all say the same thing."

They all lean in, crowding into the center of the van to see the note clearly. We look like a football team in a huddle.

DR. KELLER is printed on each and every one of the eleven notes.

"Dr. Keller?" Ramon says. "That piece of shit?"

"You've got to be kidding me," Kayla says.

Suddenly, the confined space is too close, too crowded for me to take. My head starts to spin, vision begins to blur. I shove open the van door and step out. I realize I'm hyperventilating and bend over, resting my hands on my thighs, trying to slow it down, calm myself.

Everybody else spills out after me, expressing their concern for me. I hear Kayla say softly, "Girl needs a minute."

I finally start to get back some element of control: my breathing slows, heart rate cuts back. Except, do we ever really get any control over our lives? Or is it just an illusion that helps us keep on keeping on, surviving one day at a time?

"Hey," says a voice beside me. "You okay?"

I nod at Naved. "Just needed some air."

He squats on the concrete, looking at me but not touching. "You need someone to give you a check-up, we're in the right place."

I manage a smile. "I'm good, thanks. Just need a minute."

As I straighten up, he stands up, too. He's watching me closely, genuine concern in his eyes.

"So what happens now?" he says. "I'm guessing that Dr. Keller isn't going to be too keen to cooperate with you again."

"You guess right," I say. "He'd probably rather die a long, painful death than have anything to do with me. But let's put that aside for the moment and focus on the real problem."

Naved frowns. "I thought Keller was the problem?"

"He's the lesser of the two problems," I say.

"And the larger one is?" he asks.

"Without those patients slash victims talking to us, we don't have a case."

Naved glances back at the hospital building. "We just heard a bunch of reasons why we can't talk to them. Apart from the lecture in legalese that your boss and the two bigshot lawyers gave us back at your field office."

"And yet, talk to them we must," I say, hands on my hips as I look around, squinting against the low afternoon sun as I try to figure something out.

Naved looks at me.

"What?" I ask. "Why are you looking at me like that?"

"You're not the kind of person who always colors inside the lines, are you, SAC Parker?"

I smile at him slowly. I feel a lot better now that I'm thinking about ways to get around the problem rather than focusing on the problem itself. My momentary panic attack over Keller has passed—or to be more accurate, I'm in the process of convincing myself that Keller isn't the elephant-sized roadblock he seems to be at first glance.

"No, sir," I say to Naved, grinning openly now. "I sure as hell ain't."

FOURTEEN

Seventy-eight minutes late for Thanksgiving dinner, and I'm still sitting in my car.

Our tucked-away back lane is quiet and devoid of much traffic. As seems to be the tradition now, most houses already have their holiday decorations up. I remember my great-aunt used to complain that if people kept putting up the decorations earlier each year, then one day they'd be up all year round.

That is literally true of our next-door neighbor, a reclusive man whose front yard is a tragic wasteland of overgrown weeds and whose car is little more than a rotting rust heap on deflated tires. Yet he has a long green stocking with blue and red trim dangling from his front porch. It's the worse for weather, faded and frayed, but it hangs out there all year round. Sadly hopeful. Maybe he's confused Santa with the UPS delivery driver.

All the lights are on in our place.

No decorations yet—call me a traditionalist but I follow the practice of putting them up on the first day of Advent, which is the fourth Sunday before Christmas, and happens to fall on the Sunday after next, December 3rd this year.

The flimsy drapes are drawn in the living room, and I can see silhouettes of people moving around inside. My mother-in-law Aishwarya's classical profile is unmistakable as is her ramrod-straight back and lean, tall form. My father-in-law Kundan's more aptly middle-aged silhouette is visible too, his large jowly face and mane of long shaggy hair equally distinctive. There are others in there—at least another man and a woman, and of course Lata and Natalie—but only Aishwarya and Kundan are standing by the window.

My phone pings again, for the nth time.

Lata again.

Where are you?

I sigh and unbuckle my seatbelt. Time to face the music.

For a moment I pause, my hand on the doorknob, wishing I'd asked Naved to join us. I want to talk about the Splinter case, not engage in pointless chitchat with my dead husband's family. My head is bursting with thoughts, ideas, possibilities, theories. These first hours are so precious, it feels a crime to spend them on what seems an arcane American ritual invented by white puritan settlers.

But that would be thoughtless and selfish of me. Those people in there are Natalie's family, too. And Lata's. And that makes them my people, my family. Besides, it wouldn't hurt to spend a couple hours away from the case. We've hit a blockade and while I'm determined to find a way around it, I haven't found it yet. I was diagnosed with autism and ADHD when I was twelve and one of the symptoms is my obsessive-compulsive tendencies. I need to back off.

Besides, I need a little time to assess Naved Seth, too. My first impressions of him are overwhelmingly positive but we've barely known each other for twenty-four hours. Again, because of the way my brain is built, I tend to experience instant likes and dislikes for people I've just met. Even with Amit, it was love and trumpets at first sight. With work relationships, I need to be more careful. Being in the Bureau, I know the dangers of trusting blindly. Being back on the job has made me realize how much I need this, to be FBI Agent Susan Parker, hunting down serial killers and assorted violent killers. I can't afford to screw it up again.

Aishwarya's is the first face that meets me when I enter. My mother-in-law is standing by the door in one of her designer haute couture slinky gowns, looking as svelte and majestic as a Roman statue, one arm pressed to her waist, the other holding a flute of sparkling white wine. It would have to be top-of-the-shelf for her to even sniff it. She probably brought the bottle along because Lata and I certainly can't afford champagne.

With typical Aishwarya snobbery, she looks at me and through me, offering no hint of recognition or greeting, and continues the conversation she was having with a man with a trim beard and an expensive suit whom I've only met once before. Aishwarya's brother, Amit's uncle, glances at me cursorily, giving me the quick once-over that older men always seem to give younger women, and then continues talking to his sister. He confirms my earlier impression that he's pretty much a masculine version of his sister, but with more money, power, and chauvinism.

"Hello! Here she is!"

A rousing warm welcome greets me as Kundan approaches, setting his whisky glass down and enfolding me in a bear hug.

"So good to see you, Susan, bete," my father-in-law says in his rumbling tone. "We are all waiting for you."

Kundan, with his fleshy round Punjabi face, unabashedly undyed gray hair, spreading midriff, and hearty laughter, is poles apart from his wife in every sense. He's dressed in a carelessly elegant polo shirt, jeans, and sneakers. The first time I met him, he had just retired from a long career as a corporate 'automaton', as he called it, and his first act was to throw out every suit, formal shirt, trousers, and any other officewear in his wardrobe and replace them with jeans, Hawaiian bush shirts, tees, Bermudas, flipflops, and sandals. I'm betting that the polo tee and sneakers are a concession to Aishwarya's insistence on 'proper dress'.

"How are you doing?" he asks me now with genuine concern in his kindly brown eyes. "We saw the news about the arrest. You made quite the splash! Congratulations."

"It wasn't exactly an arrest, papaji," I say, using the affectionate term that Amit himself used.

"You rescued so many victims also. Eleven, no? What a wonder. We are all proud of you."

The "we" rings a little hollow since both Aishwarya and her brother—what's his name? Sujit? Sumeet?—are continuing their conversation while looking at something on a foldable screen. But that's hardly Kundan's fault.

"You're sweet for saying that, papaji," I say, giving him a half-hug. "Give me a minute."

When I turn around, I'm face to face with Lata, whose forehead has a tiny wrinkle.

"Where were you?" she signs silently.

"I'm so, so, so sorry," I sign back, then join my palms in a namaste. The beauty of the Indian gesture is its versatility: it can be used as a greeting, a prayer, an apology, a request for forgiveness, a gesture of humility. "Did you guys eat yet?" I sign.

"Obviously not!" she signs back. "We've been waiting for you."

"Let's eat then. N's up in her room? I'll get her then help you with the food."

"I can manage the food. Just talk to Natalie, she's upset."

My heart lurches in my chest as I head upstairs. I hate disappointing my daughter, even if it's just being late for dinner.

I press the button by Natalie's bedroom door that makes a light flash inside, the visual equivalent of a knock.

Natalie is sitting up in her bed, browsing on her tablet. As I come closer, she turns it face down quickly, but not before I catch a glimpse of a news story with a file picture of Magnusson when he was alive. My heart thumps. If she's been looking at the news stories, she's probably seen the picture of Amit. I curse those damn asses at SCVPD. My seven-year-old daughter doesn't deserve to be confronted with a picture of her dead dad lying in a pool of his blood. But this is the world we live in now: everything everywhere all at once, online.

"Hey, sweetie," I sign, pretending to ignore the tablet for now. "I'm so sorry I'm late. How're you doing?"

"Were you chasing that bad man?" she asks, frowning anxiously. "The one you got the call about last night at dinner?"

I smile. "Didn't have to chase him. He was already dead."

Her frown eases but she still looks unconvinced. "You didn't have to fight him?"

"No, sweetie, I didn't fight anybody."

"So that's it? The bad guy's dead? You got him, right? It's over?"

I hesitate, wanting to explain, then decide against it. I want to erase that worried frown. "Right, sweetie. He's dogmeat."

She giggles at that. "Dogmeat? Like in a can?"

"Yup. He's in the can! Kaput! Done for. Finito!"

I tickle her as I emphasize each word, getting louder with each one. She bursts out laughing, squirming until she's about to fall off the bed. I grab her and swing her upside down, hugging her waist as I spin around, the way I've done since she was a toddler.

"Faster! Faster!" she manages to sign to me upside down.

Spinning makes me dizzy, and we both end up collapsing in

a heap on the carpet. I spot a pile of clothes and toys shoved under her bed.

"What's this?" I say with exaggerated emphasis. "Did the raccoons do this again?"

When she was a toddler, a family of raccoons terrorized the neighborhood, turning over trash cans and slipping into houses through pet doors to raid refrigerators and pantries. Terrorized might be a strong word since they never did any real harm, just made a whole lot of mess. Natalie, all of three, heard about these shenanigans and when we began trying to get her to pick up her toys and clothes, she would sometimes skip the chore. When caught out later, she claimed that raccoons were responsible.

She giggles now, pretending to be dizzier than she's actually feeling. "Yup!" she signs.

"Uh oh," I say. "Them danged raccoons have gotta be taught a lesson. What we gonna do about it, kiddo?"

She pretends to think, resting her chin on her palm and tapping her cheek. "I know!" she signs. "Let's leave some candy out for them. Then maybe they'll put the toys and stuff back in their proper places!"

"Ha ha ha," I say. "Nice try, kid, but no cigar."

She makes a face. "I don't want a cigar!"

"Nobody really wants a cigar, kid, except maybe Arnold Schwarzenegger. It's just something people say."

She frowns. "Who's Arnold Schwarzenegger?"

I sigh. "Kid, you make me feel old!"

We go down to dinner a few minutes later, still full of good spirits.

The good mood doesn't last long.

As per Kapoor family tradition, Aishwarya ignores me completely over dinner, focusing only on her daughters and her brother, with the occasional condescending instruction to her husband: *Pass the turkey to Sujit; serve Kajal more rice, she's hardly taken any; Kundan, go easy on that sauce and stuffing, remember your cholesterol; Sujit, you must try this okra—I showed Lata how to make it like this; Lata, bete, you've outdone yourself this time, it's your best turkey roast ever; Natalie, why aren't you eating? You need to eat well to grow up big and strong, bete! Here, take some more turkey. Doesn't your mother feed you anything? Look at her, Kundan, practically skin and bone.*

This last is willfully intended as an insult to my parenting. The barbs were frequent enough even while Amit was alive, although he never let her get away with them—it led to some spectacular showdowns between mother and son—but they've been flying fast and furious this past year. There were times when I actually wondered aloud to my therapist, Dr. Sharif, why in God's name I had gone and attacked Dr. Keller instead of my mother-in-law who surely deserved it more! I'd swear he actually chuckled at that, but hid it behind his notebook before I could be sure.

Iceberg, I remind myself now. *I am an iceberg.*

I ignore the monster-in-law and try to make conversation with Kundan instead. "How's Delhi, papaji? Lata said you guys just flew in this week."

"Hot as a bloody furnace," Kundan says, "when it isn't pouring cats and dogs. There used to be a time that Delhi was either hot or cold with a little wet in between. Now, the gods play hockey with the weather whenever they feel like it!"

"Climate change," Lata says. "Happening all over. We've had a helluva wildfire season this year."

"I was just telling Aish about that," Sujit says in his sonorous voice. He has that weirdly seductive way of saying even the most mundane things. Whether it's because of his famous habit for dating Pretty Young Things half his age or just his Silicon Valley creeper style, I don't know, but he gives me the willies. I feel glad he's not seated beside Natalie; he has that oily, untrustworthy aura about him. The fact that he's halfway to being a billionaire doesn't impress me one bit. There's also the fact that Amit was never too close to his uncle—he never spoke about it, but I always had the impression he'd seen or heard something when he was younger that made him keep his distance from Sujit.

He talks about the wildfires and the amount of property damage it's caused, about celebrity and movie star friends who've lost their multi-million-dollar beachfront mansions and lavish ranch houses to the flames. I can't listen to this dross anymore and cut him off mid-sentence.

"Insurance will cover those rich and famous peeps," I say, "but think of all the people who can't even afford insurance. The ones struggling from paycheck to paycheck. The homeless. The animals displaced. The pets who couldn't be evacuated in time. Like those poor horses."

Natalie signs to me: "What horses, Mom? What happened to the horses?"

I kick myself mentally for having opened my mouth. "Oh, they were just really unlucky, sweetie."

"Well, I think anyone who can't even afford insurance doesn't deserve to own a house," Aishwarya says primly, sipping her champagne. "As for the homeless, that might be the best solution for the problem, don't you think, Sujit?"

"They're a bloody nuisance," Sujit says, hacking off another generous chunk of turkey and putting it onto his plate. "Should round the lot up and deport them."

"Where, Uncle Sujit?" Kajal says unexpectedly.

Aishwarya looks at her youngest daughter in surprise. Sujit stops in the act of forking up turkey. Even Kundan looks up from his okra. On the handful of occasions that the family has been able to drag Kajal away from her coding cave in Pasadena, she's almost always silent, speaking only the bare minimum, and only when spoken to. It's the first time I've heard her voice a question that sounds like an opinion.

"What was that, Kajal?" Sujit asks, looking puzzled.

Kajal tears into him. "Where would you deport the homeless to? I mean, they're American citizens, too. Just like you and all your rich friends are, aren't they? In fact, most of them are probably born here, descended from generations of Americans. Not immigrants like us. A good number of them are probably descended from slaves, brought here by force from Africa to help the illegal European settlers cultivate the lands they stole from the Native Americans, who are the actual owners of this country. So where would you deport these poor, homeless people to?"

"Kajal," Sujit says, putting down his knife and fork, "let's not make this political."

"But it is, isn't it?" Kajal says, clearly on a roll. "It's all about politics and power, wealth and race. That's what it's always about for men like you. As long as you get what you want, you don't give a damn about the damage you cause to the world. That's why we're facing climate change today, because of men like you."

"Kajal," Aishwarya snaps. "You can't talk to your uncle like that. Apologize at once."

Kajal glares at her mother. She's all of twenty-eight and as bright as a laser, brilliant at what she does, earning more than Lata and me and Amit combined last year, probably a lot more by now. But Aishwarya talks to her like she's a troubled teenager getting out of hand.

"I'm sorry I was born into this family," she says, shoving her chair back. She throws down her napkin and walks away. Through the kitchen, I see her slide open the back door and step into our backyard, then slide it shut again.

There's a brief, awkward silence following my younger sister-in-law's abrupt exit. Then, as usual, Aishwarya takes charge again like the whipcracker she is. She resumes the conversation, switching smoothly to another topic.

I start to get up. "I should go check on Kajal."

Kundan puts his hand on mine, nodding to me to remain seated. "Give her some space. I will speak to her."

I smile. Thank God for Kundan.

The little flareup has got Natalie interested in the topic du jour. She asks Kundan questions about the weather in India, the country of her ancestors and one she's not visited yet. I facilitate by translating her signs for Kundan. He tells her about the unseasonal showers and sweltering summer temperatures in early spring and autumn, the awful air quality and smoke haze caused by the ancient practice of hazing in farmlands in neighboring states.

He even manages to make Natalie laugh with a joke about how just last week he was sweating so much, he thought he would melt and disappear!

Aishwarya is visibly upset about Kajal's outburst as I can see from her sideways glances at the back window. Kajal is visible, pacing the backyard as she talks to someone on her phone.

"Must be talking to her therapist," Aishwarya says derisively.

"Nothing wrong with that, Ma," Lata says in a quiet tone.

"We all need someone to talk to from time to time," I add, taking my cue from Lata.

"Nonsense!" Aishwarya fumes. "Ever since Kajal began going to them, all she does is swallow pills. This lithium, that fluoxetine, citalopram, sertraline. First this one doesn't work, so try that one instead, then that one, and then another. What is she? A guinea pig?"

Kundan makes a visible effort at turning the conversation to something more appropriate for a family dinner. He asks Natalie how she's finding art camp, what her hobbies are, her friends. Natalie is always happy to wax eloquent and replies enthusiastically.

"It is very good to see her doing so well," Kundan says to me as an aside after Natalie finishes.

"She's awesome," I say. "She's really taken to art as a means of self-expression. You should see what she does with gouache. It's pretty amazing."

From the other end of the table, Aishwarya makes sympathetic sounds. "Poor thing. How difficult it must be. Studying alongside other, normal children. It must be so painful."

Lata looks sharply at her mother. "Mom! Natalie is just as 'normal' as any other child. She's actually brighter than most kids her age. She's ranked in the ninety-sixth percentile in her grade."

Aishwarya pats her daughter's hand. "Of course, of course. Teachers must be feeling sorry for her. So kind of them."

Lata glares at her but holds her tongue.

She exchanges a glance with me.

I sign to her, "Iceberg!"

She signs back, "Makes me so mad, can't imagine how you deal."

I shrug and sign back, "Actually, I think I'm getting used to her."

"For real?" she signs, looking surprised.

"Sure. Just give me another couple centuries. Actually, make it a couple millennia, and no guarantees."

Lata laughs out loud.

Kundan smiles in solidarity. Natalie grins at me. I wink at her. Sujit excuses himself to take a call. Aishwarya glowers and glares and sulks.

Later, changing Natalie into her pajamas, she says, "We didn't say thanks."

I pull her favorite pajama top down over her head, adjust it, and say, "That's because we're all immigrants, none of us were born here, so we don't really celebrate Thanksgiving the way other Americans do. We just use it as an occasion to get together with family."

"I'm born here," she says indignantly.

I put my hand to my mouth. "Oh my. You're right! How did I forget that? I guess I wasn't around when you were born."

She giggles. "Silly. I came out of your stomach."

"Did you really? Sometimes, I think you just fell out of the sky into my lap."

"Mom! You're talking crazy. Babies don't just fall from the sky. They come out of women's stomachs!"

"Oh, yeah!" I say. "I forgot that. But you know what?"

"What?" Natalie asks, enjoying the banter.

"We can still give thanks, just the two of us, right here, right now."

"Yes!" she says, delighted.

She thumps down on the edge of her bed and takes my hands in hers, then closes her eyes. She looks so adorable, I can't resist kissing her on her forehead.

"Mom!" she admonishes me. "Focus!"

I straighten my face and half-close my eyes, too.

Natalie says in a solemn tone, "I'd like to give thanks for my amazing mom, who catches bad guys and locks them away forever, and for my awesome aunt who's a soldier who goes to foreign countries and fights bad guys there to keep America safe. And for my art teacher Patrick who always encourages me to follow my rainbow. And for my friends, and for giving us such good weather here in sunny California—except for the wildfires, the wildfires aren't nice, they're scary and they burn down houses and they make the air all smoky, so please make them stop."

She opens her eyes, smiling at me.

"What about the rest of your family?" I ask. "Don't you want to offer thanks for them?"

She frowns, shuts one eye, and adds, "And thanks for my grandpa. I wish he could spend more time with me because when he's here, he's always fun."

She opens the closed eye and announces, "All done. Now your turn!"

I stifle a laugh and nod, shutting my eyes and saying, "Thanks for my beautiful, wonderful, incredible, fantastic, amazing, awesome daughter, Natalie. She's the best of the best, the most awesome of awesomest—"

"Mom," Natalie says severely, slapping my face lightly, "enough. I'll get a swollen head."

"Well, thanks for Natalie. And for Lata, who helps me keep a roof over my head, the trains running on time, and without whom I don't know what I'd do. And for everything and everyone I have in my life right now. And for giving me this opportunity to prove myself again, because I really love my job and like Natalie said, I really want to catch bad guys and lock them away forever, and I'm so, so grateful to be back on the job again and I promise I won't mess it up this time."

I open my eyes. "All done." Natalie nods approvingly, hugs me, then slides off the bed. "Brushing my teeth and going wee-wee!"

As she goes into the bathroom, I turn and see Lata standing in the doorway. The expression on her face tells me she heard my little Thanksgiving prayer.

"You're back on the job?" she says. "For real? After we talked about it just this morning?"

I raise my palms. "I was going to tell you. I didn't really have a choice, Lata. It just—"

I break off as I hear the sound of angry, raised voices. It sounds like Aishwarya and Kajal in the backyard, really getting into it this time.

Lata shakes her head and raises a finger in warning. She

says stiffly, "I have to go down and deal with that. We'll talk about this later."

She's gone.

I slump down on Natalie's bed, covering my face with both hands.

Why is it that the harder I try not to mess up, the more I mess up?

FIFTEEN

The schoolteacher's house is bright and noisy, bursting with laughter and good cheer.

I know the holidays are hard for a lot of people—I can relate —and folk in the big cities like LA probably spend this weekend like any other public holiday, getting buzzed, binge-watching, or getting their rocks off in whatever way works for them. But out here in the boondocks like Santa Carina Valley, the concept of family still has meaning.

This woman's Thanksgiving family get-together is living proof of that: I mean, just look at this. She's strung up colored lights in her backyard, put up a shamiana with cushioned lawn chairs, got a barbecue going, cooler full of beer. I can glimpse at least a couple of gray-haired gents and ladies mingling with younger generations, hear their laughter, almost drowned out by the stereo playing some old Beach Boys hit kids yelling "Cannonball" as they pile into the pool. If Dominic Toretto were watching this, he'd be jealous; even the family cookouts in the *Fast and Furious* movies can't measure up.

What am I doing here again, sitting outside her house and

watching her like an obsessive stalker? I should know better. I'm back on the job. If someone calls Santa Carina Valley Police Department, I'd have a hard time explaining it away.

I tried. God help me, I really tried. I even drove down to the task force workspace, which is in the old sheriff's station, sandwiched between the Santa Carina Valley courthouse and the public library.

But except for a custodian cleaning up and an old retired cop using the restroom, it was as empty as a tomb. All the action was up at the ranch, where the task force and the volunteers were still working the scene, searching for the murder weapon and scouring the considerable acreage that surrounds the ranch house.

I sat for a while at one of the desks earmarked for me and my team, I even poured myself a cup of coffee and sat myself down, determined to get back to thinking about the problem of the patients slash victims and how to question them. I lasted maybe five minutes. Before I knew it, I was walking out to my car and barely two minutes later, I was here, in front of the schoolteacher's house again.

Because I'm afraid.

Afraid that once I get sucked back into the twenty-four-seven whirlwind of the job, I'll forget Amit.

Not *forget* forget him. I can never do that. But I might forget to remember to keep looking for those answers. To figure out what really happened. Why he did what he did.

I'm deadly afraid of that.

Because I know from experience that once this job sucks you in, it never lets you out. And if that happens, if I forget, if the job overwhelms me as it surely will, I'll lose my last connection to Amit. He'll recede into the background, like a person visible only in the rearview mirror as I drive away, until he becomes just a dot and then blinks out of existence.

I can't bear even the thought of that happening.

And so, once again, on a night when I should still be at home, making the best of whatever version of family I have left, here I am outside a strange woman's house again, doing God knows what.

The sound of a dry leaf crackling under a shoe alerts me.

Before I know it, my Glock is in my fist and I'm turned around, pointing the gun at a dark silhouette.

She's standing beside the driver's side window, holding something in her hand.

Our eyes meet.

This time, there are no headlights blinding her, and there's enough ambient light for her to see my face.

And the gun I'm pointing at her.

"Calabaza en tacha," she says.

The words make no sense to me at first, and then I see the object she's holding out to me.

It's a dessert plate and spoon, with a serving of something sweet and sticky looking.

"Candied pumpkin," she adds. "We made it for Día de Los Muertos but I still have leftovers."

The Day of the Dead. All Souls Day. That was earlier this month.

She holds the plate out, expecting me to take it.

I take it instinctively, not wanting it to fall in the street and shatter. That would be too noisy. And messy.

My gun clatters against the bottom of the porcelain plate. The spoon almost slides off. I catch it in time. It's gooey with sticky syrup.

"Please," she says, "it's really good. It's from my abuela's original recipe."

Still at a loss for words, I eat a spoonful. My mouth fills with the spicy-sweet taste of pumpkin and delicious coconut cream, among other things.

"It's delicious," I say, out of sheer habit. It sounds absurd under the circumstances but what else am I supposed to say?

"May I?" she asks, pointing inside the car.

I frown, not getting her meaning at first.

She walks around the front of the car, temporarily blocking my partial view of her own backyard where the rest of her family are continuing to enjoy the evening.

She opens the passenger side door of my Prius and gets in.

She doesn't shut the door, leaving it open as she sits beside me.

I can smell her perfume.

It's vanilla based with floral hints.

It makes me think of church and Sunday dresses, of Sunday school bible study, and my first holy communion, and more memories than I want in my head right now. It smells of goodness and youth, hope and purity. It makes me feel young and innocent. It makes me feel old and jaded.

I lower the plate to my lap. It clatters against the Glock again. I reholster the gun slowly, careful not to let the plate or the spoon or any of the sticky sweet dessert slide off onto me or into the car.

We sit side by side, watching her house.

A loud burst of laughter explodes from the house next door, then dies out almost as suddenly. The street is lined with parked cars and bright colored lights. The neighborhood is dark and quiet, and we sit in a pool of silence.

"I know you have questions," she says.

I say nothing.

"I know you have doubts," she says.

I try not to let the plate slide off my lap. It's harder than it seems. I will myself into stillness, calming my breath with an effort even though my heart is pounding.

"I want you to know, there was nothing between us," she

says. "Your husband and me. I only met him that one time, the day he came here to see me. He never called or texted me before that. I didn't know who he was. I don't even know how he found me, how he tracked me down. It was a shock. I had changed my name, you see. I had worked hard to put all that behind me. Even my husband didn't know. I had to tell him about it, of course, after that visit, because of what happened afterward. The police came, and the FBI, and there were so many questions. But the truth is, there was nothing more to it. No secrets, no mysteries. He just turned up one fine day and confronted me on my doorstep and wanted to know all these things. I told him I didn't know anything. It took a great deal of persuading to make him believe. When he finally understood, he apologized and left. That was it. That was all that happened. You have to believe me."

I place my hands on the steering wheel if only to stop them trembling. I grip the wheel, willing my heart to stop pounding.

"He..." I say, then my throat chokes up.

The spoon clatters against the edge of the plate. I lower one hand and grip my thigh tight, forcing it into stillness.

She leans over, reaching down.

I turn to stare at her.

She hesitates, then makes a gesture, asking permission.

I nod once.

She lifts the plate off my lap, tamping the spoon down with her thumb, an easy, expert gesture. She places the plate on her own lap, where it lies still, docile, calm, no longer the nervous, jangling thing it was with me.

"Please," she says, "go ahead. Ask your questions. I think it will ease your heart."

I swallow, trying to clear my throat.

"He found you, you said," I say. "What did you mean by that? Why was he looking for you?"

"I do not know that answer," she says. "He did not tell me his reason."

I feel a flash of anger. The same illogical, impulsive urge to lash out and hurt the object of frustration, like the urge I had the night before to slip into her house and attack her, force her into telling me the truth. I suppress it.

"What did he say then?" I say, keeping my voice quiet to avoid revealing the flood of emotion coursing through me. "Tell me exactly what he said."

She says, "He said, and I am trying to say the words from my memory as best as I am able, please excuse me. He said, '*I know you changed your name, and I know why. I am not here for you, I will not expose your secret. I just need to know if it is true, that he did those things to you.*'"

She pauses. "That is as best as I can remember."

I frown. "Who was he talking about?"

She's silent.

I look at her. She's staring down at her hands, folded in her lap, cradling the plate of candied pumpkin pieces. She has the glow of a happy life well-lived, the look of a settled wife and mother and valuable member of a community. I can easily picture her as a preschool teacher, nurturing a class full of inquisitive, restless, endlessly curious toddlers. She's patient and kind. I can't imagine what dark secret that matronly face might be concealing. I can't imagine this woman having any secrets. And yet clearly she does.

"My father," she says at last.

I try to process that. I recall her file by heart because I've looked at it so many times over the past months. "You mean Michael Gonzales?" I say, naming the man listed as her father in the file, her maiden surname before marriage.

She shakes her head. "That was my stepfather. My mother's second husband. My mother took his name, too. I was already eighteen then so strictly speaking, I didn't require a guardian legally, but he adopted me anyway, to make it easier to change my name permanently. To help me erase the past. I accepted gratefully. I embraced his name, his guardianship, his culture, his language. I even converted to Catholicism. Most people now assume I'm Mexican-American."

I believe her. If she hadn't told me all that, I would have assumed she was, too.

"And your real birth father?" I ask. "What was his name?"

"Henrik Deutermann," she says.

I roll the name around a few times. It means nothing to me. I don't recall hearing it before. Definitely not in connection with the Splinter case or any case I've worked before. It's unusual enough that I would remember if I had come across it. Yet, there's something about it that tingles my spine. Not the same name, precisely, but something very close to it. I try to place it, but it eludes me, on the tip of my tongue and out of reach.

"Who was he?" I say finally.

"A monster," she says.

I look at her. She sits very still, staring straight ahead, at the glimpse of her backyard visible through the gap in the trees. As if keeping her eyes on her family, on the life she has now, to avoid falling backwards into the bottomless well of the past and whatever horrors it may hold.

"I don't understand," I say.

"I cannot talk about that," she says. "Do not ask me to talk about it. Even if you take me to your FBI offices and interrogate me, I will not talk about it. It is a part of my past I have worked hard to forget. I can never go back there, not even through the path of memory."

I blink rapidly. She sounds so insistent, so fierce, it comes as a surprise. "Okay, okay," I say, backing off. "Just tell me one thing."

She turns her head slowly and looks at me.

Her eyes are bright now, brighter than they were a moment ago. They gleam in the dimness, like silver pennies.

"I will answer your one question," she says quietly, "then you must promise me one thing also."

"Yes?" I say, unsure of what she's going to say next.

"After I answer, you will leave. You will stop watching my home and my family. You will leave us alone for good. You will go away and never come back. Will you promise this to me?"

I swallow again.

"All right," I say.

She exhales slowly, as if releasing a long-held breath. She seems to calm herself.

"Very well," she says. "Ask me your one question."

"It's the same question that Amit, my husband, asked you that day. I want to know how you answered. Tell me exactly what you said, the same words."

She nods slowly, as if this sounds reasonable to her.

"I told him what I am now saying, the same exact words as best as I remember them. I said, *'It is all true, everything you must have heard or read. It is all true, except that it was worse. Much, much worse than you can know, and far worse than you can imagine.'* Those are the words I told him. That is my only answer to you as well. And now, Agent Parker, we are done. You will never come here again. You will stop watching my house. You will not trouble my family. Just let us live."

She gets out of the car, stepping out into the street in a single, fluid movement, and walks away.

I hear the squeak of a wrought-iron gate opening and then the sound of it shutting. After a moment, I see heads turning in her backyard and calling out her name. She passes through the gap between the trees, and her head tilts to look in my direction. She stares at me for a moment, then turns and says something to someone I can't see, and then laughs at their response.

Just like that, I am shut out and she has gone back to her family, her life.

Suddenly, I feel cheap and tawdry for watching their private celebration, like a lurker in the bushes.

I start the Prius, back out of the parking space, turn, and drive away.

SIXTEEN

Naved's place on Plum Canyon is in a cul de sac, backed up against a hill. Even though it's called 'Canyon', it's really just one long stretch of mountainous road with houses on either side, some climbing the hills all the way to the top. His house is way up on top, at the end of the road, overlooking not just all of Plum Canyon but the whole Santa Carina Valley, too. It has a large wooden deck on the second floor and a fabulous view. Still, it's a lonely house, almost a quarter mile from the nearest neighbor and is surrounded by empty, undeveloped lots. The house itself is oddly quiet for this holiday evening, almost no lights on except one at the top.

He comes out of the house through the side gate, shutting it behind himself.

"Hey," he says, getting into my car. "Everything all right? You sounded a little off on the phone."

"Sorry again for interrupting your Thanksgiving, and thanks for seeing me," I say.

He shrugs. "As you can probably tell, it's not like I'm having a backyard barbecue!"

"So your wife and sons aren't here with you today?"

"Alia, Jehangir, and Naushad are still back in New York," he says. "The plan is for them to join me once I'm settled."

I wait but he doesn't continue. After another moment or two, I sense that he isn't comfortable talking about it anymore. I know better than to probe. If he wants, he'll tell me in his own time.

"So, what's up?" he asks. "Did Marisol get back?"

He's talking about Marisol Mancini, our chief evidence investigator. "She's still running forensics up at the farmhouse. I hope to get something from her soon. But actually, this is about something else. I need your opinion and your advice."

He looks at me uncertainly. I can see he's curious. "Sure. What's this about?"

I tell him about the day of Amit's death and the school-teacher, mentioning my unofficial surveillance of her but playing it down a little so I don't seem like a total creeper stalking her. I also leave out any mention of my violent thoughts and impulses. Naved is a partner and among cops, that's the next closest thing to family, but there are still limits to what we tell even those closest to us. I end with a summary of tonight's encounter, repeating my conversation with her as accurately as possible.

He nods, taking it all in. "So you want me to weigh in on...?"

"For starters, I want some perspective. Am I crazy to be this obsessed about this woman and that brief meeting with Amit? Am I reading too much into it? Does it even matter what he said to her and what she answered? I just need you to tell me if I'm getting carried away with this thing. I mean, it's not like I don't have my hands full already with the Splinter case."

He nods slowly. "I get that, Susan. I can understand your concern. You had a bad shock less than a year ago. You suffered a breakdown. Got put on mandatory mental health leave. It left a blot on your record, everyone in the Bureau and law enforce-ment knows about it, it's hit your own self-esteem hard. And this obsession—I guess, it is an obsession, I can't think of any other way to describe it—does seem unhealthy at first glance. I mean, if Gantry knew you were watching this woman, he'd have your badge and you'd be out of the Bureau, probably wouldn't get a job in law enforcement again. It's a career ender."

I nod, my heart sinking. "I know, I know. I've been an ass, I admit it."

He holds up a finger. "But."

I frown.

"We're all obsessed, Susan. I mean, it comes with the territory. You hunt serial killers, the most dangerous animal on Earth. Mass murderers capable of putting dozens, even hundreds, of victims into the ground if left unchecked. You have to be obsessive to bring down a bastard like that. The Splinters of this world don't play by the rules, they don't follow the rules in the FBI employees' handbook, they don't care about people's rights and law and order. You've got to outthink them, outsmart them, and even then, it takes years and a hell of a lot of effort to bring them to justice. But when you do, you save lives. Some serial killers have killed hundreds over a lifetime. You cut short someone like Splinter's run, you save who knows how many innocents. If that's what being obsessive brings, so be it. Inshallah, we need more Susan Parkers in the world, obsessively working to keep our children and families safe from monsters like Splinter."

I stare at him, taken aback. I've only known this man for a day or so and until now, he's barely said more than a few words. But clearly, still waters run deep.

"That's quite a speech," I say.

"You asked," he says.

"So, you're saying my being obsessed with the schoolteacher *isn't* a bad thing?" I ask hesitantly.

"I'm saying look at the facts. I've only known you a short time, Susan, but I've seen enough to know that you're a good cop. Great instincts, initiative, leadership, sharp mind, great reflexes, but you know how to work the case. Trust your gut. What does it tell you?"

I think for a moment. "It tells me that there's a connection between this woman and Amit that probably even she doesn't know about."

He nods. "And he did."

"Right. I think Amit found out something, I don't know what, about her past that intrigued him. That's why he drove over to her house that day to ask a total stranger that very weird question, out of the blue. I mean, that's the opposite of Amit as a person! He was a shy guy. Even at parties, he would stand by himself all evening, sipping his drink. The first time we went out together, I had to ask him. It was the same when we got married. He proposed, but I had to literally put the idea into his head, I even pointed out the ring. In some ways he was pretty outgoing, but in others, he could be really, really diffident. I used to joke with him that it was a miracle he wasn't still a virgin!"

Naved says, "Okay. Maybe I didn't need all that information."

I cover my face with my hands, embarrassed. "I'm sorry. I open my mouth and my guts fall out."

"It's okay. I get the point. You're saying that it was very unlike Amit to do that, talk to this total stranger. So, in his own way, he was probably obsessed, too."

"Yes, exactly," I say. "That's the only way I can make sense of it. The question is, what was he obsessed with? Why did those questions matter so much?"

"Maybe start with the name she gave you? Henrik...?"

"Deutermann. Henrik Deutermann. I did a quick internet search for him actually," I say, holding up my phone and showing him. "See for yourself."

Naved stares at my screen, the blue light giving his dark

complexion a peculiar cast. I notice that the nearest streetlight is several meters away, and more than partly obscured by the omnipresent palm trees that are a fixture of the southern California landscape.

"That name," he says, squinting out at the dark moonless sky. "It sounds familiar somehow..."

"He was a psychiatrist," I say. "Disgraced. Vilified. Shunned. Creator of a controversial new form of therapy. Practiced it on American GIs first, at the US military's request no less. Some form of motivational therapy to keep up morale, it sounds like, the intention being to help untried soldiers get their heads into the right space for violent combat."

"Yes, it's all here," he says. "Sounds like he was in the business of brainwashing young minds into killing and dying for their country."

Naved continues reading: "Later, after the war, he adapted it to civilians. Then focusing largely on immigrants. Foreigners who were having a hard time adapting to life in the new country and suffered mental health episodes or breakdowns. The focus was on rehabilitation, but a number of his patients ended up becoming violent after reintegration into society. At least a few went on murder sprees."

He uses his finger to scroll down faster, skimming the rest. "Forced to shut down his private asylum in California. Black-balled. Brought up on charges, civil as well as criminal. Was able to get off because of his military connections and the government's desire to avoid a scandal. Spent his last years in obscurity. Some of his controversial methods continued to be in use for decades, some are still being used even today, but in very different forms. Like electroshock therapy, hydroshock therapy —that one sounds a lot like waterboarding—and yada yada yada. Quite a character."

"Quite," I say.

I lower the phone as he thinks about it.

"The parallels between this guy and Splinter are hard to ignore," Naved says.

"Yes. In a sense, both are therapists who seem to believe that they're actually 'treating' their victims while in fact they're doing horrendous, inhuman things to them."

"So do you think maybe your husband was onto something related to your case?" Naved asks.

"That's what I don't get. If he found out something, why didn't he just bring it to me? I mean, I know we were fighting a lot in those days, mainly over how much time and involvement I was putting into the case. He felt it was unhealthy bringing all that horrible stuff into our house. Bad for Natalie. I tried to make him understand that it was *because* of Natalie that I needed to do the job, to keep her and other little kids like her safe. It reached a point where Amit even tried to talk me into quitting, finding another line of work."

"Yeah," Naved says, looking away, "that happens. What we do, the nature of the job, it's hard on our families. Especially our spouses. They get it, but they also don't get it."

"So then, after all that, why would Amit himself go down a rabbit hole over some dead psychiatrist from sixty years ago? If he thought he'd found something about Splinter, he could have just texted me. Why go off and question a strange woman about it? And after that, why go and—"

I stop myself.

Naved gives me a moment then says, "So this schoolteacher, she's actually the daughter of Henrik Deutermann?"

"Apparently. I don't know how, since Deutermann would have been, like, sixty or something when she was born. I guess I could check county birth records to confirm it. But I did believe her."

"Sixty isn't unusual especially back then but even now. Maybe it was a second marriage to a younger woman," Naved says. "There could be lots of reasons. Besides, that encyclopedia article says Deutermann died in 1997, so it's not impossible."

"I don't know," I say, feeling hollow now that I've shared it all with someone else for the first time. I should feel lighter, unburdened, but all I feel is empty. "Maybe it has nothing to do with Splinter at all. Maybe it's something else I'm unable to see. That's why I brought it to you. To give it a fresh pair of eyes."

He nods. "Okay. Tell you what. You leave this with me."

"Leave what?" I say. "That's all I have. There is nothing else."

"Sure, sure," he says, "but it's something. Otherwise, it wouldn't bother you so much. Leave it with me. Let me work on it. I'll have to do it on my own time. When I have something, I'll come back to you. How's that sound?"

I look at him. "You'll do that for me? You hardly know me, Naved."

"I'm going to do it so you can free your brain for more important things, Susan. Let me take this off your mind, so you can focus on Splinter. Deal?"

I smile at him, even though he can probably barely see me in this darkness. "Deal, pardner."

"Great."

My phone buzzes just then. Talk about good timing. I'm struck by a pang of guilt, thinking it must be Lata, wanting to pick up where we left off. I don't know if I have the stomach for another personal heart-to-heart, so it's with a feeling of dread that I unlock the device and look at the screen.

"What is it?" Naved asks.

In response, I turn the ignition and start the car.

SEVENTEEN

The SCVPD uniformed cop who stops me at the turnoff to Magnusson's farmhouse looks at my ID and then at me. "Saw you on the internet today."

I assume he must mean file pics of me, since I haven't talked to any reporters. But when he holds up his phone and shows me, it turns out to be a shaky cellphone video of me getting out of the van in the hospital parking lot after I read the Dr. Keller notes. The Gen-Z-ers in the car must have taken it. They posted it online with a snarky caption about "Twenty-first-century Boomers and their drama!" Some sharp-eyed media maven recognized me in it and snapped it up, mixing it into the live coverage of the Splinter story. Even now, past dinnertime, there are a couple dozen media vans parked on the shoulder about fifty feet behind me.

The cop lets me through without any further ado. I'm guessing he's not one of McDougall's boys or he'd have busted my chops for longer. Naved's following right behind in his Camry.

The farmhouse looks different tonight; the crime scene lights and dozen odd crime scene technicians around the house give it a busy air. Apart from the tents and tables where Mancini's investigative team is piling up the forensic evidence they're bringing out, there are at least a dozen more tents set up to accommodate the rest of the task force and volunteers. There are figures in the fields, too, busy searching with flashlights. It would probably be a lot busier if this wasn't a holiday night.

Naved parks beside me and we both get out at the same time. I jerk my head to indicate the mobile laboratory. He nods and follows me there.

I know better than to try to enter the sacred sanctum without being invited. So we wait. An assistant emerges a few minutes later to say that Marisol will be right with us, she's just finishing up something.

Naved and I sit on the edge of the porch, looking out at the field.

"I feel like we're still missing something here," I say. "I'm not talking about forensics. I mean something about this whole set-up doesn't make sense to me."

Naved nods. "A murder weapon would be good for starters. I mean, these eleven patients slash victims. They're trapped underground in that basement by this psycho killer for weeks, maybe months. Yet somehow one of them manages to break out and kill the guy. And then what?"

"We've been presuming that he or she then went back to their cell and stayed there until we got called," I say.

"Yeah, but from the decomposition of the body, that was days ago. So this person, who's been a prisoner down there for weeks or months, brutally slaughters Magnusson then goes back down to their cell and locks themselves in? That doesn't compute."

"The cells were unlocked when we found them," I say.

"That's another thing. You and I both saw when we went down there. They were all just sitting there. They must have known their doors were open. They could have walked out at any time. Why just sit there? Not just the other ten, but the killer, too. After committing this brutal murder, getting all that rage out of their system, why go back down and sit and wait? I mean, those last few days they must have been starving. Magnusson was dead, so there was nobody to feed them, right? Why didn't they get out? Go looking around. The killer definitely did."

I nod. "And the murder weapon. What did the killer do with it? I know we haven't found it because Mancini would have texted me the instant she did. That's a number one priority."

"It doesn't make sense," Naved says.

"Well, you have to factor in Stockholm Syndrome," I say slowly, thinking it through. "We don't know what Magnusson put those eleven through. What they endured down there. Maybe they were too traumatized to leave their cells. Maybe he'd played games like this with them before, unlocking their cell doors, tempting them to try to escape, then catching them and putting them back in, torturing them. Maybe he'd conditioned them not to leave even if the cell doors were unlocked."

Naved nods. "Pavlovian conditioning. That would explain why they didn't leave. But not the murder weapon."

"Agreed. And there's something else. The notes. What's with all the damn Post-it notes? Why aren't they talking? Why won't they even identify themselves, try to reach out to their families, let them know they're all right? Have you ever known kidnapping victims to behave like this?"

"No," he says, staring into the distance in the direction of the stand of trees. "Unless they have something to hide."

"All eleven of them?" I say. "That doesn't make sense. I mean, they've gotta have families. Wives, husbands, sons, daughters, siblings, parents, friends, work colleagues."

"The phone lines have been burning up," Naved points out. "SCVPD, LAPD, all over the country, 911 is getting a record number of calls from people reporting missing family members, associates, friends. Every missing case file in the last twenty years is being pulled up and relooked at right now. I've got a couple dozen calls myself."

I nod. "My phone blew up so much this morning, I had to turn off notifications. Last I checked, my email inbox was full, and my unread texts are in the hundreds. I've been screening them and only checking the ones from the case and family otherwise I'd go blind just trying to read them all."

"And yet, those eleven patients sitting in the hospital won't let us release their pics to the media," Naved says. "Why? What are they hiding?"

"Maybe they're trying to protect the killer. They don't want him or her to get hauled up for Magnusson's murder, because he did them all a huge favor, saved their lives."

"See, that's another thing I don't get," Naved says. "You yourself said it on the drive home. Splinter's MO was very consistent in one respect: he only took down families. 'Intact families' was the phrase you used."

"Right," I say.

"So why pick up eleven individuals, abduct and imprison them for months, and torture them psychologically without killing them? It goes against that pattern. Serial killers don't do that kind of thing."

"I know," I say. "It's driving the BAU down in Quantico crazy. I was on a couple of calls with profilers today and they both said the same thing, that we need to be sure we really have Splinter, because this kind of drastic deviation is not consistent with anything he or any other serial killer has ever done before. Sure, serial killers do abduct and assault or torture victims, even multiple victims at times. But that's not what Splinter did. Splinter went after his victims in their homes, with their families. That was his perversion. This..." I gesture at the farmhouse. "This is like a whole other thing."

"What if it isn't Splinter?" Naved asks.

"You mean, a different serial killer? Or serial abductor?" I shrug. "It's a possibility. But Magnusson? One of our prime suspects for the Splinter killings? And he turns out to be a whole other serial killer but not Splinter? That's a helluva coincidence and you know what we say in law enforcement."

"There are no coincidences, yes," Naved says. "But it would explain the inconsistency in the MO."

"But not the way the victims are behaving. Or the connections to the Splinter case. Magnusson was literally our number one suspect until we studied his medical records and spoke to his doctors before ruling him out on physical grounds. No, I don't buy that. Whatever this is, however inconsistent or out of character it may seem, it's still Splinter. I mean, the scarecrow alone underlines that."

He frowns at me. "Scarecrow?"

I slap my head. Somehow, in all the hectic confusion of the past twenty-four hours, I've forgotten to tell anyone about the scarecrow.

I walk forward, beckoning to Naved to follow me. There are lights everywhere now, precluding the need for me to turn my car around to point the headlights. I wave out at the field where the silhouette still stands. We're pretty distant from it but the elevated position and the crime scene lights do cast just enough illumination to make out the general outline of those spiky points.

He looks at it, squinting. "Is that... Are those...?"

"Splinters."

He laughs uneasily. "Now that's a dark sense of humor."

I stare at the scarecrow. The flap of one sleeve stirs in the wind. The bright scene lights cast a weird light on the looming figure. I catch a glint of something metallic, as if the raised figure is winking at me.

I frown. I'm just starting to walk out there to take a closer look when my phone buzzes.

Marisol Mancini Calling.

"Come on," I say, turning around and heading in the opposite direction, back to the mobile crime unit.

Inside, the lighting is brutally harsh, a blinding white that erases every shadow, creating a clinical, almost futuristic impression of the high-tech laboratory.

Where most coroners and forensic scientists would look exhausted and bleary-eyed after working almost twenty-four hours nonstop, Marisol Mancini looks as fresh as a daisy and twice as beautiful. She claps her hands twice, softly, as we approach, then holds up her arms in a V for Victory gesture, changing it to a high five as I come up.

"What you say? Huh? What you say?" she crows.

"That you're a miracle worker!" I say, meeting her high five with my palm. The impact stings. Like many paraplegics, her torso and upper body strength is off the charts. It doesn't erase my grin though.

She frowns at Naved. "This is new?" she asks.

I gesture Naved forward. "Detective Naved Seth, ex-NYPD, now SCVPD."

Mancini gives him a keen once-over. "You are partner now with Susan?"

Naved spreads his hands. "For the moment, I guess. Right?" he asks, checking with me.

I nod. "He's my partner," I confirm.

Marisol nods. "Good enough. Come see what Mancini does," she says. "Look, look."

She makes us look through microscopes and shows us screens filled with data, as she walks us through her process. I let her go on for another minute or two before politely interrupting.

"This is great stuff, Marisol, and I know we'll get it all in your report. But right now, we're really in a rush. So could you maybe just give us the conclusions?"

Marisol clicks her tongue. "Americans, always want drive in fast lane, no time to stop and smell the science. But for you, Susan, I will cut to chase."

She says something to an associate who does something on a laptop then nods.

Marisol points at us. "You look your mobile, yes. All there."

I take out my phone and scroll till I find her email package. "Got it. Marisol, you're amazing. I'm going to look through this and get right to work, okay?"

As Naved and I leave, she calls out behind us, "Bring me murder weapon, you find, okay? I need murder weapon. What good murder case without murder weapon? Like spaghetti without fork!"

I wave back as we exit the mobile unit. I see McDougall and a couple of his flunkies watching me as I come down the ramp of the trailer followed by Naved. He's probably wondering what breakthrough I've got but is too proud to ask me outright. Technically, I'm supposed to share everything with the task force, and I absolutely intend to do just that—but first, I need to do something.

I dial Ramon Diaz.

"Ramon," I say when he answers. "We caught a break. Check your phone."

"Got it, jefe," Ramon says, and from his tone I can tell he's scrolling through it as we speak. Loud music and voices recede as he either shuts a door or steps outside. "Wow. You were able to ID all eleven!"

"All twelve actually," I say. "Marisol was even able to use

DNA from the empty room to ID the missing person. Who was probably the one who killed Magnusson."

"This is awesome, chief," Ramon's voice says over the loud music and voices in the background.

"Can you run it through Penelope and let me know what you get?"

"Already on it, boss, but she's Carlotta now, okay?" Ramon says.

"Oh yeah, I forgot. Run it by Carlotta, please," I say.

"Done deal. Call you in a few," he says.

Disconnecting, I look over at Naved. He's been scrolling for the past several minutes while I've been on the phone.

"This is incredible," he says.

"Oh, you ain't seen nothing yet," I say. "Ramon's running it by Carlotta who'll have a lot more than just IDs for us before you know it."

Naved stops scrolling and looks at me. "Penelope? Carlotta?"

I grin. "You'll see when he calls me back."

"What about the lawyers? All that stuff they were lecturing us on this morning?"

I shrug. "What about it? They were telling us why we can't question the victims slash suspects slash patients. They didn't say anything about stopping the investigation, did they?"

"No, but—"

I hold up a hand. "Look, we got this DNA from the scene. Which is routine. We ran it through the usual databases and got hits. All we're doing now is following up on that to flesh out the picture on our unsubs to know who they are."

"Unsubs," he says, "so you think—"

"I don't think anything at this point. I'm just following the evidence. Which is our job."

He frowns and thinks about it for a moment, then his brow clears. "I can't find a damn thing wrong with that."

I grin. "You see? All kosher here."

We lean against Naved's Camry, staring out at the field as we sip and wait. I look at the neat rows of dried out stalks. It's a vineyard, of course, long since dried out and sorely neglected. Do vineyards even need scarecrows? Do crows and birds in general like grapes? I'm about to ask Naved, or do a quick search online, just out of curiosity, when a uniform turns a flashlight, catching the scarecrow, and again, I see that glint I noticed earlier.

And then my phone buzzes again.

EIGHTEEN

Ramon is video calling me.

"Everyone else's on call, too, but they're voice only. I just wanted to see your face when you opened the package," Ramon says.

"Scrolling through it right now," I say.

Kayla, David, and Brine call out their hellos, then explain that they're muting their devices to avoid flooding the line with their family soundtracks. That's fine with me; right now, Ramon Diaz is the star of the moment, impressively taking the ball handed to him by Marisol Mancini.

"El Capitan," I snap off a salute to Ramon, "Carlotta exceeded herself this time. That was uber fast!"

"Made a few tweaks," Ramon says proudly. "She's quite a mover now."

I sense Naved looking at me weirdly and angle my screen to catch him as well. "Naved's here, too. The package looks huge. Why don't you run down the highlights for us, Ramon?"

"You got it, boss," Ramon says. "The first thing you gotta know is none of them are US nationals."

"How's that?" I say.

"Hold on a sec," Ramon says, "lemme see if Carlotta can do the honors. She's a *lotta* better than I am at summarizing."

I roll my eyes at the pun. "I'm sure she's a lotta better at puns than you are, dad-joke Diaz."

"Hey," he says, pretending he's hurt, "Diaz don't do dad-jokes, okay? Only bruh-jokes!"

"How long's this going to take?" I ask impatiently.

Ramon finishes tapping out something on his laptop then shoots me a thumbs up. He hits a button on his keyboard and my screen fills with a picture. Naved is leaning in to see my screen and squints at the image.

It's a scan of a foreign passport.

The image slides sideways, to be replaced by another scan of another passport. The face on this one looks familiar: a youngish, white, blonde woman about my age, with piercing gray eyes. With a start, I realize it's the same woman who insisted on walking out with the EMTs instead of being carried out. The one in the second room that Naved and I searched last night. Her name is Gennifer Mason, nationality British.

As the screen changes again, Ramon's voice speaks over the visuals. "Carlotta got these scans from USCIS."

US Citizenship and Immigration Services is the part of Homeland Security that oversees naturalization and immigration. All US tourist visas are issued through them.

"And?" I ask.

"They're all foreign nationals. Different countries. All travelling on tourist or student visas."

"All twelve of them?" I ask, glancing at Naved.

He looks as surprised as I am.

"Every last one, boss," Ramon says.

I try to process the fact that all twelve of Magnusson's captives are foreign nationals. "I don't get it. So how did Splinter pick them up? Were they all part of a tour group or something?" I ask.

"That's the thing," Ramon says. "From what Carlotta was able to dig up, looks like there's no connection between them. All different ages, nationalities, identities. She even dug deep on social media. None of them are even friends or followers of each other's accounts. Zero overlap in their digital and social lives."

"That's odd," I say. "What about their I-94s?"

The I-94 is an official USCIS document that registers every non-American's official entry and exit into and out of the United States. It used to be issued as a white card. Now it's done digitally. It's simple to look up anyone's I-94 if you have their passport number and last name. Ramon would have scraped that info digitally as well. He's very thorough.

"There is one thing they all have in common," Ramon says.

"What?" I ask.

"They all arrived in the US within days of one another. Entered through different points—Newark, Denver, Los Angeles, Chicago, San Francisco—but all within the same week."

"Weird," Naved says.

Ramon adds, "And here's something even more interesting. Within hours of entering the US, they all took connecting flights from their city of entry to LAX. Except for the twelfth guy. He's the only one who landed directly in LAX."

I try to imagine a dozen foreigners of diverse ages, genders, backgrounds, arriving across the US, then getting on flights to Hollywood, only to end up captives of a serial killer.

I frown. "So what the hell was Splinter thinking, picking these people up? I mean, even if you toss a handful of stones at LAX, you'll still end up hitting mostly people from Asia where a third of the world's population comes from. What are the odds of him randomly choosing twelve strangers, all tourists, and they all turn out to be from twelve different parts of the world?"

Naved shakes his head. "There's something very strange going on here."

"I don't make this shit up, I just pass it on," Ramon says. "But yeah, it's crazy AF."

"Very unusual," David says.

"So now they're victims slash patients slash suspects slash tourists," Kayla says. "This case gets crazier by the minute."

"Still, there's gotta be a connection between them," I say. "There's no way they're all random. It doesn't make sense otherwise."

Ramon appears onscreen again. He grins. "This is where it gets really interesting, jefe. Hold on to your hats, guys!"

He launches into a summary of the background info that he's been able to pull up on the twelve victims slash suspects. Most of it is mundane stuff. Ordinary lives, regular law-abiding citizens. Most of them with nothing more than a parking ticket or two, one DUI, one bankruptcy and a civil fraud lawsuit by a former partner which was later dropped, one defamation suit—both criminal and civil—both with judgments in the accused's favor, a couple of divorces, all minor league stuff that doesn't really rise to the extent of being called a criminal record.

"Those were the general background searches I was almost done with earlier. Then I inputted the therapy factor."

I nod. "Splinter was a therapist who targeted other therapists and their families. Good thinking, Ramon."

"Thanks, boss. First searches turned up nothing. None of them are therapists or related to therapists. So then I searched for signs of mental health issues, violence or any violent behavior in the past. Nada. Zip. Zero results. They're all pretty average, everyday people going about their regular lives. Families, kids, jobs, businesses, the usual shit. Not a bad egg in the bunch. *But*"—he holds up his finger for emphasis—"then I widened the search to FF&A."

"Family, friends, and acquaintances," I say for Naved's benefit.

"*And*," Ramon continues, "ta-da!"

"Skeletons in the closet?" I ask, hazarding a guess.

Ramon tilts his head to-and-fro. "Um, not exactly. More like they all seem to have at least one troubled person in their lives. The bipolar sister. The depressive ex-wife. The alcohol-dependent brother-in-law. The drug-*and*-alcohol dependent significant other. The unstable daughter diagnosed first with schizophrenia, later found to have been suffering from C-PTSD after a sexual assault. It's a laundry list of issues. The point is, all twelve were close to someone who's undergone extensive therapy. We're talking people whose mental health, whose *lives*, were dependent on therapy."

"*All* of the twelve?" I ask.

"Every last one."

"How did you dig up this stuff?" Naved asks. "I mean, this level of in-depth profiling? How is that even possible?"

Ramon smiles and winks, flexing his bicep in his cut-off tee shirt, then tapping his head. "Ramon got da muscle, and Ramon got da muscle! Bruh, if you think this is something, you ain't seen nothing yet. My Carlotta's gotta whole lotta game!"

"Who the heck is Carlotta?" Naved asks.

Ramon laughs at Naved's expression.

David chips in, "Carlotta is Ramon's AI chatbot. He wrote it himself, with a little help from ChatGPT."

"You mean a *lotta* help from ChatGPT," I add. "He originally called her P-NLP but later changed her name to Carlotta."

"Penelope?" Naved says.

"Personalized Natural Language Processing framework, man," Ramon says. "Think of it as my personal ChatGPT. Sweet, right? I switched her handle to Carlotta 'cause she's gotta whole lotta game!"

Naved looks impressed. "Very impressive. So you fed all the info you scraped online on the twelve into this AI chatbot named Penelope aka Carlotta, and she spat out this additional stuff on their families?"

"Something like that," Ramon says.

"But this sounds like info from medical files," Naved says. "Isn't that kind of info confidential?"

David adds laconically, "Special Agent Diaz might or might not have added some datamining code into said AI chatbot. Said code being illegal in these United States."

Ramon feigns an innocent look. "Hey, I don't know nothing about that. Some hacker must have given my Carlotta a virus. What am I supposed to do about that, huh?"

"Use it?" I say. "Okay, so we all know you're a tech whiz, Ramon, let's get back on point. Let me see if I'm getting this right. So all these twelve tourists slash victims slash patients have someone close to them back home who had psychological issues? For which, they're receiving therapy, right"

"Yes!" Ramon says. "Except you used the wrong tense, SAC Susan!"

"They *were* receiving therapy?" I frown. "And they just stopped? No, wait, that can't be right. They're all..."

Ramon grins and rolls his hands to encourage me to go on.

"Fully recovered and no longer in need of therapy?" I say, starting with the least likely option.

Ramon makes a buzzer sound, indicating I'm wrong.

"Institutionalized now?" Naved says, joining in.

Ramon repeats the buzzer sound.

I hold up my hand. "They're all either dead or as good as," I say, feeling the rightness of this even as I say the words.

Ramon points a finger at me and fast-claps, then puts four fingers in his mouth and emits a piercing whistle.

"Jeez, Ramon!" Brine complains. "You just made me spill a really great year of Pinot Noir all over myself. We talked about the whistling, remember? I have a really sensitive startle response!"

"Said the white man to the brown man," Kayla comments. "Check your privilege, Briney baby."

"What does race have to do with it?" Brine asks in an injured tone.

"Guys, guys," I say, "let's get back on track here. So all twelve had people they loved who were therapy dependent. That has to mean something. This whole case revolves around therapists. Splinter targeted therapists and their families. He made them perform mock therapy on each other before killing them. Magnusson was a therapist. He had these twelve people in cells that were some kind of therapy rooms. Now we find out that all twelve of them had close ones who were dependent on therapy."

"And just this morning, all of them asked for the same therapist," Kayla says.

"Dr. Keller," I say.

There's a long moment of silence in which I can hear the voices of the task force team members around the farm and in the fields. The six of us are quiet, our wheels spinning as we try to make sense of this new data dump.

"Um," Brine says. "Not to derail your train of thought, Susan, but does anyone see an inconsistency here?"

"What's that?" I ask.

"We keep saying 'twelve of them' and 'all twelve' and so on, but aren't we forgetting that we only brought eleven people up from that basement."

Naved looks at me just then and I catch sight of it in his expression: he gets it, too. At this moment, I feel like both our minds are running in perfect synch. Like train tracks running in parallel, side by side. It feels good. Like we're turbocharged, firing on all cylinders.

We both arrive at the same conclusion at the same time.

"There was someone else down there," we both say together.

"The twelfth victim slash patient," he says. "That's got to be it."

I think about it, looking around the farm. There are still people combing the fields with flashlights. Mancini's last comment about the murder weapon rings in my ears again.

"Ramon," Naved says, a fraction of a second before I can speak. "Could you run those twelve IDs through Carlotta and ask her to match them against screen grabs from the surveillance feed you mirrored at the hospital?"

Ramon slaps his forehead with the end of his fist. "Bruh. You a genius."

He types so quickly, all we can hear is a clattering sound as his fingers race across his keyboard. Then he sits back as twelve passport pictures flash by in rapid succession, overlaid by twelve screen grabs from the hospital rooms. One solitary passport pic blinks continually, left without a match.

"Aram Grygorian," I say, reading the name on the passport scan.

Naved and I stare at the picture. It shows an unhappy, nervous-looking man in his late forties, with thick wiry hair and bushy eyebrows.

We look at each other, both blurting out the same conclusion at the same time. Partners in perfect synch.

"The killer," I say. "He has to be the killer."

Naved nods. "He killed Magnusson, but never went back to his therapy room in the basement."

"Then where is he?" Brine asks, sounding puzzled.

I turn and look around at the sprawling farmlands stretching out into the darkness.

"He's still here," I say.

NINETEEN

Naved and I walk toward the field together in silence.

We pass crime scene volunteers carrying flashlights and kits. A couple of SCVPD uniforms exchange words and chuckle softly as we pass. I'm not sure what it is about an FBI agent and a cop working together they find amusing, but I can guess. That damn viral video from the hospital parking lot didn't help. But to hell with all that. I've got a job to do and I'm going to do it. I reach the edge of the field and start through the dried-out rows of what might once have been grapevines.

The scarecrow is at the southwest corner of the field, perched right at the point where the dirt road climbs up and curves one final time to level out onto this farmland. I stop about fifty yards or so away from it, and point.

"Isn't that a weird place to place a scarecrow?" I ask Naved.

He frowns at the raised figure then looks around the field. "I'm no farmer," he says, "but aren't they usually placed in the middle?"

"Give the man a cigar," I say, continuing toward it.

"Maybe Magnusson deliberately placed it here to scare off

visitors, not crows," Naved says as we get closer. "That same dark sense of humor we were talking about."

We're at the scarecrow now, looking up at it. It's a lot bigger than I first thought. The illusion of size wasn't entirely an illusion. It's at least twice as large as a typical scarecrow, I see now, those bib overalls as big as a small tent.

"That's gotta be his," I say, pointing at the overalls. "But there's no way in hell Magnusson could have hauled that all the way out here and then raised it up all by himself."

I gesture at the house, some hundred and fifty yards away now. "In fact, there's no way in hell he could even have gotten out here, with or without help. I don't think Magnusson could walk more than a hundred or so steps a day."

"His Fitbit must have been very disappointed," Naved says.

I burst into laughter. The sound is unexpectedly loud, carrying in the quiet night, and several heads turn to look in our direction. I cut myself off by turning it into a coughing fit.

"Nice one," I say. "Took me by surprise."

A man in an SCVPD uniform approaches and shines a flashlight in our direction.

"What are you doing?" he calls out.

I shield my eyes from the beam. "Hello, officer. SAC Susan Parker, and this is Detective Naved Seth with SCVPD. We're good, thanks for asking."

He keeps the beam on my face, switching it briefly to Naved then returning to me.

"Could you lower that, please?" I call out.

He lowers it off my face, but it stays pointed in my direction. "Sorry. My job to be checking. We are still processing the area, SAC Parker. You are not to be out here."

Odd accent and phrasing but this is SoCal, we have a lot of ethnicities on board. He's just doing his job, is all.

"I'll just be a minute, thanks for being diligent," I call out, waving.

After a beat, he turns away, switching off the flashlight and starting up the field.

When I turn to Naved, he's staring up at the scarecrow with an odd expression.

"What?" I ask.

He takes out his own flashlight and points it at the scarecrow.

"Just now, when that cop was waving his light around, I thought I saw something..."

He goes up close to the pole, shining his light upwards. I join him, using my own tactical flashlight to try and catch what he saw. Our beams crisscross for a second, and we both see it at the same time: a flash of reflection off a high-toned metal surface.

He tries to reach up for it but it's a good four or five feet beyond his reach. He crouches, about to jump to try and snag it, but I stop him.

"Not a good idea. Those things'll cut your hands to shreds. I can reach it if you boost me."

He looks at me doubtfully. "How much do you weigh?"

"Just crouch down and boost me."

He interlocks his fingers together, forming a cradle.

"Hold on," I say. I dig into my jacket pocket, hoping to find a pair of crime scene gloves. But I come up empty. The box is back in my car which is a good two-hundred-meter walk back.

"Use this," Naved says.

He hands me a white handkerchief.

I tuck it into my jacket pocket, remove my boots, and climb on his hands, using his head and shoulders for leverage. His neck and shoulder muscles strain but he manages to raise me up.

"Don't you drop me!" I warn.

Everything looks different up here. I can see over the ridge now all the way across to the road about a quarter-mile away.

The media vans are still there. I can see an anchor doing a standup with a bright broadcast light on him. A state cruiser is just starting up the dirt road, its high beams dipping and rising unevenly. Over to my left, Magnusson's farmhouse seems somehow bigger and more eerie in the crime scene lights; the fields around it are dotted with people in safety jackets shining flashlights downwards.

I'm about level with the scarecrow's chest now. The blue denim overalls are weather worn and faded. The bib is partially unbuttoned, the flap hanging down to expose a chest bursting with lethal-looking splinters, each about a foot long. They've been sharpened at both ends, tapering to needlepoints. The head of the scarecrow is made of an old tee shirt that's been stuffed with more splinters, pierced by both ends. The tee shirt has an old classic rock group's picture on the front. Splinters poke out of the lead singer's face, creating the illusion of a monstrous beast that's all teeth.

I take a moment to steady myself. If I fall forward onto the scarecrow, or even use it to try to maintain my balance, those splinters will pierce my hands and body through and through. Not a pleasant way to die.

The thing we're seeking is in the front pouch of the overalls, like a joey snug in his mother kangaroo's secret pocket. Only the tip of the metal handle peeks out about an inch. Barely enough to reflect the beam of a flashlight if shone directly on it. Barely. But enough.

Using the handkerchief, I pull it out slowly, careful to use only one hand. I'm glad I did. When fully exposed, it has one of the ugliest blades I've seen. A jagged toothy edge, curved at a wicked angle to form something resembling a predator's maw. I hold it high in one hand, resting my other hand on Naved's shoulder.

"Okay, bring me down now, slow," I tell Naved.

He does as requested, lowering me as far down as he can

manage. When I'm about three feet from the dirt, I jump off, landing with bare feet in the field. My heel crunches into dried leaves, making a crisp sound, like potato chips being crushed.

I brush them off my foot and put my boots back on.

"I think we just found the murder weapon," I say.

He shines his flashlight on it, making a sound of appreciation.

"That is one killer hunting knife," he says. "Never seen anything like it."

"I think it's custom made," I say. "Like the other blades Splinter used on those therapist families. Impossible to trace that way, and he gets the sickest design to suit his tastes."

"This has to be the murder weapon, right?" Naved asks.

I nod. "Let's run it over to Mancini right now. This could be the break we need."

"It also proves our theory is right. There was a twelfth patient down there."

"Which begs the question, where are they now? And why did they stow this out here, where it was sure to be found sooner or later? Why not just take it with them, or bury it in the woods somewhere? We're only a few miles from the Angeles Forest. There's hundreds of square miles of wilderness out there."

Naved puts his hands on his hips, looking up at the sky as he thinks. There's just enough light from the slender crescent moon rising in the west to illuminate his features. "Maybe they wanted to keep it handy? In case they needed to use it again?"

Again, our mental tumblers turn at the same time, gears meshing in synch and clicking. We stare at each other.

"Because they're still here. They never left," I say.

We both stare down at the knife together, trying to parse its secrets.

I hear a sound in the brush. Similar to the sound my heel made when it crunched that dry leaf, but heavier, like it's caused by a boot.

At almost the same time, I catch another sound I recognize, this one more ominous and deadly: the click of a revolver's tumblers falling into place just before the hammer comes down.

Without thinking about it, I shove Naved and myself to the ground. "Down!" I yell.

The gunshot meant for me passes over the back of my head, an inch from my body but close enough to singe stray hairs and etch a burning hot line across my back. The sound is deafeningly loud in the quiet night, like a cherry bomb set off at midnight.

I land face down in the field, getting a mouthful of dirt. The hand with which I'm gripping the knife is stretched out and my elbow and shoulder get solidly thumped, setting off my funny bone and almost dislocating my shoulder socket. I hear myself grunt as a second gunshot rings out. This one is lower and closer, as the gunman adjusts his aim to compensate. I know the third shot will punch through me but there's no time to turn, draw, and fire with my shooting hand all tingly.

Still, I roll over and try, letting the knife fall into the brush. My hand claws at the holster, snapping it open and my gun is halfway out when the third shot rings out followed by the unforgettable sound of a bullet hitting living flesh.

TWENTY

I lie still for one agonizing moment, certain that I've been shot.

Then Naved springs up beside me, shouting and running.

I finish pulling my gun out of its holster, only to get my hand caught in weeds. I tear myself free and get back on my feet, spitting dirt out of my mouth, crouching low and scanning.

The shooter is about fifty yards away already, Naved closing in on him.

I glimpse other figures out of the corner of my eye, coming toward us. The closest ones are a good hundred yards or more away still, and they're coming slow, unsure of what's happening. It's always like that in the first minutes of a firefight: confusion about who's shooting at whom and why, and what to do about it. In the dark, the bad guys aren't that easy to tell apart from the good.

I don't wait for them to come and help us.

Instead, I start running.

Not after Naved and the shooter.

They already have a head start and I'm unlikely to catch up quickly enough.

Instead, I run in the opposite direction: toward the dirt road.

I reach the rise and look over.

The headlights of the state cruiser I saw while perched on Naved's hands are close now, almost at the top. The driver is slowing down to take the last sharp curve.

I leap down about eight or nine feet, landing with a thump on the dirt road below the edge of the field. I stand up, holding my hands out.

Just then, the black and white ChiP SUV comes up and around the last curve, the headlights centering on me.

I hold up my shield and yell.

"FBI!"

The cruiser jerks to a halt. I can see the eyes of the startled highway cop through the windshield, reacting to me.

I hold my hands out. "Don't shoot. I'm gonna show you my ID!"

His hands disappear off the steering wheel anyway and I'm wary of them as I come around to the driver's side, holding my shield with my FBI ID out as close as I dare to get. I keep the gun pointed away from him but still ready in case I need it. Two more gunshots ring out from behind me, and I see him react to them as he takes in my ID and me.

"SAC Susan Parker in pursuit of a suspect, need your vehicle," I blurt out in rapid fire.

His eyes widen in recognition. He knows me. Either from that year-old *LA Times* article or from today's viral footage. I don't give a damn which one. At least, he hasn't taken his gun out to shoot me, and that's all that matters.

"Get in!" he says.

"Thataway!" I yell as I throw myself into the back of the cruiser because it's faster than running around to the shotgun seat. "Step on it!"

The powerful engine pushes the SUV over the last bit of slope and we're on the farm level now. I point across his shoulder. "Go!"

Credit to the guy, he doesn't hesitate or ask me if I really want to do that. He just floors it and the cruiser leaps, crashing into the field. It tears into the dried out vine stalks and tosses them aside like they were chaff. We roar through the field, ripping a swathe through it. Vine stalks, dried leaves, dirt, all go flying around and behind us, leaving a trail of dust.

Through the windshield, I can see the two figures still running across the field. The farther one, the shooter, is almost at the far end of the field now, about a hundred and fifty yards away. Naved is close on his heels, but has fallen almost fifty or sixty yards behind. The shooter probably let off a couple of shots in Naved's direction to force him to slow down.

The other cops closer to the farm haven't given pursuit yet. I'm betting they're still trying to figure out what's going on and what to do about it, instead of simply running like headless chickens across a dark field after two unidentified armed men who suddenly began shooting at each other. I don't blame them.

"Faster!" I yell at the highway cop. He's a young guy, mid to late twenties, but he's a doer not a talker, thankfully, and gives the cruiser more gas, piledriving through the field. The sound of dry brush and leaves hitting the metal is relentless, adding a sense of urgency to the chase. We're cutting across the field at a diagonal now, and it's clear that we're going to pass Naved and cut off the shooter in another couple seconds. Which was my intention when I went for the car instead of after the bastard who shot at me.

Naved turns his head to look sideways at us as we roar past him. I wave, not knowing if he can see me, but he waves back. He still doesn't slow his pace though. I admire his tenacity.

The shooter has heard and seen us coming, too, and he keeps looking back over his shoulder as we gain on him.

A muzzle flash flares in the dark as he lets off a shot. It goes wide and I worry about it going on to hit one of the volunteers by the farmhouse behind us. I'd never have done that. Basic firearms safety: check the background before shooting. Even then, each time I've used my weapon, I've had nightmares afterwards about a stray shot accidentally hitting some innocent bystander, especially a child. It's every lawman's worst fear. This idiot doesn't care though. He's just firing blindly, desperate to get away.

"Cut him off!" I tell the highway cop. I yell it too loudly, right in his ear, but bless him, he does what I say without complaining.

The cruiser swings in an arc, around the shooter who tries to veer away instinctively, pointing the gun at us and letting off another wild shot. This one pings off the top of the SUV, producing a hollow metallic sound. The cruiser comes around in a curve to present the driver's side to the oncoming shooter before screeching to a halt.

I'm out of the vehicle and running around it almost before it has come to a halt. In the distance, I see Naved off to my right now, still at least fifty yards out and slowing as he sees us. He knows the danger of crossfire and the last thing we need is to fire at the shooter, miss, and take each other out instead.

I crouch, arms flung out, gun and head aligned and as low as I can manage while still staying upright. I'm aiming for the center of the shooter's chest. He flails around wildly, trying to decide which way to go.

"Federal agent! Throw down your weapon!" I yell.

The shooter hesitates. In the ambient light from the cruiser's high beams, I see now that it's the same SCVPD cop who challenged us earlier. He's wounded. Just a flesh wound, I think, from the ragged tear in his sleeve through which wet flesh glistens in the moonlight, and the way he favors that shoulder. That must be where Naved hit him with his first shot. The shot that saved my life.

"FBI! Drop your gun!" I yell.

The highway cop is out of his cruiser and has his gun on the shooter too by now. Naved approaches at a slower, cautious jog. We have the shooter triangulated. He's not going anywhere, not without getting shot again.

The other cops by the farmhouse are too far away to be much good at the moment but they are there, too. Someone's probably called for a chopper, or maybe there's already a drone up there, circling and trying to make sense of what's happening.

The shooter has nowhere to go, and he knows it. He turns a full circle, trying to find a way out, caught like a rat in a trap.

I advance slowly, my voice hard and precise.

"Last warning!" I call out. "Lose the gun."

Even in this dim light, I can tell when the fight goes out of him. He knows he's trapped and accepts it. He raises the hand with the gun in it, lets me see and hear it drop with a dry crunch as he says, in a voice that's more shrill and panicked than I expected, "Don't shoot! Please! I'm unarmed now!"

He has an accent. I'm pretty sure it's Armenian.

He raises both hands even before I can tell him to do it.

"Keep your hands up!" I order, coming closer, my gun still held out.

Naved is maybe twenty yards away and closing faster now that he sees the shooter has been disarmed. I shift the gun to my right hand and wave him in. He nods and comes up.

I call back to the highway cop without taking my eyes off the shooter.

"Officer, hold your position. My partner over there, Detective Naved Seth of SCVPD, and I are going to put the cuffs on him. Okay?"

"Okay," he calls back.

Naved comes up beside the shooter, approaching cautiously. I move a little so I'm not in Naved's line of fire, just in case, click the safety back on my Glock, holster and secure the weapon, then come up to the shooter.

Even in the moonlight, I can see how scared he is, sweating

profusely, trembling with exertion. He looks thin, emaciated, pale, like the other eleven in the hospital. If he's an SCVPD cop, he's the thinnest, most underfed one I've ever seen. I'm guessing he took it off someone and SCVPD will find a body somewhere in the fields or woods, either stabbed to death or unconscious. I'm hoping it's the latter.

"Please," he says as I approach. "I didn't know who to trust. There was nobody to tell us what to do anymore. I didn't mean to shoot at you. I'm sorry. Please don't kill me."

"We're not going to kill you, Aram Grygorian," I say. "We just want to talk to you."

He reacts to the sound of his name, staring as if seeing me for the first time.

"You are Susan Parker?" he says.

The fact that he knows my name sends a chill through me. Then I remind myself that he's been hanging around here for at least a day and two nights, long enough to hear my name mentioned more than once.

"That's Special Agent in Charge Susan Parker to you. I'm the federal agent you just shot at and tried to kill," I say. "That's a federal charge, buster. You're going away for a very long time."

I instruct him to interlace his fingers and place them on the top of his head.

"I want to talk to you," Grygorian says. "If I know it was you, I not shoot. So many cops, not good light, I did not know you Susan Parker. I am sorry, very sorry."

"That's a first," says the state trooper. "Never heard a perp apologize for shooting at a cop before!"

"Stick around in this business long enough, you'll hear a lot worse," I say laconically as I pull Grygorian's hands back to cuff him.

"You should put him down and bend a knee," the trooper says. "I'd do it if some asshole took a shot at me. Any cop would, sure as shit."

"Yeah, well, I'm not you and I'm not any cop," I say.

He shrugs.

The trooper's right though.

Some SCVPD cops would probably keep their knee on the back of his neck for a good fifteen minutes or more just to punish him for shooting at them, but I hate that kind of action. I take no pleasure in causing unnecessary pain to others. I've caught the guy and that's enough.

Besides, Grygorian is so pathetic and weak, even my 125lbs would probably crack his ribs.

I read him his rights. Once I'm done, the trooper wanders back to his SUV to answer his radio. Naved and I start walking Grygorian back to the tents which are buzzing with SCVPD as the news of the arrest spreads.

Naved looks at me. I know I must look a mess, dirt all over my face and hands, leaves in my hair, barefoot, sweaty.

"You all right?"

"I'm okay, I'm not hit. You?"

"I'm good. I thought he got you with that first one."

I can still feel the burn along my spine, like a flaming rod touched once, but lightly. The smell of burnt hair is still in my nostrils, despite the stronger odor of dirt.

"It was close," I say.

"I should have shot sooner. Should have seen him coming. I was facing him. You were looking in the opposite direction. I shouldn't have let him get off even those shots," Naved says.

"Shoulda woulda coulda," I say, putting my hand on Naved's shoulder. "Don't beat yourself up about it. You got down when the going got rough, that's all that matters. Besides, we got him."

"Thanks to you," Naved says. "That stunt with the state trooper's SUV was fucking awesome. If you had just run after him like I did..." He shakes his head. "You're something else, Susan Parker."

"Just doing my job, Detective Seth," but the compliment warms me.

"Please," Grygorian says suddenly, twisting around to look at me with his large eyes. "We talk, yes? I have information. Very useful. Worth your while."

"Sure, sure," I say, still upbeat from surviving the near-death encounter and the successful chase. "You can talk all you want to the Santa Carina Valley Police Department. They'll be the ones booking you and charging you. Sing all you like to them."

Grygorian turns his head to stare in the direction of the ranch house. The cluster of SCVPD cops around Chief McDougall are all conferring, while the chief appears to be busy on a call. He holds up a finger, telling them to wait one moment, while he listens to the person on the other hand.

"Please, if they arrest me, I be dead man in one day, maybe two. He will send others for kill me. He knows I will talk. I betray already. I do as he want, I kill fat doctor. But then I break his rule. I leave therapy room."

"Who?" I ask.

Grygorian shakes his head nervously, scanning the dried out rows of vine stalks. "Not here. How you say? Fields have ears. We talk private. I tell you much. Yes?"

Naved and I look at each other.

"Can you believe this guy?" I say, gesturing at Naved with my hand which Grygorian can't see since he's in front of me. "He's giving me a full statement right here."

Naved gets the message: *keep playing on.* "Sounds like he's making stuff up to try to save his skin," he says.

"I tell truth," Grygorian says. "Please to believe! Take me safe place. Not police."

"Relax, bozo," I tell Grygorian in a cheerfully cynical tone, playing my part to the hilt, "you'll probably be taken to the hospital, like the other eleven patients."

At the mention of the other eleven, Grygorian grows more

agitated. "No, no, no!" he says. "I cannot! No take there. I go, I am dead man. Please, Susan Parker. *You* take me."

"Hey, hey," Naved says, gripping Grygorian's bony arm to steady him. "Calm down. Nobody's going to hurt you. You'll be under police protection."

McDougall finishes talking and gestures to his men. Two of the plainclothes detectives, senior bulls both whom I know, split off from the group and start walking toward us. They have less than a hundred yards to cover. They're heavy-set, middle-aged men, not in the best of shape, and take their time. They can see that the suspect isn't going anywhere.

"Lawyer," Grygorian says suddenly, as if struck by inspiration. "I want lawyer. You have to get lawyer for me. It is law, yes? Get lawyer!"

"See those two men over there, walking toward us?" I say. "They're cops. They'll get you someone from the public defender's office. Though it may be a while, this being Thanksgiving."

"Please, Susan Parker," Grygorian says, looking and sounding like he's on the verge of tears now. "I beg you in the name of your dead husband. Amit Kapoor. Yes? For his sake, do not do this."

At the sound of Amit's name in this man's strange accent, my heart stops.

"What did you just say?" I ask him, dropping all pretense now.

Naved stares at Grygorian but I can sense that he's watching me. He's afraid that I'll lose my cool.

Grygorian looks at me, nodding pitifully. "I know he die, yes? Police call suicide? But it was not suicide. Your husband not kill himself."

I stare at Grygorian, feeling heat rise up inside me like a match flaring. "You can't possibly know that."

"You take me safe place. I tell you what I know. Please. I have family also. Two daughter. Wife. I want go home to them.

You are only hope, Susan Parker. That why I write your name on yellow note, stick to door."

Naved looks at him. "You wrote that note?"

I glance over Grygorian's shoulder at the two approaching cops. Fifty yards and closing.

I make a snap decision.

"Naved," I say quietly. "Go get your car. Meet me at the top of the dirt road. *Now.*"

Naved looks at me, sees my face, then starts jogging without another word or question. He jogs toward the two approaching SCVPD cops who stop, thinking he's coming to them. When he runs past them, they turn and watch him, calling out to him. Naved continues to the Camry without answering.

I don't wait to see the rest, I've already started walking away, turning to the right toward the top of the dirt road, away from the ranch house, away from the two approaching cops.

"Walk fast," I tell Grygorian.

Grygorian doesn't need urging. He keeps pace with me, moving quickly. He stumbles a time or two, like a man at the end of his tether, but gathers himself together and manages to go on. He walks like a bundle of bones in a sack moving independently of one another, but he and I are a good deal faster than the SCVPD cops.

The two of them probably start to realize something is off by now. They call out my name and title, trying to pick up their pace.

I ignore them.

Naved is in the Camry now. He drives past the two cops who slow down as they see him pass them by and now they're sure something's wrong. One of them starts talking on his radio, while the other one picks up the pace, jogging toward Grygorian and me.

The SCVPD cop is less than ten yards away when Naved brings the Camry to a halt beside me.

"Get in," I order Grygorian.

We both pile in, both of us in the back seat.

"Go," I tell Naved.

Behind us, I can hear the cop shouting. Other cops have noticed, too, and several of the younger ones are starting to run.

Naved floors the Camry, taking us down the dirt road in a bumper car rollercoaster ride.

The suspension takes a couple of bad ones, but the car keeps going. I hope his ride is in better shape than my poor Prius because it would be really embarrassing if we break down now. But the Camry gets us down the arroyo and to the paved road. The media vans are out in force, probably buzzing with word of the chase and gunshots, but I doubt they'll have the news of the arrest this soon, especially since we haven't actually *made* a formal arrest.

"Get your head down," I order Grygorian. To Naved, I say, "Keep going. Don't stop, no matter what."

I shove Grygorian's shaved head down into the footwell of the rear seat, while I do the same on my side. Bright camera lights shine into the car, turning the interior day-bright and I can hear reporters yelling even through the closed windows. Then we're past the media gauntlet and hurtling down the road.

TWENTY-ONE

We pull into Naved's driveway. We need a place where we won't be disturbed for a short while at least, and where we can secure Grygorian. When Naved offered, I didn't think twice.

I help Grygorian out of the back seat. He straightens up and looks around fearfully. His face looks like a bony Halloween mask; the fear in his eyes is real.

"You sure there's nobody home?" I ask Naved for the second time.

He nods, then realizes I might not see it in the dark. "Just me."

We go in through the side gate which lets out a long, sustained squeak and a clang as it shuts behind us. My neighborhood is quiet, but this is dead silent. Being at the end of the cul de sac, on top of the hill—or is it a mountain?—the nearest through road is several hundred meters away, and it's never very busy even in business hours. Right now, the only sound audible in the distance is the wailing of the coyotes, and about five miles away in Canyon Country, the hooting of a goods train as it passes through Santa Carina Junction, just as they have since the railroad reached here a hundred and seventy years ago in the Wild West era.

The house has that silent pallor of uninhabited places. It's a fairly typical four-bedroom Spanish style hacienda, two stories, wooden flooring, red terracotta tiles with solar panels, the usual arched entrances and little flourishes. We enter through the back door which looks out onto a backyard and swimming pool that looks disused. Two bright yellow plastic ducks float on the still surface.

Something rustles in the bushes by the back wall, and I glimpse a furry shape with a tail leaping to the wall and disappearing over it. Raccoon? Coyote? Fox? Bobcat? Take your pick. Maybe even a young mountain lion looking for easy pickings.

The people I know who live up in these hills make sure to keep their pets indoors: dogs, especially the little ones, are like catnip to the local predators. Lata's last girlfriend knew someone from Plum Canyon who was bit on the butt by a mountain lion when they were hiking in the mountains in the open area, a large undeveloped space meant for hikers and trekkers. People have been crowding the animals out of their habitats for centuries, and out here on the edge of civilization, some of them are fierce enough to bite back.

Naved offers us water, drinks, food. Grygorian drinks greedily, water sluicing down his long pale throat as his large Adam's apple bobs. He finishes almost the entire bottle. Naved sticks some burritos in the microwave while I hit the restroom and take a look around. The house is filled with pictures and stuff belonging to other people, a family. They look Hispanic to me, not South Asian like Naved and his family. There's no sign of him or his anywhere. I guess he's house sitting for someone else, or maybe just borrowing their guest room till he finds a place of his own. It's not really my business but I'm concerned about someone else walking in on us.

"So you're sure nobody else is expected?" I ask Naved while

Grygorian scarfs down the burrito like it's the first food he's had in a year.

Naved glances at the mantel shelf covered with pictures of what is clearly not his family. "Belongs to a friend," he says. "They're on a long vacation in Oaxaca, visiting family there. I have the place to myself until the second week of Jan. Just till I find my feet and an apartment."

I nod. I notice he didn't say "a house" or mention his family.

I glance over at Grygorian, seated at the kitchen island, polishing off the first burrito and looking like he's capable of burning through the second. "Thanks for going along with me on this."

Naved is silent for a moment. "You sure this is a good idea, Susan? I mean, McDougall is mad as hell. My phone's blowing up with messages and missed calls."

"So's mine. That's only to be expected. This is a big arrest for McDougall, a huge break for SCVPD. Especially after all the egg on his face from having a serial killer and a farmhouse dungeon filled with abductees right in his backyard. He probably thinks I'm trying to steal the glory from him by bringing Grygorian into federal custody. I'm betting he has his people racing to LA even as we speak, lights and sirens going full blast."

"And he's probably already called your boss," Naved says.

"Yeah, that too," I admit. I don't mention that I've already ignored a missed call and a text from Gantry.

"So what's the plan here, Susan? I mean, what's the end game? Why did you ask me if I could bring him here? Why not take him down to the task force workspace? Or the sheriff's station? Or even a federal facility where we'd have a proper interview room, cameras, witnesses, the works."

"Sure, sure," I say. "But then we might as well have handed him over to McDougall's bulls right there on the farm."

"So why didn't we?"

I smile at him. "I have a plan. You heard me calling Kayla

and asking her to patch the others into the call too, back in the car. You heard what I told them all to do. They're on it. You've seen my team work. They're damn good at their jobs. Wheels are in motion as we speak. Don't worry. Play along with me and before the night's done, we might just make everyone happy. But before we do that, I need to know what this guy knows."

Naved looks at me for a long moment, then at Grygorian, who has indeed managed to demolish the better part of the second burrito while we've talked, and then sighs.

"Okay, Susan. I'm trusting you. But you know this means my badge and career if things go south."

"And mine, too," I say. "You've trusted me so far. Trust me a little longer, Naved."

He nods.

We give Grygorian a bathroom break and Naved finds him something to wear from his own wardrobe. Grygorian looks weird in a sweatshirt, pants, and sneakers. I can hardly recognize the man we chased across the vineyard. Only his sunken cheeks, hollowed-out eyes, and the loose way his clothes hang off him are a reminder of the weeks he spent in Magnusson's therapy room.

We take a seat on the large, comfortable couches in the high-ceilinged living room.

At my insistence, Naved reluctantly took the cuffs off Grygorian earlier so he could eat and drink freely and I told him to leave them off while we talk. I don't think this guy is going anywhere right now. All he wants is to be here and talk to me. I'm burning up with curiosity.

"Mr. Grygorian," I say, "you clean up nice."

He twitches, glancing nervously around. He looks jittery, crossing and uncrossing his long legs. "I am sorry," he says. He gestures in my direction. "For the shooting at you. I was not knowing it was you. I think it is one of them, come to kill me. I shoot first, in self-defense."

I hold up a hand. "Mr. Grygorian," I say. "You recall that back in the vineyard, before we got into Detective Seth's car, you asked me to get you a lawyer. My team is working on that right now. I need you to know that if you choose to speak to me without that lawyer present, you may incriminate yourself. Do you understand what that means?"

Grygorian says petulantly, "I do not care legal. It is not of consequence. I am fearing for my life here. You are only one who will help me, Susan Parker."

I look at Naved who shrugs as if to say *It's your party*. I tell Grygorian to go on.

"They will be looking for me even now," Grygorian says, addressing me directly across the coffee table. "If they find, they will kill. They do not hesitate. I need you help. It is only way to stay alive for me."

"Who's trying to kill you?" I say, leaning forward.

He gestures wildly. "Splinter!" as if it should be obvious.

"Splinter is dead," Naved says. "You killed Dr. Magnusson—"

Grygorian flaps his hand at him. "Magnusson only front. He caretaker. His name on farm, it is perfect place for Splinter therapy. That is only reason he chosen."

"You're claiming Magnusson was a front?" I say. "For whom?"

Grygorian shakes his head, his unruly hair flopping from side to side. "I do not know name. I not see his face. Only hear voice. Maybe voice also modify. He use, how you call it, virtual avatar? Like him on screen, but not his real face. He speak, but not real voice."

"This person you're speaking of, is that the real Splinter? The serial killer who murdered all those families?" I ask.

Grygorian stares at me with a puzzled look on his face. "You do not understand this yet? You are not understanding?"

"What do you mean?" I say.

"*Splinter* kill those families, all those people," he says.

"Yes, that's what I'm saying. Splinter killed them all. I'm asking you a simple question: if Magnusson wasn't Splinter, then who was? Was it this anonymous person whom you saw in a virtual avatar?"

Grygorian shakes his head again. "You still not getting this. Magnusson not Splinter. He cannot be Splinter. He only a tool to oversee therapy. A helper." He gestures, trying to think of the right word. "How you call them? Ass-ociate?"

He emphasizes the first three letters in the word 'associate', either deliberately or ignorantly, it's hard to tell. He's quite agitated and only getting more upset by the minute.

"You're saying Magnusson was an associate of Splinter?" Naved asks.

Grygorian groans, gets to his feet and starts pacing in a random pattern around the room, gesturing and talking. "Not of Splinter! Nobody can be associate of Splinter! Splinter is Splinter."

Naved and I look at each other. This is getting really weird. Right now, I'm glad we're both armed but Grygorian doesn't seem violent or hostile, just frustrated. The language problem isn't helping either.

"We want to understand you," I say. "We're doing our best. Please calm down and try to explain it to us. Make us understand. We want to help you."

That has an effect. He stops pacing and looks at me. Abruptly, he sits again. "You must do this something for me. Soon, it must be. It is only way they might agree to let me live."

I nod. "That's why we're here. I'm listening. But first, you agreed to give me some information. You said you were going to tell me something about my husband's death."

Grygorian stares at me directly for the first time since we've been here. He has a peculiar look on his face. I don't know him well enough to be able to read it accurately.

Suddenly, he buries his face in his hands. Without seeing his face, I can't tell what he's feeling or expressing. It's an oddly unsettling moment.

Naved and I look at each other.

I shrug.

I get a text message from Kayla:

> Reaching u in 7. Bohjalian en route.

> > Gr8. Use side gate, back door.

I add the code for the back door that Naved gave me and hit send.

Kayla sends back a thumbs up emoji.

I see that I have several more missed calls and unread texts. The only one I choose to tap on is from Lata.

> Got news update. Shots fired at Splinter ranch. U ok?

> > I'm fine, unhurt, all good

> Prolly won't be home tonight.

> > Ok, u do what you have to do. Don't stress about me and N. Ok?

I sense the anxiety between those simple words.

She's telling me she understands from her own combat experience how important it is for a soldier in the field to know they have the full, unconditional support of their family and loved ones. That they can't afford to be distracted by personal doubts and worries when they're under fire and in life-threatening situations. She gets it. It doesn't mean she's not still mad at me for accepting the return to duty and diving in like this off the deep end—exactly what I promised her I *wouldn't* do—but she understands and supports me. It fills me with a warmth so empowering, I feel like I could climb mountains on that energy alone. It also brings moisture to my eyes which I have to blink back.

I heart you, I send back, using the pulsing red heart emoji in place of the word.

She sends back the same pulsing heart emoji too.

Grygorian keeps his face buried in his hands this whole time, not looking up or reacting. When his face finally emerges, he looks red-eyed, as if he's been crying.

He can't seem to make eye contact with me now.

"Grygorian," I say again, gently but firmly. "We had a deal. You would give me one piece of info upfront, I would do this favor for you, provided it's not illegal, and afterwards, you'll tell me the rest. That was the deal, wasn't it?"

I ask the last question of Naved who nods, backing me up.

I continue, "You said you know that my husband Amit Kapoor's death was not a suicide. It's time for you to start talking now."

Grygorian looks miserable. He stares down at the floor between his feet as if he wants to dive into it and disappear.

He sits that way for several minutes.

Disgusted, I stand up. "This is going nowhere. Let's get him into custody."

It's a bluff and Naved knows it, but pretends he's about to stand up, too.

Grygorian's head jerks up in panic. "No! No. You stay. I need help from you."

"Then start talking or I walk," I say.

He grimaces, makes several faces, as if trying to work himself up, and finally says, "Your husband, he left-handed, yes?"

I answer cautiously, "Yes."

"Then how he shoot himself in right temple?" Grygorian asks, addressing the question downwards, as if ashamed to look at me.

I blink several times. Naved looks at me, catching my reaction.

I say to Naved quietly, "I kept pointing that out to SCVPD. They kept deflecting. Said it wasn't relevant, people do strange things in those last moments. They just wouldn't agree that it mattered."

Naved nods in understanding. "It didn't fit the narrative, so they brushed it under the rug."

To Grygorian I say, "That's something you could have gotten anywhere, off the internet maybe. There are a lot of podcasts, bloggers, vloggers, all speculating about every Splinter murder. Even I've talked about it publicly."

Grygorian frowns, thinking. "The house," he says at last.

"The murder house? What about it?" I say sharply. Now that we're on point, I'm impatient to get something out of him. We're already off to a bad start with that left-handed thing. I'm not going to have him lob some scrap of rumor he picked off the web and pass it off as new info. If he's messing with me on this, I'm not going to take it lying down.

Beside me, I feel Naved stiffen. Maybe he's also getting irritated with Grygorian for wasting our time.

Grygorian flaps his hands. "He die in Splinter murder house, yes? No?"

"Yes," I say.

"And you thinking that no, he did not kill self, he was kill by Splinter. Yes? This is your theory, I think?" Grygorian asks me directly.

My heart flips. "It's one possibility."

"Because he die in Splinter murder house, yes?" Grygorian says.

I shrug. "It is a big coincidence."

Naved leans forward. "Are you trying to tell us that it was Splinter that killed Amit Kapoor?"

Grygorian waves his hand, as if saying bye-bye. "Impossible! Splinter not possible to kill Amit Kapoor. Because Splinter not here in America that time."

"You sound very sure of that," Naved says. "How can you be so sure?"

Grygorian spreads his large hands, almost as if he's miming every word as well as speaking it. Natalie would find him very entertaining, I think unexpectedly, and suddenly that helps me see the man in a different perspective. Not as a lying criminal trying to bullshit his way out of a situation, but as a scared, nervous victim trying to make himself understood in a language that isn't his mother tongue.

"Because it cannot be. Splinter always foreigner, not American! Splinter who kill that family? That Splinter already have return home."

Grygorian mimes a plane taking off then uses his long, spindly fingers to indicate numbers. "Whoosh! Fly only one week after murder. Amit Kapoor come to house two, maybe three months afterward? Splinter long gone before that. Not in US! So. See? Impossible!"

Naved and I both look at each other. I see my impatience mirrored on his face, as well as the personal irritation that I know I'm feeling.

"How could you possibly know that?" I ask Grygorian.

"Unless you've met Splinter and he's told you this personally? Is that what happened?" Naved asks.

Grygorian puts his hands on his head, covering his face partially this time. Again, the same gesture of shame. "I cannot tell you. I say too much already."

I decide to switch tack, trying a less confrontational tone. "Grygorian, listen to me. If you're worried about being charged as an accessory because you were in contact with Splinter, we might be able to help with that. I can put you in touch with the Bureau's legal team and the state's attorney. My people are already on it even as we speak. It's all being set up. We can try to get you some protection, maybe even immunity, depending on how much you can tell us. But you have to tell the truth right now."

"I am only telling truth!" Grygorian yells. It's almost a wail. He's starting to remind me of a six-foot-plus toddler now, terrified of being punished for something bad he's done. But his fear is real, and there's no question that the threat he fears is real, too. "Nothing but truth I tell you. Why you not listen! You must help! Or they kill me!"

I decide to take this all the way. I move over to sit on the couch adjacent to his. I put my hand on his elbow. "Okay, okay. Calm down. I'm going to ask you this one question now, and I need you to tell me the truth as simply as you can. Do you understand?"

He seems to calm down a little.

He looks at me with red-rimmed eyes. Closer now, I can see that his tears are real. Whether from the effects of all that he's been through, or because he's genuinely terrified for his own life, he's shaking with fear.

"Yes," he says vehemently. "You ask now. I tell. Ask question."

"Okay," I say and take a deep breath. "You said that Splinter killed that last family that lived in the house where Amit was found. You're right about the timing. Amit died seventy-three days after that murder. The crime scene investigation had been completed and the house was deserted by then, only a patrol car left outside, and police tape around the house. The police and the FBI think that Splinter came back, found Amit there and killed him. I don't believe that and now, you say that isn't what happened."

"Yes, yes," Grygorian says, nodding vigorously. "Not

possible for Splinter kill Amit Kapoor. Splinter already gone from USA."

"Are you saying Splinter fled abroad? After killing Dr. Rao and his family?"

"Yes," he says, looking happier now that I'm accepting his version. "Splinter go abroad."

"Do you know if Splinter is still abroad now? Or if he's returned to the US since then? Anything you say could be helpful."

Grygorian looks at me with the same look of frustration. "I try explain before, but you still not understand. Splinter kill. Then Splinter go, fly outside US. Gone. Whoosh. He never come back. Same like other Splinter murders. Each time, Splinter go in house, kill family, then whoosh, leave US, go home. You see?"

I frown, seeing the inkling of an idea emerge. "Are you saying that Splinter is a foreign national? That he lives some-where else and only comes to the US to commit these killings?"

Grygorian smiles for the first time. It's a strange, bashful grin. His upper teeth are crooked and overlap, adding to the overgrown toddler look. "Yes! Yes! Splinter always foreign national. Always come US. Kill. Go home. Never come back again. Always. Every time. I say that already, did I not?"

I look at Naved. His eyes are wide. He nods at me slowly. This is big. The biggest break in the case we've had until now.

"Okay, Aram," I say, using his first name. "You're doing great. Now, I need to ask you one last question."

He nods vigorously. "I answer. Then I tell you what you do to help me? Yes? This deal?"

I nod too. "Deal."

He grins again. "Ask question."

"If my husband didn't kill himself, and if Splinter didn't kill him, then who did?"

Grygorian shakes his head slowly, a sad expression

appearing on his elongated face. "Wish I could tell. But I do not know this answer."

I'm disappointed. "But you said—"

Grygorian replies very soberly and sadly, "I tell I know Amit Kapoor not die suicide. And I tell you Splinter not kill Amit Kapoor. That I am sure. Exact who kill, I cannot tell sure. But I can tell someone you ask who will know answer. You must ask the Therapist. He know everything because he the one plan everything, tell everyone what to do. Okay? See? I already tell everything I know. Now nothing left. Because I trust you. I think you deal fair. Now you must promise help me. Protect me from Splinter. Otherwise, Splinter come kill me also."

TWENTY-TWO

It's early Friday morning. I'm sitting in the task force workspace which occupies the old sheriff's station in downtown Santa Carina, right next to the courthouse and public library. My team is with me. Kayla, David, Ramon, Brine, and of course, Naved.

A cluster of SCVPD's finest is gathered at the far end of the premises, watching a live news report on a wall mounted flatscreen TV. The report itself is being broadcast live from right outside the building. The bright broadcast lights creep in around the edges of the closed windows and doors, seeping in to fill the already illuminated workspace with day-bright luminescence. Kayla just informed us that social media is blowing up. It's easy enough to imagine all those American people in their homes nationwide, all of whom have had a bellyful of turkey and family and are eager for a distraction from their real lives.

Onscreen, currently being telecast live across all the major news and streaming networks, Chief McDougall is standing beside two other people in front of this building. The good-looking man in the expensive suit is Andrew Bohjalian of Bohjalian Legal, the high-priced high-profile defense attorney I had Kayla call in to represent Aram Grygorian. The third person is Deputy US Attorney Masaba Ibrahim who looks none the worse for wear despite being hauled out of bed at an unearthly hour on Thanksgiving night.

McDougall has just finished announcing the finding of the twelfth Splinter victim and the recovery of the murder weapon that killed Magnusson, believed to be the man who kept the twelve people imprisoned at the basement of the old ranch farmhouse under deplorable, inhumane conditions. The words 'therapy rooms' are mentioned more than once. Everyone is being very careful about the phrasing and emphasis, careful not to label Grygorian as a murderer while artfully leaving no doubt that he killed Splinter. By the time they're done, it comes off as yet another victim rescued from the horrific serial killer. Almost every network uses Magnusson's file pic with the words "believed to be Splinter" without compunction.

When McDougall re-enters the task force workspace and passes by my team, he looks as pleased as the cat that got all the turkey. For once he doesn't give me the evil eye.

As far as he's concerned, all is forgiven between us.

By giving him all the credit for bringing in Grygorian and letting him save face for having nurtured a serial killer in his backyard, I've risen several notches in McDougall's estimation. Pissed off as he was when I took off with Grygorian from the ranch, this actually played out far better for him. Had I simply handed Grygorian over at the time, McDougall wouldn't have been able to deny the fact that Naved and I (and that state trooper, who's completely swept aside and sidelined in this) nabbed Splinter's killer. We would have gotten all the credit.

This way, he gets to shine. When I had David speak to him a couple hours earlier, that's how he sold the proposition to McDougall.

McDougall, being the consummate politician, quickly saw how this worked out in his favor and as far as everyone is concerned, my brief escapade with Grygorian never happened. Officially, the conversation Naved and I had with Grygorian never happened either, but since we have a recording, we could bring it back into the picture anytime we choose. For the moment, we're holding it back. I didn't even mention it to Gantry when I talked to him earlier. I simply explained our disappearing act as my taking "abundant caution" due to Grygorian's perception of an imminent threat.

The way I described it was intended to make Gantry believe that Grygorian was in actual mortal fear of being shot by the cops and had asked both for a lawyer as well as protection, both of which are technically accurate facts, and so I drove around with Detective Seth until Bohjalian and his associates arrived to take custody of Grygorian. Gantry bought it either because it was credible, or because there was no advantage in busting my ass over what turned out to be nothing.

And because McDougall's happy, Gantry is happy, too.

"So let me get this straight," David says, frowning as he works through it in his slow, methodical way, "you're saying that Magnusson, who was once a licensed psychiatrist and a practicing psychotherapist, was only the caretaker of sorts. Overseeing the incarceration of the twelve abductees. While the real kidnapper was this faceless Therapist person. Who was the one behind it all, pulling Magnusson's strings, torturing the twelve abductees during their imprisonment in these 'therapy rooms', all the while appearing only as a virtual avatar on the screens installed in these rooms. But this "Therapist" was not Splinter either. Splinter is a foreign national who flies into the US, slaughters targeted victims—each one himself or herself a therapist—along with their families, after forcing them to endure unspeakable tortures, and then flies back home to his or her homeland after the deed is done? And this is how all the Splinter killings were committed?"

I nod slowly. "That's pretty much it."

David shakes his head. "Unbelievable."

"It's kind of genius, actually. If you think about it," Brine says. "He's got all the authorities here in the States running about like headless chickens looking for him while he's already done and dusted, cooling his heels on some beach drinking pina coladas."

Kayla elbows him hard enough to almost knock Brine off his tilted seat. "Don't stereotype. You don't know who he is or even if he's a he. He could be some revolutionary who thinks of himself as an activist-hero working to right social injustices for all you know. Sometimes, shit gets pretty crazy when dudes get fueled by righteousness."

"Since when does torturing kids and butchering families count as social justice, K?" Ramon says. "Nah. Dude's messed up in the head. I make him for a former patient who didn't like the meds he'd been scripped and went loco. He ain't no hero, not in my book."

"Kayla, you have a point about the stereotyping," David says, the geriatric millennial of my youngish team, "but there's really no use speculating about any of this. All we really know is that Splinter is a foreign national. For all we know, he could be any one of the twelve victims slash patients we brought out of those therapy rooms."

Everybody is silent for a minute after David says this.

They all look at each other, then at me.

I nod. "Already there, guys. The connection's too obvious to ignore. It can't be a coincidence that Splinter happens to be a foreign national and that the twelve 'patients' down in that basement were foreign nationals, too. We can't ignore the likelihood that one of those twelve could be Splinter."

Naved's the only one who isn't buying this line of reasoning. "That doesn't make sense. If Splinter's the mastermind behind this whole set-up, why would he subject himself to that kind of degradation and subhuman treatment? Why incarcerate himself in a therapy room alongside all the others?"

I shrug. "So he can hide in plain sight? Right now, even if we assume that Splinter is one of those twelve, we still can't be certain which one he is."

Ramon raises a digital pencil. "Actually, Carlotta can answer that one. She says he's not any of the twelve. She checked their I-94s already, remember? Every time they entered or exited the United States, it would have been noted on their I-94s. For one of the twelve to be Splinter, they would have had to be present in the United States during Splinter's previous kills. But when Carlotta searched, she came up with zip, zilch, nada. The twelve are all first-time visitors to the US. Carlotta told us that right at the top."

Naved points to Ramon. "There you go. That proves conclusively that Splinter is *not* one of the twelve."

"But then what's their connection to Splinter? Or Magnusson? Or this mysterious Therapist, whoever *he* is?" Kayla asks.

"I don't know," I say, "but there has to be one."

Naved shakes his head. "I'm not convinced, Susan. Grygorian was half off his rocker. He could have just been feeding us a line to get us off his back."

Brine nods vigorously. "I'm with you. There's something hinky about all this. I mean, look at the guy, Grygorian. A couple hours ago, he was impersonating a cop, hiding out in plain sight, armed and willing to kill. Now, he's lawyered up, under the wing of the great Andrew Bohjalian, who's foregone his usual six-figure retainer to rep Grygorian pro bono. By the time this is over, Bohjalian will probably get Grygorian off with a slap on the wrist, even though he's committed a string of crimes, including first degree murder, attempted murder of a federal officer, and who knows what else."

I frown. "So what are you saying? That he made the whole thing up? He's lying?"

"Or he's just plain loco, jefe," Ramon says. "You gotta consider the possibility."

Even Kayla nods. "The man needs help," she says. "Can't blame him for saying whatever keeps him out of trouble. I mean, it makes a nice story, but it does smell funny."

"And the fear of Splinter coming after him? Of being killed?" I ask. "Those are just, what, paranoid delusions?"

David says, "You said it."

Kayla nods. "He could just be a paranoid schizophrenic off his meds."

"I don't buy that," I say. "I don't buy any of it. I believe Grygorian. I think he's telling the truth."

"What truth is that?" Naved asks. "I mean, think about it, Susan. All he's done is muddy the waters. If we buy his whole crazy spiel, then what do we have?"

"A new suspect, for one," I say. "This 'Therapist' he spoke of. He sounded scared to death of him. Who's that guy?"

"A virtual avatar who only appeared on the screens in the therapy rooms?" Kayla says. "That could have been anybody. Could have been Magnusson himself."

Brine points at Kayla. "That actually makes a whole lot of sense. Captor as well as therapist. Magnusson nabbed them, locked them up, and performed his own sick version of therapy. It's his way of continuing to practice even after his license was taken away. No, you won't stop me from doing my job. I'm Splinter! I treat anyone I like. I even treat other therapists and their families! Nobody stops me! Nobody!"

"Thanks for the dramatic input, Brine," I say, "but we just talked about that. Magnusson couldn't have been Splinter. Magnusson was born right here in the US. Splinter's a foreign national."

"Says who?" Ramon asks. "Grygorian? See, jefe? You're already falling for his line of BS. I ain't buying it. I think

Naved's right. This Grygorian dude was just mouthing off to save his own skin."

"That's what I'm saying, too," Naved says, "Grygorian's version of reality doesn't gel with the rest of the evidence. It just doesn't add up. We put aside his rant and it all makes sense. Magnusson was Splinter. Magnusson abducted the twelve tourists—"

"So why tourists? Why all foreign nationals?" I ask. "And we still haven't answered how Magnusson was able to do all that with his physical condition."

"He could have had an accomplice," David says, "an able-bodied associate who did all the heavy lifting."

I raise my hands, growing frustrated with the lack of support. "Like who did you have in mind?"

Almost in chorus, Ramon, Kayla and Brine all say together, their voices overlapping: "Grygorian!"

Naved gestures. "Grygorian could have been the associate. We know he's killed already and was capable of killing again. It's sheer luck and your good reflexes that saved you from being his next victim. It makes sense that Grygorian and Magnusson acting together were actually Splinter."

David nods. "That makes more sense than the spiel Grygorian gave you. I'm sorry, Susan, but that's just the way I see it, too."

"I don't know," I say. "I don't agree. I think Grygorian's telling the truth."

Naved leans forward. Gently, he says, "Or maybe you want to believe that because he said what he said about Amit's death. Maybe that's clouding your judgment a bit?"

I stare at him.

I look at Naved and the others. I know I must look mad. I *am* mad.

Not all the team knows the full story about Amit. About the schoolteacher and what Naved and I talked about earlier tonight. They only have the recordings and transcripts of Grygorian's Q&A with Naved and me. Naved and I never touched upon the Amit parts in the convo with Grygorian, and the others know better than to bring it up unsolicited.

But Naved knows everything I know about Amit's death.

What is Naved really thinking when he tells me I'm being misled by my emotions?

Does Naved mean that Grygorian was just making that up to save his own skin? That he doesn't actually know anything about Amit's death?

Or is Naved saying that he was just humoring me earlier, by pretending to go along with my crazy, grief-riddled conviction that there was more to Amit's death than everyone else believed, and that he's now trying to bring me down to earth again, telling me to get real, let it go, focus on the case, not bring in my personal feelings and confuse it all up.

The problem is, my personal feelings are all I have. They're the only thing that differentiate me from Gantry, McDougall, the other SCVPD bulls in this task force workspace. They're what makes me me, Susan Parker. If I let go of them, then I'm left with nothing, just procedure and protocol. I'm no different from any other suit in the Bureau.

"I need some air," I say.

Nobody stops me or comes after me.

I walk out of the building, fighting back the tears that threaten to overwhelm me, telling myself to get a grip, and emerge into the cold, bracing November night.

It's quiet outside.

The lot is deserted at this hour.

The media cameras and vans are all gone, except for a couple of stringers parked across the street who are probably sleeping in their vans rather than driving all the way to Los Angeles and then back in a few hours.

The SCVPD bulls and McDougall left a few minutes ago.

I'm tempted to get in my Prius and go for a drive. Drive it off. Just like walking it off, but it burns fewer calories, and probably isn't better for your blood pressure.

But it's already late, really late, and where am I going to go?

Home's just four minutes away at this time of night. I don't want to take this confusion and emotional mess home to Lata and Natalie who are almost certainly peacefully asleep.

If I drive in the opposite direction, it would feel too much like running away. I can't do that again. I have to stay and face this to the end, whichever way the chips fall.

If this were Los Angeles, I'd drive to the nearest all-night diner or coffee shop, not because I need the caffeine—if anything, I need to be decaffeinated—but just for something to do, something to drink while I think. But this is Santa Carina Valley. The "late night" coffee shop, Medal Coffee, shuts at 10 p.m., and that's only because Marge, the octogenarian owner, takes pride in continuing her late husband Emory's tradition. Marge would have locked up four hours ago. And it's another four hours before anything opens up in this sleepy, suburban burgh. So there's literally nowhere to go.

Naved finds me twenty minutes or so later, pacing the parking lot, going nowhere, getting nowhere.

"Hey," he says when I stop walking.

He holds out his palms as he comes toward me.

"Look, I'm sorry if that hurt you," he says quietly. "But I had to say it. Out loud. Because I know the others won't say it. They're too loyal to you, too afraid of setting you off."

I exhale. "No. No. You were right to say it. I was buying Grygorian's spiel too easily. I should know better. I've done a thousand suspect interviews before. They always lie. Yet here I am, not just buying into his story lock, stock, and barrel, but even trying to sell it to you guys. What was I thinking?"

Naved looks relieved. I think he was afraid that I might lash out at him. I'd lay even odds that he was hesitant to come out here until Kayla and Ramon encouraged him, seconded by David and backed up by Brine. But he was still nervous.

"Okay, good," he says, sounding as relieved as he looks. "I was afraid you might—"

I wave his explanation away. "The thing is, Naved. Even if Grygorian was lying about everything, there was something about the way he talked about it all. About the Splinter killings. About the whole operation. Something that smelled true. Sure, it smelled hinky, too, I won't deny that. But there was some truth in it. You saw him. He was scared shitless. That wasn't a lie."

Naved shrugs. I can see he doesn't agree but doesn't want to disagree outright with me either. He probably thinks I'm just having a hard time accepting that it was all BS and trying to let me come to that conclusion myself when I'm ready. "Sure, sure. But how do we separate the truth from the bullshit? Susan, we can't afford to go off on a tangent. Not now. Not when we've practically closed the whole Splinter case."

I frown. "Closed? How do you figure?"

Naved shrugs. "Look around. McDougall and the SCVPD practically took a victory lap tonight. Magnusson AKA Splinter is dead, killed by one of his own victims, who's lawyered up and will argue, convincingly, that it was self-defense and/or justifiable homicide, or even plead temporary insanity maybe. Either way, the big bad evil witch is dead. The victims are rescued. We've got boatloads of evidence from the farmhouse, to use Mancini's phrase, and once the lawyers sort it all out, we'll have the first comprehensive video record of a major serial killer's methodology and who knows what else. The academicians and retired BAU profilers will be writing books and papers about this for decades. You could write a book about it! You could make it your ticket to fame and riches. It's happened before. There's nothing more left to investigate."

I hear every word he says but even before he finishes, I'm still shaking my head.

"No, I don't believe it," I say. "This can't be the end. Splinter's too smart to get offed by one of his own victims. There's too many unanswered questions. If his MO was home invasions of other therapists with intact families, torturing and running his own 'therapy rooms' on them and ending with the brutal, vicious slaughter of the whole family, then why did Splinter change and start abducting tourists? Single tourists, too, not families. Why bring them to his farmhouse and keep them there for months? He would have known he was risking exposure by doing that. And for what? He didn't even kill them. You heard Dr. Singer at the hospital. They aren't permanently harmed. That's not like Splinter at all. He had plans for these twelve. What were those plans? Why these twelve people? We know they all had very different profiles, other than each of them having had a loved one who underwent therapy and things went spectacularly badly, so they each had a reason to hate therapists. What are the odds that these were twelve random people Splinter picked? A billion to one? No, Naved. He picked these particular twelve people for a reason. And then there's the therapy room door."

"The door?" Naved asks, looking puzzled.

"Those doors all locked electronically, remotely. Yet when we arrived, they were all open. Why? Who opened them? When? Why did only Grygorian get out, kill Splinter, then hang around the farm? Why didn't the others get out, too? Why didn't all twelve of them get the hell out of Dodge? What's with all the weird silent patient behavior? Why the Post-it notes? Why did Grygorian ask for me? Why are they all asking for Keller now?"

I shake my head. "No. There's too many questions still unanswered. This is definitely not over yet."

"Susan," Naved says gently. "You've worked on cases

before. You know that there are *always* unanswered questions. It's the nature of the job. Sometimes, we learn the answers months or even decades later. Most often, we never know. That's just how it goes. When the perp, or unsub as you call him, is apprehended, then that's enough to close the file. We got Splinter, AKA Magnusson. It's over. Let it go."

I look at him for a long moment, then say sadly, "I can't."

"Can't or won't, Susan?" he asks.

I shrug. "Take it however you like. I'm not going to walk away until I can make sense of it. If you want to continue as my partner, you're going to have to live with that."

He sighs. "Okay, let's say I go along. What would we even do next?"

"For starters, we talk to the families. Ramon and Kayla are already working on that. They should have something soon."

He looks at me searchingly. "You want to see if what they say matches Grygorian's version of events, don't you? That's what this is really about, isn't it? You're just not ready to let go. You still believe that you can find out what happened to Amit. I'm not saying that's all you want, but it's a part of it, isn't it? Be honest with me, Susan."

"Sure," I admit. "I want to know. But I also believe that the two cases are connected. Amit's death is somehow linked to Splinter."

Naved looks around at the nearly empty lot, the quiet street, then into the distance where even on this moonless night, you can still make out the outlines of the Santa Carina mountains against the deep blue night sky.

"All right," he says.

I didn't need his approval, but it makes me feel better that he's willing to continue on this path.

At least for now.

TWENTY-THREE

Ramon shoots a finger at me to let me know that the video feed is on.

I nod and slip on the headphones.

I hope this interview goes better than the previous ones.

The idea of talking to the friends and family of the Splinter victims slash patients seemed like a good idea but the first two people we spoke to seemed disinterested, even a little rude. The language and cultural barrier probably didn't help, and a lot of people are intimidated by the idea of talking to the FBI, or the "world police" as one Thai lady just called me a few minutes ago, but I was really hoping for more. At least with this next one, one of those problems will be eliminated since the person is in the UK. And a bonus: he happens to be a cop, too.

"DC Hallett, thank you so much for agreeing to speak to us," I say.

The thirty-something dark-haired man nods on the video chat screen. "Glad to be of assistance to the FBI, Special Agent Parker. Please, call me Tom."

"Thanks, Tom. I'm Susan."

"Susan, how can I be of assistance?"

"Tom, you've already told my associate Agent Regis that you were a colleague of Gennifer Mason at the Gloucestershire Constabulary."

"That is correct, ma'am. Genny and I practically grew up together. We were neighbors in a hamlet only a few miles from Birbury Village. We're fairly isolated out here in the Cotswolds and so we look out for one another. The Halletts and the Masons have known each other for, oh, I don't know, generations, I'd suppose."

"So you and Gennifer were friends even before you became colleagues?" I ask.

"Aye, ma'am. Except for the last couple of years, we were pretty close."

"What changed in the last couple of years, Tom?"

"Well, it's a sad tale, by any reckoning. Like I said, it's a hard life out here. A good honest living, but hard, nonetheless. Genny and her older sister Gwen, that's Gwendoline Mason, relied a great deal on one another. You see, ma'am, their mother was diagnosed with cancer several years ago, while Genny was only a young lass. She was eleven at the time, if I recall rightly. The two of them did their best, but it was hard going. By the time the cancer was detected, their mum was already fourth stage. Too far gone. The doctors said no point in chemo, it would only worsen her suffering. They prescribed pain medication and that was about it. She passed only a few months after. From there on, it was just Genny and Gwen, the Mason girls as we called them. Gwen was nineteen at the time, so she became Genny's legal guardian. Otherwise the council would have taken Genny, I reckon."

"Where was their father in all this?" I ask.

Tom shakes his head slightly. "Oh, he was a right old bugger. Long out of the picture. The old story, went out for a pack of smokes, never seen again. Genny said she and Gwen always suspected their mum knew where he was but if she did, she never told either of them and neither sister cared to go a-searching for him. As I recall my dad telling me, they were well rid of him. Word was that he was a soldier who suffered trauma from a grenade and was never right in the head afterward. My dad said he went doolally and likely ended up in a mental asylum someplace. Only they don't call them that anymore, do they?"

"Psychiatric ward would probably be the modern term," I say. "So there was a history of mental illness in the family?"

"Oh, yes, ma'am. Not long after Gennifer started here, Gwen began suffering from mental health issues."

"Did she receive treatment locally?"

"Yes, ma'am. We have here what we call the NHS, the National Health System. Public healthcare services for all."

"I'm familiar with the NHS. Go on, Tom."

"As I recall, Gwen was passed from hand to hand by a series of therapists, all prescribing different medications, most of which caused side effects that were worse than Gwen's symptoms. The episodes escalated until Genny began to grow fairly desperate. That was when she told me she was planning to remote consult with a psychiatrist in Chicago."

"I see. How did that go?"

"It was a bloody disaster, ma'am. That was when things went from bad to worse."

"How so?"

"Well, for one thing, Gwen became fatally depressed and ended up throwing herself off a bridge, breaking her neck in the fall. She was declared dead in the ambulance."

"That's very sad. But how was her death related to the Chicago therapy?"

"Well, ma'am, post-mortem tests revealed that Gwen had developed Type B diabetes unbeknownst to either of the Mason sisters, and that would have been a contra-indication for the medications that the Chicago therapist had prescribed, likely causing her final, tragic episode. Gennifer tried suing the Chicago therapist but had no luck there as the pre-existing condition of diabetes had not been disclosed to him and the document he had made Gwen sign affirmed that she understood the risks of the medication and that she didn't have any of the contra-indicated conditions, diabetes being one. It was a whole lot of legal gobbledygook that drove poor Genny up the wall, I can tell you. I've never seen her as mad as she was that day."

"When was this?"

"Almost two years ago. After that, she was surly and brooding all the time. There were a few incidents."

"What kind of incidents?" I ask.

"She used excessive force in one instance and was down-right rude to a member of the public who registered a complaint that went on her record."

"And then what happened?"

"Well, ma'am, that's where I more or less lost touch with Genny. As I recall, she took a long leave of absence from her job and never returned. I thought she might have gone abroad, across the pond as they say."

"She came here? To the United States?"

I already know this, of course, but I want to see if he knows.

"Well, I can't say for certain, ma'am. It's just a feeling I had, based on things she'd said."

"Such as?"

He hesitates. "Well, ma'am, as we're both in law enforcement, I suppose I should say that this was a comment made after she was, shall we say, in her cups."

"She was drunk."

"Aye, ma'am. Drunk and mad as hell. She spent a great deal of time in those two states before she went away."

"What was the comment she made, Tom?" I ask.

"She was angry with the Chicago therapist, with the whole profession, it seemed. She might have said something on the order of some of those blokes deserved to, ahem, have their tickets punched."

"Are those her exact words, constable?"

Again, reluctance on his part. His eyes shift. "I might not be recalling them exactly. Somewhat to that effect."

I'm guessing Gennifer said something a lot worse than punching tickets. Probably something like all therapists should be bloody strung up. But I don't press it.

"And you think she might have come here to the US, to what, Tom? See the Chicago therapist? Berate him personally? Maybe even... punch his ticket?"

He sucks in a breath. "I hope not, ma'am. She's not a bad sort, our Genny. We talk about her in Bixbury, the Mason sisters and all the rotten luck that befell the family. There's still a place for Genny here, if she ever wants it. We're a small community and always short-staffed, and I for one would be happy to see her again. She was a good copper, was Genny. Makes me sad to think of all she had to endure. They had it tough, those Mason girls."

"Indeed they did, Tom." I think for a minute, trying to form a picture of the gaunt, intense-looking young woman who insisted on walking out of the farmhouse rather than being carried out on a stretcher like all the others. I feel like I have some insight into her as a person now. The hard childhood, the family tragedies, the frustration and rage she must have felt at watching her mother and then her sister both dwindle and die while she stood by helpless. The NHS and all the doctors in the world unable to do diddlysquat to help them either.

"Tom, you mentioned two incidents she was involved in before leaving the force. Could you tell me something more about them?"

"Oh, well, yes, one was an altercation with a therapist she happened to meet on her day off in the local market. The lady, Dr. Rivers, was quite upset over it, said Gennifer had all but accused her of being a 'murderer with a medical degree' or some such."

"And the other incident?"

Tom nods. "That one was with an elderly gent who had been reported missing by his family. Genny was supposed to go over to the mental health specialist who had been treating him and instead of simply taking down his statement as she ought to have, she ended up assaulting him."

"So that was also a therapist?"

"Indeed, ma'am."

"And during the time of these two incidents, did she have similar altercations or fights with other civilians?"

"Not at all, ma'am. Genny could be the sweetest, kindest girl. That was why it came as quite a shock when she went off the deep end as she did. Surprised us all, it did."

"So you would say these were aberrations? That her anger was directed specifically at therapists? Because of what had happened with her sister?"

"Quite definitely, ma'am."

I think for a moment then look at Naved and the others. Nobody seems to have anything to add.

I'm about to sign off when a thought occurs to me.

"One last thing, Tom. I'm assuming your job requires you constables to be quite fit and active, right?"

Tom grins. "Oh yes, ma'am. Although it's more running and chasing down than shootouts in the streets. Not as exciting as you lot over there."

"Oh, you'd be surprised, Tom. Most of our job is paperwork and online searches. I rarely get to draw my gun in the course of duty. So you would say that Genny could handle herself in a violent situation?"

"Our Genny could toss me over like a sack of potatoes," Tom says. "Did, too, more than once! As you Americans might say, girl had some moves!"

"Right. That's all I have for you, constable. Thank you very much for your time. I really appreciate your cooperation."

"My pleasure, ma'am. And if I may say something?"

"Of course, Tom. Go ahead."

"I know you wouldn't be calling all the way from California if something hadn't gone wrong with our Genny. I'm a copper, I know how these things go. But if there's any chance you can help her out, well, she's a good girl, our Genny. Life did her wrong, that's all. It would be a tragedy if she ended up on the wrong side of the law. That's all I have to say, ma'am."

I end the video call and look at everyone.

"That was interesting," I say.

"More than the others," Naved says.

Constable Tom was the third video call we've had with family or friends of the twelve. Naturally, we couldn't tell anyone why we were calling or even that their relative or friend had been found. The previous four conversations weren't of much use: even though they all spoke English reasonably well, they simply didn't know anything. They basically repeated what we knew already from Carlotta's background deep dives. Constable Tom Hallett was the first one to actually provide some psychological insight and context.

"You want Ramon to line up the others we spoke to?" Kayla asks.

"You spoke to them. Are they likely to give us something useful?"

She shakes her head. "Pretty much like the earlier ones. No more good-looking British cops!"

"Then let's skip them. I think we have as much as we're going to get."

Brine yawns. "Sorry!"

"Don't apologize," I say. "We're all running on fumes. Let's close shop for now. Why don't we all go take a few hours, go freshen up, grab a shower, breakfast, meet back here around, let's say, nine?" I suggest, getting up.

Everyone responds positively to that.

"Kayla," I say apologetically. "I need you to do one more thing before that."

"You want me to call Keller, smooth the way, fix up a meet," she says confidently, one step ahead as always. "Already done, and done, and done. We're seeing him at 8 a.m. at his office, before he starts seeing patients for the day."

"That's in Westwood, all the way in LA. Couldn't we see him here in SCV? He consults at the hospital, doesn't he?"

"He does and I did ask, but no, he only comes to Silas MacKenna thrice a week or if he's called in on an emergency, and only in the afternoons. The rest of the week, he practices at his own place. You know the one."

I do and Kayla knows it. It's where I assaulted Keller. I was hoping to meet in more neutral territory, but I guess beggars can't be choosers.

"I guess we'll have to make that work," I say, a little disappointed—and irritated.

"You forgot to say, thank you Kayla, you're amazing, Kayla, I don't know what I'd do without you, Kayla!" she sings out.

I grin. "Thank you, Kayla. You're amazing, Kayla. I don't know what I'd do without you, Kayla."

She winks. "You got it, chief."

Naved waves goodbye as we both get in our cars. We leave the lot together, and are together all the way up Bouquet Canyon Road until I turn left at Saugus Drive and he continues up to Plum Canyon. The high school girls' track team goes by the Mormon church on the corner, a gaggle of some thirty-odd teenage girls in tee shirts and shorts, all jogging spiritedly. Well, almost all. A few stragglers look like they'd much rather be home, still in bed. I don't blame them. So would I.

When I walk in, Lata and Natalie are already up. I smell

pancake batter in the kitchen. Lata hears the door open and comes out holding a spatula.

She raises an eyebrow at me. "You all right?"

I shrug. "Nothing a shower and a stack wouldn't cure."

She looks at me with that searching gaze that pricks my conscience. I'm tempted to tell her about Grygorian and what he said about Amit. But I know that would be exactly the wrong thing to say. For now, at least, probably because she knows I got shot at last night, Lata's not going to give me a hard time about breaking my promise and reversing my position on the job. I don't want to ruin it by making her think I'm falling down the rabbit hole all over again.

"You sure you're fine?"

I nod. "Copacetic."

She buys it, relaxing. "Okay."

As she starts to turn away, she calls out, "Blueberries?"

"And chocolate chips!" I call back as I go up the stairs.

I peek into Natalie's room, expecting to find her dressing. I'm surprised to see her sitting on her bed, wrapped in her towel, looking morose.

"Hey, sweetie," I sign and say simultaneously as I go to her. "What's up, big girl?"

She looks at me glumly and signs, "I forgot something."

"Was it something for camp, sweetie?"

She shakes her head.

"Well, what was it then?" I ask.

She looks at me with big, sad eyes. "When we gave thanks yesterday, I forgot to thank God for taking Papa to heaven and keeping him happy there."

Another pang of guilt sears my heart. In that first fateful talk when I tried to explain to Natalie why her father wouldn't be coming home anymore, she asked me if he was in heaven. Not knowing what else to say, and not wanting to deny it and get into a lecture about belief systems and religions, I simply said yes. She then asked me if God took him there because Papa was such a good man, and I said yes to that, too. Then she asked if he was happy there, and of course I had to say yes again. In for a dime, in for a dozen. Someday, maybe I'll try to explain it to her better, when I'm a better person, a better mom. But for now, it's the best I could manage.

"That's all right, sweetie," I say now. "We can still thank him."

"But Thanksgiving is over, Mom," she signs in agitation, "it was yesterday."

"Sure, honey," I say, stroking her head gently, "but you know how we celebrate Christmas Eve and then the next day is Christmas Day and there are actually twelve days of Christmas?"

She nods.

"So it's just like that. You can give thanks all of today, too, if you like. In fact..." I'm about to add that she can give thanks all year round if she wants, but decide not to push my luck. Even child psychology has its limits. "In fact, let's do it right now. Let's put our palms together, close our eyes, and thank God for keeping Papa happy up there in heaven."

"Okay," she signs, smiling.

We close our eyes. Or she does. I open mine to watch her. She squeezes her eyes tightly shut, pressing her palms together so hard I can see the ends of her fingers turn white. I taught her to resist the impulse to sign her prayers because God hears us even if we only pray silently in our minds, but it takes an effort, which is why she presses her palms so tightly together, to keep her natural instinct to sign under control.

When she opens her eyes, she looks much less anxious and glum.

"Now shall we get dressed for camp?" I ask, holding up her favorite outfit. Even though schools are shut all this week, Natalie gets restless sitting at home and asked us to send her to a

Thanksgiving Art Camp. It's a thrill to see the projects she comes up with.

She grins.

Over breakfast, she chatters, hands working furiously as she signs and stuffs syrup-drenched pancake into her mouth, chewing and talking at the same time—one of the 'superpowers' she has, which speaking people can't do.

Lata watches us discreetly from where she's leaning against the kitchen cabinets and sipping her filter coffee, a faraway look in her eyes. I wonder what she's thinking about—or feeling—and make a mental note to make some time for me to ask about *her*, and how *she's* doing.

Under Lata's watchful eye, I manage to put two whole pancakes away, with blueberries and chocolate chips, and two mugs of steaming hot, delicious filter coffee.

After breakfast, I insist on dropping Natalie off at art camp.

"It's on my way," I say.

Before she gets out of the car, Natalie turns to me once again.

"Mom," she signs, "what if I don't want Papa to be *too* happy in heaven? Does that make me a bad person?"

"Why do you say that, sweetheart?" I ask.

"Because maybe if he wasn't too happy, he might not want to stay," she says, looking down at her shoes.

It's a confession that she's obviously been working herself up to for some time.

It rips into my heart.

I pull her into me, hugging her tight. "Oh, my sweetheart," I say, then sign into her palm, the way I used to when she was a toddler. "Nothing you say or feel or think can ever make you a bad person. And that's not a bad thought at all. In fact, I wish he could come back. I wish it every single day, my love."

She looks at me. "But he can't, Mom. Once people go to

heaven, they never come back. It's a one-way trip, like a one-way ticket to the moon. That's what Dadu says."

Dadu is what she calls Kundan. It's the North Indian word for grandfather. Despite the flood of grief washing through me right now, I'm still able to find amusement in his use of the old '80s song lyrics to explain heaven to his granddaughter. One way ticket to the moon indeed! Bless you, Kundan. When it comes to explaining complicated adult stuff to kids, simplest is best.

"Dadu's right, Natalie. Now, you have a good day at camp, okay?"

"Okay, Mommy. Oh, there's Sanaya and Aiden and Fiona! Gotta go, Mommy! Bye. Love you!"

"I love you, too, my heart," I sign back, but she's already gone, ponytail bobbing as she flies across the lawn to join her friends who have stopped and are signing excitedly to her. I feel happy that she has friends who made the effort to learn ASL just so they could communicate with her. I take a moment just to bask in the joy of being Natalie's mother, and also just being.

As my daughter's ponytail bounces away, I promise myself that I will find Amit's killer—I'm convinced he was murdered—and bring him to justice.

Or, failing that, I'll give the bastard a one-way ticket not to the moon, but straight to the other place.

He deserves it for having deprived my daughter of a dad.

TWENTY-FOUR

About an hour later, freshly showered and changed, fortified by a third strong mug of Lata's filter coffee, I park in the visitors' lot of the Keller Wellness Recovery Center in Westwood, sandwiched neatly between the lavish estates of Beverly Hills and the gleaming office towers of Century City. I take a moment to center myself before getting out of the Prius. When I do, I'm instantly made aware of the difference in my social and financial status to the clientele that frequents the facility. My poor Prius looks like a homeless waif surrounded by the shiny bright Lexuses, Mercedes, Audis, Porches, Bugatis and Puganis.

The foyer and reception impress the same air of careless luxury upon me, reminding me that I could do with a new suit. Better yet, a new me.

Naved is waiting for me in the foyer.

"You up for this?" he asks, looking at me with an overly casual gaze.

I smile sweetly at him. "I'm not going to lunge across the desk at him and slam his head down on the floor, if that's what you're worried about," I say.

He raises his eyebrows and nods. "Good to know."

We walk to the reception, introduce ourselves, are told we're expected, given the requisite visitor patches to stick to our jackets, and wait for the elevator which arrives almost instantly. Naved and I step on.

As the doors close on us, I add a coda to my last remark, "But you can't blame me for wanting to do it."

Naved turns and looks at me, then laughs out loud.

He's still laughing when the elevator doors open on our floor. "You are quite a character, Susan Parker," he says.

I smile back at him. "Why, thank you, Naved Seth."

I feel good going into this dreaded meeting. I would be lying if I said I was looking forward to seeing the man again. I would also be lying if I said I wasn't anxious or stressed about it.

But I'm able to manage that stress and anxiety, look past our bad history together, and focus on the goal: finding the truth about Splinter and, I believe, the truth about Amit's death.

I just know the two are directly connected.

And some inner instinct tells me that Keller might be the key to finding that connection, and by doing that, finding the truth.

Don't ask me why I believe this. I just do. Don't you sometimes have a feeling that's so strong, so overwhelming that you simply cannot shake it off until it's been fully explored? Like a door in your house you've never seen before that suddenly appears one fine day. What do you do? You open it, of course. It's creepy, it's scary, and you're terrified of what you might find behind it. But it's your house. You can't *not* open that door. I'm convinced that what lies behind this particular door, metaphorically speaking, is truth. Horrifying or gratifying, it doesn't matter. I want the truth and I'm ready to face it at last.

We're met by an executive assistant who looks competent enough to be a qualified psychiatrist herself. With crisp, businesslike efficiency, she walks us into the inner sanctum. The tastefully appointed offices of Dr. Keller, psychotherapist. She leaves us there.

Before we enter, I tap the sign on the door and remark to Naved, "Ever notice that if you leave just two spaces in the word 'psychotherapist', you get 'psycho the rapist'?"

Naved looks at the sign then at me. He doesn't say anything.

I shrug and push the door open, preceding him into the room.

Dr. Keller is seated behind his desk, looking at his phone. Once again, I can't help but be struck by the John Cassavates resemblance. I mentioned it once to Kayla, after she and I had been to see Keller for the first time to recruit him as a consultant, but she didn't see it at all. The fact that she hadn't seen any of those 'white bread' movies as she called them might be one reason, but it might just be me.

A little below average height, slender through the shoulders, slightly hunched over, that long, clean-shaven jaw a little too long for the face to be considered good looking. On a stand by the door, I noted his trademark brown trilby, which I recall as being the same as the one he wore back then.

Everything about this room, this man, brings back the humiliating, embarrassing memory of the worst day of my career as an FBI agent.

The office is as large as I remember, spacious and sprawling as only West Coast offices can be.

Keller registers my approach as I come in through the door, from his desk almost twenty feet away by the far corner, backed by a floor-to-ceiling wall-to-wall glass window.

Keller's eyes take me in, reading my face, body language, intent with that hard-edged diamond glint that I remember finding so infuriating. Gray gimlet eyes. Boring through to my insides.

Iceberg, I think, using the breathing exercise Dr. Sharif, my therapist, taught me in those months after my Keller episode. *I am an iceberg.*

"Special Agent in Charge Susan Parker," Keller says. "You look well."

He says this in a tone that suggests the exact opposite. It's annoying how he does that: says one thing while meaning something totally different.

"Dr. Keller," I say, not offering a hand to shake. Getting this close and talking civilly is testing enough. I don't need to complicate matters.

Keller looks me up and down in a way that makes my skin crawl. "Lost a little weight, I see. Perhaps a little sleep-deprived, too? How are your sessions with Dr. Alamdar Sharif going?"

"Good," I say. "He cleared me to come back to work."

"Interesting," he says, then like the pretentious ass he is, doesn't offer anything further. Again, he manages to inflect that single word with more malice than an actual critique.

Naved steps forward, offering his hand. "Detective Naved Seth, SCVPD. I'm working with Special Agent in Charge Parker on the Splinter case."

"Ah. Yes. Of course. The Splinter case. There's been quite a bit of noise about that in the media." Keller glances at me. "Not all of it good."

I ignore the jibe. "Dr. Keller, I'd like to start by thanking you for agreeing to see me at such short notice."

"I was expecting it," Keller says matter-of-factly.

That takes me by surprise. "You were expecting me to call?"

"Of course. I'm attached to MacKenna's psychiatric department, as you might recall from our brief encounter there yesterday. It was only logical that I would be called in to consult on the matter. Dr. Singer has already availed of my services in that regard, naturally."

I frown. "In what way?"

"Assessing the patients. Evaluating the optimal available options. Recommending a course of treatment. The usual."

I stare at Keller. He stares back with that curl in his cheek suggesting a snide hint of a smile. "You've already met with them?"

"As I just said."

I feel a spike of anger. "Why wasn't the Bureau informed? I'm in charge, I should have been told. My associate Special Agent Kayla Givens has maintained a line of communication with MacKenna Hospital. She hasn't reported anything about this."

Keller leans back in his chair, looking smugly satisfied at having gotten to me this quickly and easily in the conversation. "MacKenna Hospital doesn't owe you any explanation or report, Parker. Neither do I."

Naved glances at me then speaks up. "Dr. Keller, these aren't typical patients. They are also suspects slash victims of a vicious serial killer and as such, they're also considered persons of interest as well as witnesses to possible crimes. The Bureau has jurisdiction over them. Any contact with them or interaction should have been reported to SAC Parker."

Keller shifts his attention briefly to Naved and doesn't look impressed by what he sees. "Well, Detective Seth, those are questions you should take up with the hospital's general counsel, or my lawyers if you wish. But in the interim, Dr. Singer, his staff, and I intend to continue doing our jobs. And that means treating patients as patients, regardless of their status in the eyes of any third party."

"Did any of them speak?" I ask. "Did they say anything to you during your time with them?"

Keller looks down at his phone. "As I said, Parker, you can pose any questions you have to the lawyers."

"So you won't even tell me *if* they spoke?" I ask, incredulously.

I glance at Naved to see if he's getting this. He moves his head slightly from side to side as if affirming my reaction: *Can you believe this guy?*

Keller looks up at me disaffectedly. "I'm not obliged to tell you anything, Parker. Perhaps you've heard of patient-doctor confidentiality. It's a legal stricture that grants any physician—"

I hold up my hand. "Please, don't lecture me on confidentiality. I'm not asking you what they said. I'm asking *if* they said anything. That information is not protected under the law."

Keller gives me the smallest of smiles. "Matters of law are best left to the lawyers, I think. As far as I'm concerned, anything that transpires between me and my patients is confidential."

I stare at him. He looks back at me with amusement, phone still in hand.

"Dr. Keller, I came here to ask you to consider consulting with us on the Splinter case, as you did once before, by agreeing to see these eleven patients," I say. My voice is calm and measured, even though my pulse is pounding.

"And as I've already told you, I'm already seeing them. In fact, Dr. Singer and the hospital were quite pleased when I suggested I take charge of them personally. Given all the harassment from law enforcement and the glare of media attention, I think they're very happy to have this problem taken off their hands. These eleven problems, to be precise."

"Taken off their hands how?" I ask, my gut curling with a gnawing suspicion.

Keller finishes typing something on his phone and looks up at me. "They're being transferred here as we speak. Already en route, in fact."

I stare at him, not trusting myself to speak.

I consider my options.

There's no point repeating the same things I've already said or losing my temper. Even though I'm mad as hell at his attitude, at the casual way in which he acts as though this is *his* case now and he's the one in charge. Nor have I failed to notice his disrespect of me when he addresses me as just 'Parker' without using my title.

Something occurs to me then. The glimmer of a thought, originating from the one trump card I still hold in this case, even if nobody else considers it a trump card.

"So that's all twelve of them, did you say, Dr. Keller?" I say calmly.

He stops typing on his phone suddenly.

He puts the phone down on his desk.

He looks up at me.

"I believe I quite clearly stated 'eleven patients'," Keller says stiffly.

I nod slowly, as if thinking about that. "Of course, of course. Because you only have access to the eleven patients that were admitted to Silas MacKenna. Not the twelfth one, whom I only retrieved from the scene yesterday. Is that right, Dr. Keller?"

Keller stares at me coldly. "Are you asking a question or stating a fact?"

"Both, actually. I'm stating the fact that you only have eleven of the twelve individuals that we retrieved from Magnusson's farmhouse. And I'm confirming that you don't have access, exclusive or otherwise, to the twelfth individual. You don't, do you, Dr. Keller?"

He stares at me for a long moment before saying, "No."

I nod. "Yes, yes, of course. Because that individual is being treated as separate from the group. He's been quite forthcoming, you know. About the events that transpired during his incarceration there in one of those, what do they call them, Detective Seth?"

I turn to Naved, who takes my cue and plays along.

"Therapy rooms," Naved says.

"Therapy rooms, yes." I address Keller again. "In those

horrible therapy rooms where they were all apparently tortured and treated to inhumane conditions and treatment. Oh yes. Grygorian has been very forthcoming about his suffering and the individuals responsible for it."

I pause and add, "That is his name, Dr. Keller. Perhaps you hadn't heard yet. Aram Grygorian."

Keller stares at me without expression. "Is there a reason you're telling me all this, Parker?"

"But of course, Keller," I say. "I'm sure your other eleven patients are just as forthcoming as Grygorian is, and that you'll impress upon them the importance of cooperating with the authorities."

"I am under no obligation to impress any such thing upon them," Keller says coldly. "My only obligation to them is that of any doctor treating his patients, which I intend to do to the best of my abilities."

"Yes, yes, of course you will," I say, rising from my chair. "But you will bear in mind that they are persons of interest in a criminal investigation and that if they possess any information pertaining to crimes past, present or future, then you are legally bound to pass on that information to the authorities, which in this case means the Federal Bureau of Investigation, as represented by me personally, Special Agent in Charge Susan Parker."

Naved stands as well, following my lead.

"You will remember that legal obligation, won't you, Keller?" I say.

Keller remains seated, saying nothing.

"Was that a yes?" I ask. "Detective Seth, did you hear him say yes?"

"Yes," Keller says, with quiet ferocity. His eyes flash brightly, hinting at his own anger. He gets up slowly, and for a moment, I think he's going to be the one to lunge across the desk this time, but of course that's just wishful thinking.

"Good day, then. Don't bother getting up. We'll show ourselves out. We have to follow up on all those leads we received from Grygorian, you see. Busy-busy!"

Naved waits patiently until we're out in the parking lot before turning on me and asking, "The hell was that?"

I shrug. "He Kellered me, I Parkered him."

TWENTY-FIVE

If Gantry looks surprised to see me sitting on the couch in his reception area when he arrives, he doesn't show it. Instead, he breezes past me without so much as a good morning and goes into his office. He even manages to keep me waiting another eleven minutes before his executive assistant looks up from her phone, smiles, and tells me I can go in now.

"SAC Parker, you better have good news for me," Gantry says even before I reach his desk. He makes it sound like a threat.

"Sir, I believe I do."

He waits, expecting me to go on unprompted.

Instead, I take a seat in the visitor's chair, cross my legs, and smile at him.

He stares at me, not wanting to concede by asking me what my news is and deflecting instead.

"Good work on arresting the killer," he says. "I think I already congratulated you last night."

"Thank you, sir. We've also linked him through forensics."

I explain about the fingerprints and DNA of the shooter that we found on the murder weapon, on Magnusson's body, and the dining table. "He has a lawyer on board now, and the lawyer has indicated that he's willing to cooperate in exchange for fair treatment."

Gantry nods. "Bohjalian. Yes, I heard. Are they looking for a plea deal?"

"I'm not entirely sure, sir. I think they're still debating the best strategy. Grygorian is not contesting the fact that he killed Magnusson. But I checked with legal and PR and the general mood is—"

"That no jury is likely to convict a victim who turned against his captor and took down the most notorious serial killer in recent history, yes, Parker, I've been kept abreast by the GC's office," Gantry says. He adds curtly, "Good work."

"Thank you, sir."

Gantry instantly loses interest, his eyes changing focus as his ever-wheeling mind turns to other concerns.

"If that's all, SAC..." he says.

"Actually, sir, I still haven't given you the good news."

He blinks, refocuses, and stares at me. It's not easy to surprise Gantry but I've just managed to do that. He assumed, of course, that my 'good news' was apprehending Grygorian and linking him to Magnusson's murder.

"And?" he asks, unable to restrain his curiosity this time.

"Well, sir, I'm hoping that we might be able to get statements from the other eleven victims as well. That will help us build a more cohesive, corroborative picture of what actually happened in that farmhouse."

Gantry stares at me.

"I thought I was very clear yesterday at the hospital, SAC Parker," he says. "So was the hospital's general counsel. You are not to have any contact with those patients until and unless the hospital officially grants you permission. As far as I know, that hasn't happened yet, has it?"

He knows damn well it hasn't. If and when Silas MacKenna

184

Hospital decides to grant us access, they'll contact Gantry first. Maybe even the director back in Washington, DC. They won't get in touch with a special agent in charge. The system doesn't work that way.

"No, sir," I say pleasantly.

"Then what makes you so certain that they're going to talk?" he asks. "Have you been consulting a psychic? Tarot cards? Or did you read it in your chai leaves this morning?"

I bite the inside of my lower lip so he won't see me do it. I'm tempted to call him out on that last one. By substituting the word 'chai' for 'tea', he's cleverly mocking my Indian parentage. But I know, and he knows I know, that if I call him out on that comment, I can't just let it go; I'd have to report it to HR and that would open an inquiry ticket, and I'd have to follow through on that over the course of a lengthy, excruciating process. And at the end of it, it could be argued that Gantry himself drinks 'chai'—from Starbucks, but it's still 'chai'—so he was simply referring to the word for tea that he himself commonly uses, not being culturally insensitive or making a derogatory comment about my identity and race. While I'd have dinged my career file considerably, adding to my notoriety, he'd walk off without so much as a slap on the wrist.

But this morning, even cultural gaslighting isn't going to get under my skin. I let the comment pass, denying it power simply by not letting myself be provoked.

I say instead, "Well, sir. I know that Dr. Keller is the leading expert on this, and he's cracked some really tough ones before. So I have good reason to be optimistic, I think. Wouldn't you agree?"

His eyes narrow. "Did you say 'Dr. Keller'?"

"Yes, sir."

"You mean *your* Dr. Keller?" he demands.

I shake my head. "He was never my doctor, sir."

"You know what I mean, Parker," he snaps. "I'm talking

about the Dr. Keller you assaulted in his clinic last year. The one who took out a restraining order against you."

"Ah. Yes, sir. That is exactly the Dr. Keller I mean," I say calmly.

"How the hell does he factor into this case?" Gantry asks.

"He'll be consulting for us. As he did before. He has a history with the Splinter case, as you know. He's familiar with all the details. Who could be better?"

Gantry folds his arms across his chest. "I can think of several excellent psychiatrists, none of whom you have a history of assaulting before."

"Yes, well, Keller's already on the job. I handed in the paperwork to your EA for your signature, sir."

Gantry stares at me. "Did you say Keller is consulting for us again on the Splinter case?"

"Yes, sir."

"Since when?" he asks.

"Since this morning, sir." I check the time. "He's already transferred the eleven patients to his private facility in Westwood. Keller was already a consulting doctor with the department, so it was really just a formality. But I made sure all proper channels were used. We crossed our t's and dotted our i's, sir. You need have no concerns on that front."

Gantry stares as if seeing me for the first time. He leans back in his chair. "How did Dr. Keller suddenly decide to come in on the case? Did Dr. Singer call him in?"

"In fact, he did, sir. So, you see, Keller was already on the case, so to speak. This way, he'll be reporting directly to us rather than the hospital now."

"When you say, 'us', SAC, you mean—?"

"Me, of course, sir. Since I am in charge of Splinter."

Gantry's eyes narrow. "I'll bet Keller will have something to say about that when he finds out."

"Oh, he's already aware, sir," I say coolly. "He seemed quite comfortable with it when I met him."

"You called him?" Gantry says.

"I met him in person, sir. At his private facility."

Gantry stares at me for a long moment. "*You* met with Dr. Keller?"

"Yes, sir. Earlier this morning, in fact. About a half hour ago."

"And he agreed to meet with you?" Gantry asks, now with open skepticism. "*In person?*"

"Oh, he was quite pleasant, sir," I say. On that one, I'm not being entirely honest. But it's essentially true: Keller did agree to meet me in person, and he was reasonably pleasant—or as pleasant as Keller is capable of being. I'm tempted to add, *about as pleasant as you usually are, sir,* but bite my tongue.

Gantry shakes his head slowly. He doesn't actually say *I'll be goddamned* aloud. He doesn't need to: it's written all over his face.

"You didn't clear that with me," he says. "That's a major decision, Parker. That's a direct contravention of the command structure. You're still under my command. Why didn't you clear it with me?"

I smile sweetly at him. "You told me I didn't have to, sir."

"When was that?" he asks, coming forward again, hands together. Ready to get in my face given half a chance. "I don't recall giving you carte blanche!"

"But you did, sir. Yesterday. At the hospital."

He frowns.

I say sweetly, "I asked you to intervene with the hospital yesterday, and you said, and I quote, sir, '*That sounds like a "you" problem, Parker. It's your case now.*' Don't you recall saying that, sir?"

He knows damn well he did. In front of a dozen plus

witnesses. He can't take that back now; if he tries to walk it back, it will undermine the hard, what-I-say-goes-don't-make-me-repeat-myself reputation he's built over his career. Besides, I believe he meant it when he said it. He just didn't expect that I would use it to my advantage; he expected I would flounder and flail about and face-plant. But I didn't. I turned it into a win. That's the part that's galling him now. And there's nothing he can do about it. I've got him over a barrel this time and he damn well knows it. Booyah!

Deputy Director Gantry smiles the slow, shark-like smile I've come to know so well over the years. I can't say I've missed it, but it does bring back memories. Not good ones.

"Well, SAC Susan Parker," he says. "It looks like it's winner winner, chicken dinner for you today. Congratulations."

I don't miss his use of that word "today". He didn't need to say it, so if he did, he's telling me something. He's telling me that I may have won today, this Friday of Thanksgiving week-end. But every day isn't Friday.

I'll take it.

Today.

TWENTY-SIX

I'm pulling out of the FBI parking lot onto Wilshire Boulevard as Ramon calls.

"Hi, boss," Ramon's voice says. "I think I got something."

"Give it up!" I say.

"You on your way here, right?" Ramon says. "I'll show you when you get here. Save you the trouble of pulling over to read the whole package."

"To hell with that," I say as I merge into traffic. "It'll take us at least..." I check the map app. The loading symbol comes on for a moment, circling for several seconds. "Hang on, my phone's acting up."

Finally, it stops circling the drain and shows me a live map reading with ETA. "Should take me about twenty-two minutes to get there. I'm not waiting that long. Send it to me and Naved on the group chat. He'll read it while I drive and share the highlights."

"You got it, boss," Ramon says.

As Naved's phone starts pinging with incoming attachments, Brine's voice comes back on. "Hey, Susan?"

"Shoot," I say.

"You're not going to like this," Brine says tentatively.

"Give it to me." The gloat-session with Gantry has given me a little armor. I'm ready for a small dose of not-great news.

"Someone leaked pics of Grygorian and at least one outlet has already used it to ID him and run a story."

I slam the heel of my hand on the steering wheel, accidentally hitting the horn. It blares, startling the driver of the Audi A6 in front of me on Lankershim. He raises his hand in a *WTF?* gesture as he looks up at me in his rearview. I raise my palm in a *sorry* gesture back.

"How bad is it?" I ask Brine.

"Um, about as bad as it can get. They have Grygorian's passport pic, a pic of the murder weapon, and the inside track on the body and the basement therapy rooms, the therapy notes and tapes..."

"Damn, that's everything," I say, hearing my voice go shrill as it does when I start to lose it. "How the hell did they find out about those? No, wait, don't answer that. It was McDougall."

"It has to be SCVPD," Brine says, agreeing, "because it sure as hell wasn't one of ours. The way the story's spun, it makes the local PD look like they did all the heavy lifting."

"Definitely McDougall," I say. "This is his way of sticking it to me for taking off with Grygorian."

Naved looks at me. "What did I say about treading lightly?"

He's right and that only makes me madder. I slam my hand on the steering, again hitting the horn. This time, there's a pink Jeep Explorer in front of me with a heavily dolled up life-size Barbie at the wheel. She shoots me the finger with one hot-pink-painted fingernail, her blue eyes glaring at me in her rearview. I shoot her a finger back. "This is his way of taking back control. I bet the story spins it to look like he singlehandedly ran down the killer and wrestled him to get the knife away."

"Um, not quite that far," Brine says. "But yeah, it does leave enough gaps to let the reader assume, wrongly, that his people made the arrest. The story has his picture with all his pet officers, and it's a live shot from the scene. He had to have posed for that. You can see the farmhouse behind him. For what it's worth, they used a stock pic of Naved. I think it's from his driver's license. Tiniest size possible, but it's in there."

"Look, I don't care about McDougall and SCVPD stealing the glory. I practically handed it to him on a platter last night. It's the giving out of case details that worries me. I don't want to spook Splinter who's probably watching every news update in real time right now," I say as I get on to the freeway.

Brine doesn't say anything to that. Even Naved stares straight ahead. I know my team well enough by now to know when they're trying to avoid hurting my feelings by keeping their mouths shut.

"I know you guys think I'm chasing a spook," I say. "But believe me, Splinter's still out there and this is still an active case, far as I'm concerned."

"Yeah, well, I guess McD doesn't think so. Besides, he wouldn't do this unless he has the blessings of people upstairs."

Of course. "That's it. McDougall had to have checked with Gantry first before leaking the story and pics. He had to have known the Bureau's legal stance on this. That's the only explanation. He puts on that cowboy posture but he's too much of a politician to just go shooting wild."

"Anyway, the story doesn't mention anything about the forensics Mancini showed you and Naved yesterday. So they still don't know that the other eleven are foreign nationals, too," Brine says.

Thank God for Mancini and her tight lips. "Did David dig up anything more on that?" I ask, not really expecting anything this quick, but hoping anyway.

David's voice speaks next: "That's what Ramon's been waiting to tell you, boss. We've been working nonstop on this.

And I think we've got something. As in 'by Jove, I think she's got it.'"

"By 'she', he means Carlotta," Ramon says with the pride of a happy parent. "She gotta lotta it, jefe! You goin' to be very happy, you hear this!"

"Okay, okay," I say, pushing McDougall and his political one-upmanship out of my mind and focusing on Splinter again. "Give it to me, guys! Don't leave me hanging."

My phone screen lights up on the dashboard.

Bohjalian Calling.

Naved looks at me, asking permission to take the call so I can concentrate on driving. I nod.

"Actually," I add, "just hold that thought for a sec, guys. Bohjalian's calling. I gotta see what he wants. Putting you on hold."

Naved switches calls. There's a moment when the screen flickers weirdly, then resets and resolves.

"Counselor? I have you on speakerphone. I'm in my car, Detective Seth is with me. You met him yesterday when we handed over custody of Grygorian to you."

"Ah, yes, good morning, Detective Seth, SAC Parker. That's precisely why I'm calling you."

"Everything okay, counselor?" I ask.

"Oh yes," Bohjalian says in his famous upbeat style. Around town, the word is that his favorite phrase is 'We got this!' "I'm actually calling on behalf of my client. He would like to see you."

Naved and I exchange a glance.

"Me, counselor?" I ask, just to be sure.

"You in particular, SAC Parker," Bohjalian says. "But if you wish to bring Detective Seth along, that would be fine."

"What is this about, counselor?" I ask.

"I'd rather not say over the phone, SAC."

"So you want to meet up in person?" I ask.

"Yes. My client wishes to speak with you in person. He assures me it will only take a few minutes. It shouldn't take long. What does your day look like at present?"

I check the time, then the freeway ahead. "Actually, I'm halfway to Santa Carina, counselor. When would your client like to do this?"

"Sooner would be better, I believe," Bohjalian says. "And that's quite perfect. My client is, in fact, situated in Santa Carina."

"He is?" I say, surprised.

Naved looks surprised, too.

"Yes, SAC. I own an apartment there. It's in Newhall, near the old Newhall Station. Are you familiar with it?"

"I'm familiar with Newhall. Text me the address."

Bohjalian pauses for a moment then says, "Done."

The message pops up on my screen. Naved taps it for me. I glance at the street.

"I know the street and neighborhood, counselor. I can be there in... twelve to fourteen minutes."

"Perfect," Bohjalian says. "The building is gated. Once you reach it, just ping me. I'll have my associate text you the gate code. It changes every hour otherwise I'd have texted it right now. Take the elevator to the fourth floor, it's Apartment 404."

"Got it. I assume you will be there, too, counselor?" I ask.

"Of course. I'll see you soon."

I end the call and look at Naved.

"What do you think that's about?" I ask.

He shrugs. "Maybe Bohjalian talked Grygorian into dropping the BS and telling us the truth?"

I shake it off. "Never mind that. I want to know what Ramon found out. Could you get him back for me?"

"Still here, jefe!" Ramon's voice says.

"'We also serve who only stand and wait,'" David's voice says. "And research. And do our due diligence. And—"

"I get the picture, David," I say, laughing. "Now please, spill the beans. I'm dying here. What did you two find out?"

"We three, jefe," Ramon says. "Don't go forgetting my best girl!"

"Okay, okay. So tell me!" I say impatiently.

"So I had Carlotta dig deeper into the twelve," Ramon says. "This time I widened and focused the search. That part was actually David's idea."

"I told him to search all the law enforcement databases in each of the twelve countries," David says. "Using keywords corresponding to Splinter's MO in all the known kills so far."

"Brilliant," I say. "What did Carlotta come up with?"

"You're not going to believe this, jefe," Ramon's cheerful voice says. "She brought back seven hits so far."

I look at Naved, who mouths, *WTF?* That's exactly how I feel, too.

"Ramon," I say, excited now, "let me get this straight. You're saying you found police records of seven previous murders that correspond to Splinter's MO in seven different foreign countries? Which just happen to be the same seven countries that seven of our twelve victims are from?"

"That's about the size of it, jefe," Ramon says.

"How close are the MO matches?" Naved asks, leaning forward. I can see he's excited, too.

"Almost identical," David replies. "All the heads of households were therapists with intact families. Home invasion in every instance. Torture and depravity, all the disgusting brutality we've come to expect from Splinter. Photographic and videographic evidence of the 'therapy sessions' with each family. Every member of every family killed, including infants and pets."

At that last detail, I wince. "Fucking evil bastard," I murmur. Aloud, I add, "Go on, David."

"That's pretty much it, Susan," David says.

"About the timelines of each of these seven murders," Naved asks. "Were our seven victims in their respective countries at the time when the killings happened?"

"Nope, Mr. N," Ramon pops back in, "all seven were hit after our peeps flew the coop."

That's weird. "So you're saying these killings all happened in the last few months? While these seven were in Magnusson's basement here in the US?"

"Roger that, jefe," Ramon says. "Also, before you ask, coz I already checked, none of the seven victims had any association with the seven therapists or their families. Carlotta dug deep but came up with nada on that."

I shake my head. This is all too weird and getting weirder by the day.

"Guys, I'm pulling off the freeway now. Only a few minutes to Bohjalian's place in Newhall. Let me finish with Grygorian and then we'll circle back to you. Brilliant work. Great lateral thinking."

"One last thing," Naved says, and I nod, indicating he should go ahead. "The remaining five victims..."

"No Splinter-style murders in their burghs," David says then pauses. "Not yet."

That last part sounds ominous.

It's a reminder that despite what the world thinks, this is still a very active case, and a very active serial killer.

I carry that thought with me as I drive the rest of the way to Bohjalian's apartment.

TWENTY-SEVEN

As reported by Bohjalian, the building is a gated one. It's also one of the swankier condominiums in SCV. Located about a mile down a quiet lane that leads nowhere beyond. The rest of the lane is lined with senior living apartment communities and a smattering of empty lots. The nearest stores are a good mile or so away, along the road that leads to Stevenson Ranch. Clearly, the developers chose it for its private location as well as the view of the mountains, several of the taller ones already bearing a dusting of snow on their peaks.

All the buildings in this part of the lane have their own parking, and there are no commercial establishments nearby, so the solitary late model Ford Ram truck stands out. It's black, the windows tinted almost as darkly as the paint job, making it impossible to see who, if anyone, is sitting inside, but the engine is on, because I spot a curl of smoke from the exhaust pipe.

"Bohjalian's not taking any chances," Naved says.

The door to the apartment is opened by the same female associate who texted me the gate code. She's dressed in a suit not quite as expensive as Bohjalian's, but still top shelf. So is the male associate standing a few feet behind her.

"Hi, I'm Daria," she says, showing us in.

"Aslan," says the associate.

I notice the security screen by the door with split-screen views of the front door, the lobby, and the outside gate.

Bohjalian is standing in the living room, texting.

Grygorian is seated on a couch, leg jittering at ninety miles an hour. He leaps up at the sight of us.

I can hardly recognize the man we talked to only a few hours earlier. Amazing what a shower, some sleep, and a couple hot meals can do. Only his sunken cheeks, hollowed-out eyes, and the loose way his clothes hang off him are a reminder of the weeks he spent in Magnusson's therapy room.

"Mr. Grygorian," I say. "Good to see you again."

He twitches, glancing nervously around. He looks jittery, crossing and uncrossing his long legs. "Thank you," he says. "I am pleased to see you again, Susan Parker."

I don't bother reminding him of my title, but the easy use of my name still makes me frown.

Bohjalian finishes texting and looks up. He turns on his brilliant Hollywood smile as he greets us.

"Detective Seth. Special Agent in Charge Parker. Thank you for making time to see us. I know you must have your hands full. It's much appreciated."

"That's fine, counselor. So you'll appreciate that we don't have much time to sit around and chitchat. It would be great if we could get straight to the point."

"Of course," Bohjalian says. "My client wishes to share some further information with you."

I look at Grygorian who nods vigorously.

"Yes, yes, Susan Parker. I remember something I forget tell before. I tell you now, yes?"

"I'm listening," I say.

"Magnusson, he have father," Grygorian says.

"People usually do," I say dryly.

Grygorian misses the irony in my response, but Bohjalian gives me a little headshake of disapproval while he continues texting.

"Father big deal. He start one of first hospitals in country for treatment of, how you say, psychotric, psychitric patients?"

"Psychiatric patients," Bohjalian provides helpfully, his thumbs not slowing for a second.

Grygorian points at Bohjalian. "Yes, yes. Psychitric patient. He invent new treatment method. Very, how you say in English..."

Grygorian says something to Bohjalian. Daria, the female associate responds this time, in English: "Controversial."

"Controversal," Grygorian says. "Bring big success in start. Make father famous. World fame. Very success during World War Two and some years. Military make contract for therapy treatment. But later, times change. Father methods bring big trouble. People dying, killing. Hospital shut down. Magnusson father lose license. Cannot practice therapy treatment. Very angry. Make own family patients, treat them same therapy."

Naved and I exchange a look.

"Magnusson's father used his controversial therapy methods on his own family?" Naved asks.

Grygorian nods vigorously. "Wife and two son. Wife not like. She try leave. Father violent to her. He perform therapy treatment on both son. Elder son Magnusson."

"Magnusson had a younger brother?" I ask.

That's news to me. None of our searches ever showed a sibling for Magnusson. Only a wife, now ex-wife, and a daughter, both of whom moved away to Ohio soon after BAU identified him as a possible victim slash suspect. That was just over a year ago. As far as I recall, we found nothing of interest in his early life—or nothing that raised red flags at least. All this is news to me.

"Yes. He also have sister," Grygorian says.

I think of what the schoolteacher told me, sitting in the car outside her house. I also picture her face and Magnusson's features—at least the ones of him when he was younger and carried less facial weight. A thought strikes me. "Was she from a different mother?"

Grygorian's eyes widen and he nods vigorously as if this was obvious. "Yes, yes. From another woman father sleep with but not marry."

"But this woman put his name on the birth certificate anyway," I say slowly, piecing it together. "Which is why her birth surname would be the same as Magnusson and his brother."

Again, Grygorian agrees vehemently.

Naved and I look at each other again.

Bohjalian looks up from his texting, sensing something.

"The father's name," I ask, "what was it, do you remember?"

Grygorian shakes his head. "He never say."

That's disappointing.

"Why did Magnusson tell you his life story?" Naved asks with a trace of suspicion.

Grygorian shrugs. "He only tell in last few days. When he know he dying soon. Cancer spread." Grygorian runs his hands around his own body, like a mime artist. "Everywhere. No chance save. Magnusson want confess, I am think. Need priest. But no priest. So he tell me."

"By me, you mean just yourself. Not the other eleven down in the therapy rooms?" I ask.

"Yes, yes."

"Why did he single you out from the twelve?" Naved asks, still sounding skeptical. "What was so special about you?"

Grygorian shakes his head and goes silent for a moment.

"Aram?" I ask.

Bohjalian looks up from his phone and says something in Armenian to Grygorian.

Grygorian raises his head, looking morose. His eyes look damp.

He continues with a different tone. The anguish is evident in his voice. "Grygorian only one fail therapy. Too much resist, Magnusson say. This happen sometime if patient will too strong, how you call in English. Conscious?"

"Conscience?" I suggest.

"Conscience, yes. Too strong, Magnusson say. Conscience stronger than want to revenge. Magnusson say Therapist angry with me, want terminate my therapy."

"What did that mean, 'terminate' your therapy?" I ask.

Grygorian looks at me. "Kill."

"What else did Magnusson tell you, Aram?" Naved asks.

"Therapy treatment they use on us is base on father's method. Not same exact, but better. How you say... It is Darwin word..."

"Evolved?" I suggest.

Grygorian claps his palms. "Evolve. Brothers evolve father method. Create new therapy treatment. Guarantee work." He laughs nervously. "But no work Grygorian, yes? Grygorian only fail patient they treat! They say, fail, I say success. Grygorian survive their therapy treatment method. Grygorian say no to kill target they assign to me. I resist. Grygorian strong Armenian. Resist tyranny, fascism. Resist Therapist. Resist!"

He looks pleased. For a moment, the worry lines leave his face, providing a glimpse of what he must have looked like as a young man. I wonder if his daughters look like that.

Naved glances at me before stepping forward.

"Aram, why didn't you tell us this information earlier? It's a hell of a lot of information to suddenly remember," he says.

Grygorian looks nervous again. His forehead crumples back into its perpetual pack of lines. "So much happen in therapy room," he says. "So much do to me. I not remember everything all once. It come to me slow. This come to me, I think, this help

Susan Parker. Maybe she use to catch Therapist. Stop killing Grygorian."

Bohjalian puts away his phone at last. "SAC Parker, as you can see, my client fears for his life. He hopes that this information will prove useful enough to your investigation to enable you to catch and stop Splinter the serial killer."

Grygorian groans. "Not Splinter," he says. "No can stop Splinter. Splinter everywhere. Everyone. I only ask stop Therapist. If Susan Parker stop Therapist, then Splinter stop automatic. No Therapist, no therapy, no Splinter."

I frown. "Aram, are you saying that Splinter and the Therapist are two separate people?"

Grygorian spreads his hands, looking exasperated. "Of course separate. Therapist Magnusson brother. I tell you this already."

"Actually, you haven't, Aram," Naved says. "You've told us a lot of things, but we can't verify most of them. Magnusson for instance. You say he told you all these things, but we can't exactly question him to confirm, can we?"

Bohjalian holds up his hand. "One moment, detective. Are you implying that my client is lying?"

Naved shrugs. "I'm just saying there's no way to accurately confirm what he's told us."

"Now, hold on a minute, Detective. I've seen this kind of thing before. What if Magnusson changed his name?" Bohjalian asks. "Presumably so did his brother and their half-sister. It should be possible to crosscheck dates and birth certificates with county records to pinpoint that, surely? I know I could have a researcher look into it, but I would expect the FBI to be capable of doing some simple research themselves."

"We can do the research, counselor," I say, "you need have no worries on that account. But it would help if we had something more specific. Aram, if I tell you a name, could you confirm that might be the name of Magnusson's father?"

Bohjalian sighs. "He's already told you that Magnusson never mentioned a name. Any name."

"Even so, counselor, I'd like to run one past him, just in case." I look at Grygorian. "Deutermann. Henrik Deutermann."

Grygorian screws up his face, trying to think. Finally, he shakes his head. "Sorry. No remember this."

"Who is Henrik Deutermann?" Bohjalian asks with typical lawyerly caution. "Is he a suspect?"

"Let's just say that he's a person whose history corresponds in some details to what Aram just told us about Magnusson's father," I say. "One more question."

"Yes, SAC Parker?" Bohjalian asks.

"Dr. Keller," I say, watching Grygorian's face closely. "Why didn't you ask for him?"

Bohjalian frowns. "Dr. Keller, the psychotherapist that you —" He mimes a punch.

I wince mentally. "All the other eleven asked for Dr. Keller, Aram. He's treating them all. Talking to them in private therapy sessions right now. You're the only outlier. How come you didn't ask for him, too?"

Grygorian joins his hands together in the universal gesture of mercy. "No more therapy. No more Therapist! Grygorian only want go home to family. No want revenge. Revenge lead Grygorian to this much trouble. Grygorian good Christian. Forgive and forget. Just want live life with family now. Nothing else."

"Revenge," I say, seizing on the word. "You mean revenge against the therapist who misdiagnosed your sister and prescribed the wrong antidepressant? She ended up more depressed instead of less, and killed her husband, her son, and herself. That's why you wanted to take revenge on her therapist, isn't it, Grygorian? But he's in Vladivostok, isn't he? So how does it work? Why come to the US to become a guinea pig in Magnusson's basement? Is that the deal Splinter offered you?

You participate in this therapy while he goes to Vladivostok and kills the therapist who screwed up your sister's life? Tell me, Aram."

"Don't answer that," Bohjalian says sharply. "SAC Parker, I'm disappointed. You should know better."

"You not understand still," Grygorian says. "Splinter not here. Splinter everywhere. Splinter come to kill Grygorian next. Soon he come!"

"Then tell us who Splinter is, Aram," I say, ignoring Bohjalian's protests. "So we can stop him."

"Only way stop Splinter is stop Therapist," Grygorian says.

Bohjalian takes him by the hand, like a child, and leads him out of the room. Even though Grygorian has a good foot and a half on Bohjalian and could probably take him apart even in his weakened, malnourished condition, Bohjalian is clearly the man in charge. He returns several minutes later while Naved and I both look at each other, bursting to discuss what we've just been told but not wanting to do it in front of Bohjalian's two associates.

When Bohjalian returns and informs us that the interview is concluded, we don't protest. We thank him and leave, telling him we'll be in touch, and that he should do the same if Grygorian remembers something else that could be of use.

Naved and I both exchange a look to show that we're in mutual agreement about not speaking in public. We can barely wait to get back in the car. I'm already dialing the team even before I get in.

"Guys, I think we just caught a major break in the case," I say as Brine answers.

TWENTY-EIGHT

"You're right, Susan," David says. "County records show a Henrik Deutermann was the original owner of the land. After his death, the property passed to his widow and sons. The mother was apparently declared non compos mentis or mentally incompetent around the same time and died shortly thereafter. The sons Wolfgang and Hans set up a trust. The Wolfgang Trust LLC, which continues to hold the title till today. That's the company that Magnusson 'rented' the ranch from."

"That explains the one dollar a year rent," I say. "So that means Magnusson's birth name was probably Wolfgang Deutermann."

"Right on, jefe," Ramon says. "County birth records show three children whose birth certificates named Henrik Deutermann as the father. Wolfgang Deutermann. Hans Deutermann. And Sarah Deutermann."

A spark, long since smoldering in the back of my brain, ignites. "Ramon, run a quick check for this name." I tell him the name of the schoolteacher. "I think maybe she was born Sarah Deutermann before she changed her name."

Ramon comes back in barely a minute. "Right again, Susan! You're on fire today, boss."

"But who is she?" Kayla asks.

I look at Naved who nods slowly. "It's not important. Let's focus on the Deutermann brother. Hans Deutermann. What did he change his name to, Ramon?"

After several minutes, Ramon comes back sounding frustrated. "No can do, jefe. Dude must have done some kind of fancy legal rigmarole. Even Carlotta can't find any record of Hans Deutermann changing his name."

I frown. "But legally, there has to be a record, right, David?"

"There are ways around it. It's not easy, but it's not impossible. If he did change it, he went to a lot of effort and expense to keep it hush hush," David says.

I clench my fist in frustration. "It's all right. You're doing great so far. Ramon, run one more search for me, will you?"

"Anything, jefe."

"Check back on the ownership of the last murder house."

"The Dr. Rao house in Santa Carina Valley?" Ramon asks.

"That's the one, Ramon."

"That's easy peasy tacos 'n' cheesy," Ramon says. "It's owned by a company called SK Realty LLC, incorporated in Fremont, California."

I look at Naved who shakes his head. The name doesn't ring any bells.

"Who owns that?" I ask. "Is it by any chance the same trust that owns the Splinter ranch?"

"Strike-out, chief. SK Realty is owned by another company called SK Global LLP, also incorporated in Fremont," Ramon says.

"And who are the owners of that one? If you have to, go up the chain till you find an actual human name."

"No need, jefe," Ramon says, "SK Global LLP has only two partners. Sujit Chopra and Aishwarya Chopra."

That hits me like a sledgehammer.

When I don't say anything for a long minute, Ramon asks, "That all, boss? You want me to run any more? Ask me something hard, will you? Carlotta needs the exercise!"

I'm gripping the steering wheel tightly, staring dead ahead.

Naved leans forward, speaking into the phone. "Ramon, we need a minute to process this. We'll call you back. Thanks again for all the great work. You guys are amazing! I wish I'd had a team like you back in New York."

After he disconnects, he sits silently, waiting for me to break out of the shell shock that I'm wrapped in. While he waits, he uses his phone.

"Chopra. That's one of your husband's family names?" he asks at last, still looking at his phone.

"It is," I say softly. "Amit's mother and maternal uncle. They were Chopras. She became Kapoor after marrying my father-in-law Kundan Kapoor."

"Probably doesn't mean anything, Susan," Naved says. "It took me barely a minute to find SK Global. They own a whole bunch of companies, mostly tech and biochemical, but some other areas, too. I'm guessing they needed to diversify their portfolio. That's pretty common, to safeguard against certain sectors crashing. They're Indian, Dr. Rao was Indian, they probably rented out a lot of properties to Indians. Probably an Indian-origin realtor involved. Also pretty common. It doesn't mean anything nefarious."

"You're right," I say. "But it still... kinda shook me."

"Of course," he says. "It's just a coincidence, that's all. Nothing to do with Splinter. Just a coincidence."

I nod slowly. What he's saying makes sense to my head, but my guts still feel twisted up into a knot. *Snap out of it*, I tell myself. *Don't fall down the rabbit hole and get lost again, like you did after Amit died. Stay on course. Focus, Susan!*

"You're right," I say again. "It doesn't mean anything. Sorry I spaced out."

"No apology necessary," Naved says, looking relieved. "But this is huge, Susan. The Deutermann family. This helps us make a lot of sense of the whole Splinter case. It's a major break!"

"And it just fell into our lap," I say. "Thanks to Grygorian."

"Well, yeah," he says. "But it checks out."

"So now you think Grygorian's telling the truth?" I ask. "Just last night you said he was lying through his teeth. All of you said that."

Naved throws up his hands. "We had no way to verify any of that, Susan. We do now. It checks out."

"So, if he's telling the truth about this Deutermann thing, then he could be telling the truth about Amit's death being a murder, too, right?" I ask.

Naved chews his lower lip and nods. "I take him a lot more seriously now," he admits. "I think the guy really is scared for his life. He had nothing to gain by bullshitting us this time. So yeah, to answer your question, I think he could have been telling the truth about Amit's death not being a suicide."

My heart leaps. It's not enough to counter the shock I felt when I heard Aishwarya and Sujit's names, but it helps. It gives me hope.

"But, Susan," Naved says. "We can't drive in two directions at once. Let's focus on Splinter for now. Once we've wrapped it up, we can turn over Amit's case again. I've already promised you I'm going to do everything I can to try to find the truth, and I meant it."

"That's fair enough," I say, knowing he's right. We're too close to get sidetracked.

"Good," he says. "Good."

We're both silent for a minute, then I reach a decision.

"Who are you calling?" Naved asks.

"The team," I say. "We need to meet face to face. Crack this together."

Less than an hour later, we're all in the workspace again, chairs facing inward in a rough circle. Brine miraculously produces snacks and beverages again.

"So I get that Magnusson was actually the elder Deutermann son," Kayla says. "He and his brother carried on their father's work by developing his therapeutic approach further."

"The word Grygorian said Magnusson used was 'evolved'," I say, sipping at a filter coffee Brine has somehow managed to conjure up. It's not as good as Lata's homemade brew but it'll do. The taste and odor of chicory itself soothes and calms me. "Sounds to me like they improved on his method by using modern chemicals and tech."

"That's what I thought, too," Naved says. "And so, if Magnusson was the caretaker of the twelve people in the therapy rooms, then that would mean his younger brother—"

"—was the Therapist," I finish. "Grygorian kept referring to him as the main guy. Like the puppet master. He's very convinced that if we stop the Therapist, we'll stop Splinter, too."

"Hold the bus," Kayla says. "So you're saying that the Therapist isn't Splinter either? And Magnusson wasn't Splinter, too. So who is Splinter?"

I look at Naved. We both shake our heads.

"That's the part we're having a hard time figuring out," I say. "Right, Naved? You were there. Could you make sense of what he meant? Splinter come to US, Splinter kill, Splinter fly home to country. What the hell was he talking about there?"

Naved shrugs. "I think he's saying that Splinter is a foreign national who flies around the world committing these murders. Or at least that's the way I understood it."

Ramon laughs. "Sounds a little woo-woo to me, jefe. You sure this Grygorian dude has all his marbles?"

"He did undergo horrendous trauma down in that therapy room," David says. "And he was disturbed enough to stab Magnusson what, how many times, K?"

"Fifty-three times," Kayla says. "Boy had some serious rage."

"Also, he can't really know who Splinter is," Brine says.

Everyone looks at him.

He shrugs. "Just saying. I mean, look at the timelines. The Splinter killings we know of here in the US. Even without the seven we found in other countries with a similar MO—"

"Which could be the work of copycats," Kayla says.

"Even without considering them," Brine says, "Grygorian wasn't here in the US when any of the Splinter killings happened. We have his I-94. He was half a planet away. So how could he really know who Splinter is?"

I nod. "Good point, Brine. Excellent point, in fact. Maybe Grygorian is giving us good intel on some things, maybe not so good on others. That jibes with the trauma he's suffered."

"We should run this Deutermann lead down," Naved says. "Take it as far as it goes. There has to be a way to track down the younger brother."

"So how do we find who Hans Deutermann is now?" I ask. "Any ideas?"

We toss around a few thoughts, Ramon feeds Carlotta a few more suggestions, but several hours later, we still have nothing concrete.

"Okay," I say at last. "Let's take a break for dinner then get back on it. We need to crack this."

Everyone looks at each other.

"What?" I ask.

Naved looks at me.

"Maybe we call it a day?" he says gently. "Go home, get a good night's sleep. Start over again tomorrow morning?"

"You haven't slept in two nights, Suse," Kayla says, touching my shoulder. "You're running yourself ragged again, girl."

I look around at them. "You're right. We could all use some shut eye and a decent, homecooked meal. Okay, let's call it a night."

Walking out to the parking lot, Naved says, "And that goes for you, too, Susan. Take the evening. Refresh. Recharge. You need it. Besides, whoever Splinter really is, I don't think he's going to be making any moves tonight. He knows we're sniffing his trail. He's probably holed up someplace, biding his time until the heat blows over. If he's even here in the US, that is."

I shake my head. "It's not Splinter I'm worried about," I say. "It's the damn Therapist. He's the key, remember? We stop the Therapist, we stop Splinter."

TWENTY-NINE

"Hey, wasn't expecting you so early. Everything okay?" Lata says, when I walk in. She's sitting in the living room with her laptop and looks surprised to see me.

"Just need a quick rest," I say. "Figured I'd use the time to hang with Natalie."

I raise my hand before she can speak up. "And, I know, I know, we need to talk, too. I owe you an explanation. It's just been really crazy the past couple of days."

I slump down on the couch. Lata comes over.

"I can only imagine," she says. "You only came home to shower and change this morning, and I could see how exhausted you were already so I didn't want to get in your way."

"I'm really sorry," I say, "for jumping straight in and not giving us a chance to talk about it first."

"You didn't have time," she says, "I totally get that. Don't stress."

"No, it was my bad," I say. "I owed you an explanation. After we talked and I promised."

Lata waves me off. "No, no. Listen to me. I can see you're stressed about that. Don't be. I know what I said and at the time,

I thought it was the right call. But after seeing the way you've been working these past two days, the incredible amount you've accomplished already, I take it all back. Ignore everything I said that day. I was wrong."

"Really?" I say, incredulous.

"Totally!" she says. "Look, Suse. I'll be the first to admit it. I was still thinking of you as the old Susie. The Susie who... well, I don't want to drag all that up again. But you know what I mean."

I do. She means the Susan Parker who lost it after Amit's death, who went at Dr. Keller like a bat out of hell, who seemed hellbent on destroying herself, her life, her career, her family.

"I know you're not that person anymore," she says. "You've changed. For the better. And it makes me so happy and proud to see that."

It's on the tip of my tongue to tell her that I wish I was as sure as she is about that. That I sometimes feel as if that old Susie never really went away. I worry that the new Susie is just a glazed mask that will crack at some point—revealing the darker, scarier Susie that's still inside.

"I... did not expect that," I say. "You sure, Luts?"

She takes my hand and squeezes it lightly. Lata still keeps up with her training, so I feel the power behind that squeeze. "Of course I'm sure. I know you. I can see how good this is for you. You needed this."

"What I need is a shower, a change of clothes, and about twelve hours' solid sleep," I say. "All of which I know I'm not gonna get, except maybe for the shower and change, which I'll grab right now. And then maybe the three of us can do something together. How's that?"

"It sounds awesome," Lata says, standing with me, "but tonight's Natalie's night with my parents, remember? They're taking her to see the musical at Pantages, and then she's staying over at the hotel with them. They'll drop her off tomorrow."

"That's tonight?" I say. "Damn. I totally blanked on the date. *Aladdin*, right?"

"*Frozen. Aladdin* was last year."

"Right." I look around, suddenly at a loss. I rushed back here, dropping Naved off at the Santa Carina impound lot, excited at the prospect of surprising Natalie, maybe taking her out someplace special, or just spending time with her. Now, I literally can't think of how to spend the rest of the evening and tomorrow morning.

An idea occurs to me.

"Maybe we can go, too," I say, pulling out my phone. "There's still time for us to get to Pantages. Let me check if there are tickets. They're probably sitting in the front row center, am I right? Aishwarya won't settle for anything less than the best seats in the house."

I've just opened the Broadway in Hollywood website and start to scroll. Lata's hand covers my screen, forcing me to look up.

"What?" I say.

"Look at you. You haven't slept in two nights. You've been shot at, chased down armed killers across cornfields, been working nonstop for almost forty-eight hours. Have you even stopped to eat a proper meal? I don't mean a working meal where you and your team eat while you talked about the case, I mean just pushed everything aside and enjoyed the food? No, don't answer that. I know you haven't. You've been dealing with the usual Bureau politics, the typical men's club shit, lawyers and psychiatrists, coroners and corpses. Talking about autopsy findings and crime scenes. You must be exhausted. Just looking at you makes me feel exhausted, and I've spent three nights on nightwatch in the mountains of Kandahar surrounded by hostiles. Give yourself a break, Susan. Take the evening off. The weekend, if you can. Go up, shower, change into something comfy, pour yourself a glass of wine, kick back, relax. You've earned it."

"Sure, sure," I say, still resisting. "But you know how your mom can be at times. I worry about her saying the wrong thing or getting on her high horse and triggering Natalie. If I'm there..."

"You're always going to be there for Natalie. I get it. She's with her grandparents. Okay, so I know my mom isn't perfect, far from it. But even you'll agree that my dad's a pretty great grandpa, right?"

"Natalie loves him. She says he always makes her laugh until snot comes out," I say, smiling at the memory of that very literal event.

"So she's in good hands. And I told Mom to be on her best behavior or she'll have me to answer to."

I nod. Lata's the only one of the three siblings—now, two— who can correct her mom with a few quiet words. Aishwarya bristles but doesn't lash out; like all bullies she always knows when she's met her match.

"A shower and a glass of wine does sound pretty good," I say. "I can wash my hair. I kept the shower cap on both days but I'm starting to feel itchy in there. And it was a vineyard by the way."

She looks at me. "Huh?"

"You said cornfield earlier. I chased the shooter across a vineyard, not a cornfield."

She rolls her eyes. "Language Nazi!"

I wink. "Hey, we still have any of that really great Malbec you brought back from Temecula?"

Lata smiles. "Two whole bottles. I'll put one on ice right away while you go shower."

"And how about a couple of your awesome chicken satay sticks? Maybe a paneer satay stick, too? With onions and green peppers?" I say, instantly salivating at the thought.

Lata laughs. "I would love to stay in all night with you and help you kick back, sis-in-law, but I have a date."

I step back and look her up and down. "I thought I noticed something. You hit up the salon, didn't you? And you did your hair!"

She flashes her nails, then pulls up her skirt and shows me her toenails. They're painted deep purple and are sparkly. "Picked up a new outfit, too!"

"Whoa," I say. "Who's the lucky girl?"

She twirls, smiling mysteriously. "You don't know her. We just met."

"Wait a sec. Is this the one you met on that, whatsitcalled, Qupid? LesDance? I forget the name. The lesbian dating app?" I ask.

"Well, yeah, but sometimes you really do strike gold," she says defensively. Lata has a history of picking the wrong women; on the plus side, she's quick to break it off when things get funky. On the negative side, she's *too* quick to break it off sometimes and ends up regretting it later.

"Is that what you did? Strike gold? Boy, she must be some-thing special!" I say.

"Well, it's our third date," she says. The only time I've actually seen Lata shy is when talking about her girlfriends.

"That's practically an anniversary! I'm so happy, Luts!" I say, meaning every word of it.

"Thanks. So... I still have an hour before I have to leave, and I'm not driving tonight, for obvious reasons. I'll hang around and have one glass of wine with you. Just one! If you really want satay, I can order in from the Thai place you like," she says.

"Nah. They won't have paneer. Or the onions and peppers," I say. "It's cool. I'll order in later. Right now, I'm just looking forward to that shower and putting my feet up. Maybe watch something mindless and stupid, vegetate."

"Great plan," she says. "Now get your butt upstairs and wash the nasty serial killer stink out of your hair."

Twenty minutes later, freshly showered and feeling a little dizzy at the prospect of an entire evening off, but also a little guilty at not being with Natalie in what could be the only free time I get for a while, I come downstairs in my bathrobe with a towel on my head like a maharani's turban. I feel a hundred times better. The only thing sweeter than having a productive couple of days doing something you love is having some much-needed R&R time to unwind after.

Lata put on music, dimmed the lights and poured me a glass of my favorite red. She's guzzled half her own first glass and is curled up on the La-Z-Boy.

"Hey, we were just talking about this one today!" I say as I walk over to the record player.

It's a cheap turntable in a briefcase housing, playing off a Bluetooth speaker. By a weird coincidence, the song playing is "Mad World". Such weird-good lyrics. The memories this song brings back!

I take a sip of the Malbec as I watch the vinyl disc spin. The light reflecting off the grooves creates a hypnotic effect.

"Amit and I got this when we first moved in together," I say. "We were living in a tiny studio above someone's garage: every time the owners parked their cars or drove out, the whole apartment would shake like it was falling apart, and stink of gasoline fumes."

Lata chuckles. "I remember him telling me about that place. The owners were a couple of old conspiracy theory nuts, right?"

I roll my eyes. "Oh yeah. They believed everything was the government's fault. Moon landing. 911. You name it. I bet they had a field day with the pandemic."

I touch the edge of the turntable. I'm not the kind of person who gets sentimental about things. After being digested through the foster care system and regurgitated, you learn not to get too precious about stuff that you're inevitably going to be parted from, sooner or later. But this turntable is a connection to Amit, to the time we had together, to the dreams and hopes of my younger self. Touching it, I almost feel like I'm touching him.

"In one of the foster homes I was in, they had this vintage Grundig. Record player and radio console, housed in a wooden cabinet on four splayed legs. It was ancient. My foster mom had this same song, on a record, and that's where I first heard it played. I must have been only a few years older than Natalie."

I remember talking about it to Amit. We talked about the sound of vinyl and how nothing compared. It made him nostalgic for the Victrola his family owned back in Delhi. And for the Hindi film albums his dad, Kundan, used to play—which of course, his mom Aishwarya hated him playing because she thought playing film songs sounded cheap.

I remember Amit jumping out of bed naked once to take the needle off an old Bollywood record he'd hunted down on eBay when the garage apartment started shaking. I remember laughing at him standing there, checking the grooves on his precious album, looking like he'd almost died.

Lata says something which I don't catch.

"Sorry, wool gathering. What'd you say?" I ask.

"I said that must have been the original Tears for Fears recording. On their 1982 album."

"Sure. Not that I knew much about music then. But I knew this song was special. My foster mom at the time played it over and over. I was only with her for a few months, but she was one of the nice ones. I wish I could remember her name but there were so many. Anyway, the song stuck."

Lata pats the couch next to the La-Z-Boy. "Take a load off."

The couch feels delicious. I stretch out. Lata gets up,

unfolds a shawl, and spreads it over me. "Thanks," I say, snuggling in.

We sip wine and listen to music as the night deepens.

I sing aloud with the lyrics, finding an echo to my own deeply held sadness in the bittersweet lyrics.

"'*Mad world!*'" Lata joins in.

"I miss him," I say unexpectedly. "Oh, God, how I miss him, Lata."

She's silent for a long moment, then says, "I miss him, too, Suse."

"Why?" I ask her, ashamed-not-ashamed of the tears welling up in my eyes so easily, like a reservoir that will never run dry. "Why him?"

Lata sits up in the La-Z-Boy and puts her arm around me. "Because the universe sucks sometimes."

A familiar tone cuts in. It's coming from upstairs.

"His Majesty, your phone, has summoned you," Lata says as I push myself off the couch. She adds, "Hey, I'll be heading out in a few. Dunno what time I'll be home. You sure you're good to stay alone tonight?"

I make a circle with my thumb and forefinger and smile at her over my shoulder. "Copacetic."

My phone is still in the bathroom where I left it. The room was so steamed up when I came out of the shower, I didn't see it, and I was feeling so relaxed and refreshed that I totally forgot about it. Out of sight, out of mind. That's a rarity for someone as obsessive-compulsive as I am. The screen is still steamed up and I bring it into the bedroom and sit on the edge of the bed. The cool air evaporates the condensation, and I can now read the screen.

The missed calls are from Naved, Marisol, Brine, and Ramon. The texts are from Kayla, Ramon, Marisol and Brine. I debate whom to call or text first and settle on reading the texts first in reverse order.

First up, Kayla:

> Keller set up sessions with all eleven starting
> Monday: 30 mins each + daily group session
> with all 10.

Kayla, five seconds later:

> DON'T contact him!

This is followed by a series of Japanese oni emojis.
Ramon:

> Hey, call me. Got something.

Marisol:

> U r around? Heer at crime sceen?

Marisol, a few minutes later:

> Txt me asp.

For someone so meticulous in their forensic work, Marisol
Mancini texts like an over-excited teen.

Brine:

> How you doing? Got the paperwork in order
> finally! Need to run a few things by you before I
> file. Routine stuff. No rush, can do tomorrow or
> even Monday. Enjoy your evening, boss!

My first call-back is to Marisol. It goes to voicemail. She's
probably elbow-deep in guts or peering through a microscope.
"Hey, Susan here returning your call. I'm in Santa Carina, but

not on scene. If you need me, I can swing by anytime—let me know."

Ramon answers on the fourth or fifth ring of my Facetime call. He's in a tank tee in his garage gym at home. Spanish hip hop is blasting so loud, I can see the oil and coolant cans in the background actually jump when the bass kicks. He turns it down and wipes sweat, grinning down at me. "Hey, boss. That's a new look for you!"

I touch the pink towel-turban on my head. "You like it?"

He laughs. "Maharani Susan, yo! Suits you, jefe."

Ramon is pressing up what looks like at least 230lbs on the bench. There's a thin sheen of sweat on his face, neck, shoulders, and arms but he's not really straining. He finishes and looks over at me. "So, what can I do for you, boss?"

"You remember that cousin you told me about?"

Ramon pretends to think. "I have a lotta cousins, chief. Which one you need?"

It only takes a minute or two.

I've just put my phone down, as Lata pops her head in. "Hey."

"Hey," I say. "You heading out?"

She trots into view, holding out her arms to display her dating look. "Whaddaya think?" she asks, then quickly adds, "Be kind!"

"Always, yaar," I say, and give her the once-over. "Wow."

She looks up at me with a nervous frown. "Seriously?"

"Seriously, wow. If it was me, I'd want to put a ring on that!" I say.

She rolls her eyes. "Thank God you play for the other team. It's just a date, Suse. I'm not looking to settle down! I already have a family, and one's quite enough, thank you."

I walk over to give her a sisterly hug and a peck on her cheek, careful not to muss up her makeup. "You look beautiful. Go get 'em, tiger!"

She looks at me with genuine concern. "You sure you're good to stay alone?"

I wink and grin at her. "I'm still sober! So I've got some drinking to do. Two bottles, did you say?"

She wags a finger. "Go easy, okay! You know what Sharif said about booze acting as a trigger."

"He said 'regular intake of substantial quantities of alcohol,' not a few glasses of Malbec, sis-in-law. Now, get outta here. Go enjoy your night!"

She prances away, waving her fingers over her shoulder. "Be good. Don't spend all your time on your phone. And don't work the case. You need some downtime, remember!"

"Yes, Mom," I sing-song. "Okay, Mom! I will, Mom! Goodnight, Mom!"

She shoots me the finger from the bottom of the stairs, then turns it into one last wave. The front door opens then shuts, and she's gone.

I finish changing into a pair of old cotton sweatpants and a favorite tee shirt and go downstairs. I pour myself a big glass of wine and sit back, putting my feet up on the hassock.

The house feels weird without Natalie and Lata. I can't recall the last time I was here home alone with both of them gone.

Not since Amit was alive.

No, I admonish myself, *I am not going there.* No, sirree! No slipping back into maudlin memories.

I try watching something on TV, but my mind keeps wandering.

At some point, my phone pings.

A text from Kayla.

Get laid tonight, boss. Get those endorphins flowing!

221

Following the text is a meme of two persons of indeterminate gender doing the same natural act. There's a caption:

Lady's pick! Choose your flava, girl!

I laugh and text back:

> Got a spare bf or gf to share? I'm fresh out!

The response comes back instantly: a whole line up of figures, all genders, all going at it. It's so over-the-top I can't help bursting out with laughter.

Still laughing, I text:

> High hopes, girl. I haven't been laid for a year! Baby steps.

> Now, get back to enjoying your night and lemme chill.

She sends me a series of kiss emojis, signing off.
I shake my head at the outrageous emojis, still grinning.
I'm still grinning when my phone screen lights up.

Kundan Calling.

A dagger of ice pierces my heart. Natalie!

THIRTY

My father-in-law's genial face pops up on my screen. He's in the hotel suite he and Aishwarya always stay in when in LA, I can tell from the swanky background.

"Kundan?" I say. "Is Natalie okay?"

"She's fine, bete," he says in his jovial, chortling voice. "Nothing to worry about. She is a little upset, that is all. She wants to speak to you. One moment, please, I will put her on the video."

He turns the phone to capture Natalie.

Like most children born deaf, Natalie's voice suffers from her inability to hear herself. Most of our speech, the unique way each of us talks aloud, comes from imitation of our parents and elders, as well as a constant series of minor self-corrections in our early years. We teach ourselves to speak the way our family speaks by listening to them, repeating what they say, then listening to ourselves. Unable to hear anyone, Natalie's voice sounds strange, unmelodious, weird to most hearing-gifted people. To me, it's the most wonderful voice in the world, but hearing it always alerts me to the fact that she's either very, very upset or very, very happy and unable to contain herself.

"Mom!" she says in her version of a wail. "Mom." She then launches into a frenzied litany that devolves into hitching, crying noises.

"Natalie, what's wrong?" I say, my heart racing in panic. She looks unhurt, there are no visible signs of injury or any trauma. She's clearly been crying and from the high color in her cheeks, she's been upset for a while.

She gestures furiously, not signing so much as ranting. Her movements are too quick and mostly cut off by the frame because Kundan is unknowingly holding the phone too close to her face. Like most hearing-gifted, he's forgotten that I need to see her full frame in order to interpret what she's signing.

"Baby, slow down. Slow down! Hang on, I need to tell Grandpa something. Kundan? Kundan?"

Kundan's face appears again as he turns the phone back to himself. "Yes, bete?"

"Hold the phone at a distance from her, so I can read her signs," I say.

"Achcha. Of course!" he says, then turns the phone back to Natalie. She hasn't stopped signing and I catch the end of her sentence.

"What was that, Natalie? Slow down, please. I can't understand what you're saying," I say. "What happened with Grandma?"

"She was mean to me," Natalie signs.

I feel a flame of anger spark in me.

"But what happened exactly? Can you tell me, please? Calm down, and sign slowly so I can understand you, my darling," I say.

Natalie explains to me, through a long-drawn-out signing, that she was getting bored of the show and wanted to leave in the middle but Aishwarya told her that it would be interval soon, and they could leave then if she wanted to. But after the interval, she made Natalie sit through the second half and by then, Natalie was *really* bored and just wanted to go home. Aishwarya spoke to her firmly and told her that she needed to behave herself and sit and watch the whole show like a good little girl. Something about how much Aishwarya had paid for the front-row tickets so that Natalie would be able to lip-read the actors and she should show her gratitude instead of grumbling all the time.

"I want to come home, Mom," Natalie pleads with me. "Please could you come and pick me up? Please, Mom? Please!"

"Of course, sweetie," I say, indignant at Aishwarya's high-handedness. "I'm actually not very far away. I can be there in... fifteen minutes."

Natalie's face breaks out in a smile. She mouths: "I love you, Mom!"

"I love you, too, sweetie. Now, put Grandpa on. And go get your stuff, I'll be there very soon."

Kundan looks a little sad. "Bete, I'm so sorry. I tried to make Aishwarya understand but you know how she gets."

"Kundan, she's just seven."

"I know, I know. I was ready to bring her back to the hotel or take her to get ice cream. I told Aishwarya, but she said she was not going to sit alone. She paid for the tickets, and she would not let the money go to waste."

As I get ready, a thought occurs to me. I wasn't keeping count of how many glasses I drank but it was easily more than three. The last thing I need is to be pulled over and arrested for a DUI.

On impulse, I dial Naved, putting him on speakerphone while I change.

"Susan?" he says on the third ring.

"Hey," I say. "I'm so sorry to disturb your evening."

"That's all right. What's up?"

"I have a little family emergency. I need to get my ass to the city, and I've had a couple glasses of wine so I don't want to drive."

"Would you like me to take you?"

"Have you been drinking, too?"

"Um, I don't drink."

"Oh, that's good. But I really don't want to interrupt your evening. I could just call a rideshare."

"No need. I can drive you."

"You're sure?"

"Absolutely. I'll be there in ten. Less, actually. I'm already dressed."

"Thanks, pardner. I owe you."

I disconnect.

Seven minutes later, Naved pulls up to the curb outside my house. I get in.

"Thanks again," I say. "I really owe you one."

"Hey. What are partners for?"

My phone buzzes again. It's Kundan.

"Kundan, I'm leaving in a minute, I should be there in twenty minutes at this hour, no traffic. I'll text you when we're close and you can bring Natalie down to the lobby. My partner's driving me."

He looks a little confused. "Your partner?"

"Work partner, Detective Seth," I clarify. "We're in his car."

I tell him the make and color of Naved's Camry.

Kundan says, "At least come up for a minute when you arrive. I feel so bad about all this."

"Kundan, do you really want me to come up to Aishwarya's suite tonight? You think that's a good idea?" I ask.

Kundan sucks in his breath. "Ah. Samjhe. I get the point, bete. No, you are right. Better that you and Aishwarya don't come face to face. Not tonight at least. Otherwise, calamity will be unleashed! I will bring Natalie down to the lobby when you call me. See you."

I disconnect and pound the dashboard hard with the phone still clenched in my fist. "That woman! Who the hell does she think she is?"

Naved says quietly, "She sounds like quite the character."

"Oh, you have no idea," I say, trying to calm my breathing. "She's a total... I don't even want to say the word. It's hard to believe she could produce three amazing children like Amit, Lata and Kajal."

"So this is the famous Delhi socialite Aishwarya Kapoor, right? Sister to the tech millionaire Sujit Kapoor?"

"Yeah, that's them. The dynamic duo," I say, fuming. "One worse than the other."

"They inherited money, correct? But Aishwarya had control of the trust because she's older, so she was the one who backed Sujit's early tech projects which paid off big-time. That makes them business partners, if I remember?"

I give Naved a side-eye look. "Are we really doing this Forbes interview now? Really?"

Naved glances at me, sees my furious face. "Um. I'll shut up and drive now."

"Good idea," I say.

When we're about thirty seconds away, I call Kundan and say, "Please bring Natalie out now, Kundan. We're arriving."

My phone starts to buzz in my fist just as we're pulling into the hotel lobby. I glance at the screen and see it's Daria, Bohjalian's associate. What does she want at this hour? I ignore it and get out of the car just as Natalie comes running to me and slams into my arms.

"Oh, my baby, are you all right?" I ask her, signing and speaking both at once as I always do.

She signs back furiously, "Grandma is a mean woman!"

I sigh. "Yes, she is. I'm so sorry you had to go through that, sweetie."

"I'm never going to go with her again. Ever!" Natalie signs.

"Okay, okay, calm down now. You're with me. We're going home. Calm down."

Natalie looks at the car and does a double take. "This is not your car!"

"I know, sweetie. It's my partner Naved's car. He's driving us home."

She twists her neck and looks in curiously at Naved, who dips his head so she can see him more clearly. He smiles and does a little wave.

"Hi, Natalie," he says. "I've heard a lot of good things about you!"

She stares at him, then smiles shyly. She looks up at me. "He's nice," she says. "And nice-looking!"

I give her a little tap on the butt. "Natalie Nelly Parker, get in the car."

She gets in the back seat and says, "There's no child seat."

"I know, sweetie, we'll have to buckle your seatbelt tight and make do for now," I say.

"Isn't that against the law?" she asks.

"Not if you're eight years old, which you will be in just a few months, or four feet nine inches tall. Lucky for us, you pass the height test," I say, buckling her in securely.

"But last time we measured, you said I'm only four feet eight inches!" she says.

"Well, that was a while back, and you've grown since. But in case anyone asks, I won't tell if you won't. Deal?" I say, patting her chest to make sure the seatbelt is tightly strapped.

She grins up at me. "Deal!"

I bend down and kiss her on the forehead, the cheek, then on her lips. "I love you, baby doll."

"I love you, Mommy doll," she says.

"Now I'm going to sit up front with Naved, but I'm right there, okay?" I say.

She nods and gives me two thumbs up. She's thrilled at being able to sit in the adult seat, not in a booster seat.

I turn back to Kundan, who looks forlorn and sagging.

"Susan, bete, I am so sorry," he says.

"It's not your fault, Kundan," I say. "I don't know what I was thinking, letting Aishwarya talk me into letting you guys keep Natalie for the whole evening. It's one thing watching *Frozen* at home. She can press pause anytime if she gets bored and pick it up later. But in a theatre, sitting for two and a half hours can get tiresome. And forcing her to stay. That's unforgiveable."

His face crumples. "I feel so embarrassed. I tried to make Aishwarya understand but you know how she gets. I think Natalie has inherited her stubbornness from her only!"

"Oh no," I say as I open the front passenger door. "She gets it from me. Just wait until the next time Aishwarya wants to spend time with her granddaughter, see who's the stubborn one. Goodnight, Kundan."

"Goodnight, bete." Kundan bends down and waves to Natalie in the back seat. "Goodnight, Natalie!"

Natalie, in a much better mood now than she was twenty minutes ago, smiles and waves back. "Goodnight, Grandpa!"

As we pull away from the hotel, Naved says, "So I guess we're heading back to Santa Carina now."

I'm about to answer when my phone buzzes in my fist again. There's a voice message from Daria the lawyer. I hold it to my ear and listen to it, curious. It's barely a few seconds long and is truncated.

"That's weird," I say to Naved.

"What's up?" he asks.

"Daria just left a voice message for me. She texted me, too."

"What does she want?"

I read out the text to him:

> Text me when you reach here, I'll send you the gate code. It changes every few hours.

"What does that mean?" Naved asks. "Is it from before? Delayed message delivery?"

I scroll through my messages. "Nope. This is just now, less than five minutes ago."

"And the voice message?"

I play it for him, keeping the volume low to avoid disturbing Natalie, who looks like she's on the verge of dropping off to sleep.

"Hello, SAC Parker? I just spoke to the client. He's a little nervous. Could we maybe reschedule this for tomorrow morning? Thanks."

Naved frowns. "What's that about?"

"I have no idea," I say. "But I'm going to find out."

I dial Daria but her number's busy.

I call Bohjalian. He answers on the first ring.

"SAC Parker?" he says, sounding a little terse. "I've already informed my associates that you're coming. As I said before, I'm a little tied up this evening."

"I'm sorry, counselor," I say, "but did we have an appointment?"

"Well, you're the one who asked me to set up another meeting with my client. You should know!" he says.

"Counselor, I think there's been some mistake. I haven't called or texted you since we met earlier today."

Bohjalian goes silent for a moment, then says, "You didn't text me about half an hour ago?"

"I most definitely did not," I say, looking at Naved. He raises his eyebrows, trying to figure out the other side of the conversation.

"SAC Parker, I think we might have a situation. I'm going to disconnect now and call my security team. Goodnight."

And just like that, he's gone.

Naved sees the change in my face and asks, "What's wrong?"

"How much farther to Santa Carina?" I say, checking the freeway. "Drive faster. Head to Grygorian's."

He accelerates. "What's up? What did Bohjalian say?"

I reach down for my hip holster and pull out my Sig Sauer, checking the clip and chamber. "Someone's coming for Grygorian. We have to get there first."

THIRTY-ONE

I keep trying Daria's number. It rings but there's no answer.

Naved is talking to SCVPD and asking them to dispatch backup to the location.

Finally, just as we're coming off the freeway at Newhall, Daria answers.

"Hello?" I say. "Daria? Can you hear me? This is SAC Parker."

There's a faint gurgling sound that makes my throat clench.

I turn up the volume, pressing the phone tightly to my ear, trying to catch every sound. When Daria speaks at last, she sounds like she's talking underwater.

"...*shot me... gone... upstairs...she... Aram...*"

"Daria," I say quietly so Natalie doesn't hear. "Listen to me. We're going to be there in less than thirty seconds. Hold on. Help is on the way."

There's no answer. I look at my screen. The line's disconnected. I have no idea if she even heard me.

I speed dial Kayla. She answers on the third ring, her voice rich with the sound of laughter, and I hear music in the back-

232

ground. But when she hears my tone, she snaps alert at once. I tell her what's what then hang up.

"Kayla's calling in the cavalry," I tell Naved. "But it's going to take a few. You know the drill."

Naved nods grimly, taking a curve at sixty. "Ditto with SCVPD."

An active shooter on scene means that law enforcement's first priority on arrival at the scene will be life safety. They'll secure the scene first and lock it down before checking on any wounded. Depending on the situation, they might even wait for SWAT. That's a minimum initial response time of five to six minutes, plus an additional wait time for SWAT. It could be twenty minutes or more before they're ready to move in and actually start sorting out the good guys from the bad. If the shooter is already in the apartment, they could be long gone before even the first responders arrive. FBI will take longer since the field office is thirty miles further away than SCVPD.

"What about—?" Naved jerks his head back.

I glance back at Natalie.

She's fallen fast asleep, mouth open as happens when she's been crying. What am I going to do? I'm heading into an active shooter situation with my daughter in the back seat!

I try to think of options. Nothing comes to mind that would be quick enough. Kayla's already scrambling the team, but knowing where they stay, there's little to zero chance that any of them will arrive before the cops. Naved and I are on our own for the moment at least.

"You stay with her in the car," Naved says, reading the answer in my eyes, "I'll go in."

I want to argue but I can't. A glance back at my daughter's face as she sleeps in the back seat is enough to pierce my heart. No way can I risk her life, not for all the Grygorians in the world. Or all the Splinters. "Okay," I say without argument.

Just as we're arriving, my phone pings again.

It's a text from Bohjalian, just four digits, nothing else.

"The gate code is 7368," I read aloud.

Naved nods, acknowledging.

One more turn and then we're there.

Naved brings the Camry to a halt sideways to the gate, deliberately blocking it. He jumps out and checks his surroundings.

We both see the black Ford Ram at the same time. Both front doors are open and even in the darkness, I can see part of a body hanging out, fallen into the street.

Naved approaches till he's close enough to be sure that both Bohjalian's private cops are dead. He looks back at me and makes a throat-cutting sign. I nod, pointing at the building. He nods back then returns to the gate. He taps in the code he heard me say aloud. The gate slides open automatically and he slips in and runs to the lobby. I watch him till he reaches the foyer and slows, moving cautiously with his back to the wall, gun held down in both hands. He peeks around the wall into the building lobby, then disappears.

I sit back, exhaling. I'm pumped with adrenalin, eager to run after him and do my job. But I can't leave Natalie alone. Not with a killer or killers out here.

I feel something hit my seat and look over my shoulder. She's come awake and has just kicked the back of my seat. She grins at me sleepily.

"Why are we stopped, Mommy?" she asks.

Of course. With our backs to her, she wouldn't have been able to catch any of our conversation. Besides, she fell asleep. She has no idea what's going on.

I try to compose my face into a casual smile. "Naved has something to take care of. He'll be back soon then we'll be on our way."

She nods agreeably. Then she yawns. "Sleepy," she signs.

"Go back to sleep, sweetie," I say. "We'll be home soon."

She yawns again, then nods. She's asleep again in seconds. I hope she stays asleep this time.

A gunshot rings out from somewhere inside the building. It sends my pulse rate racing again.

I reach for my Sig Sauer instinctively. Keeping my back to Natalie, I slide the gun out and lower it to the seat beside me. Holding it ready for use, but keeping it well out of sight.

Another shot. This one from a higher floor. I can't be sure, but it sounds like a different weapon. Again, I look back at Natalie instinctively, but of course she hasn't heard a thing. I'm relieved to see that her eyes are already closed, and her head is down.

My mind races with my options. I have none, not until someone else arrives at least. I can't just leave Naved stranded here and take off. He might already be hurt, bleeding, and the arriving cops won't know who he is. I can't leave Natalie alone in the car either and go inside to back him up.

Is this Splinter? This isn't his style. Guns and subterfuge. He deals in home invasion and torturing families with blades and sharp objects.

Who has enough vested in this to want to kill Grygorian? Why? To shut him up? From saying what? Identifying Splinter? That's the only thing that makes some sense. If Grygorian can identify Splinter, then it's worth Splinter taking this risk. It would explain his abandoning his usual MO, too. This is a one-time cleanup job, closing loose lips. Splinter wouldn't hesitate to take down two young lawyers as collateral either. Or an SCVPD cop, for that matter.

No more shots since that second one from upstairs. I can hear sirens in the distance. I check my phone. It's been barely four minutes. I see texts from Kayla from a little more than four minutes ago.

SCVPD+Ambulance en route, ETA 2 mins.

> Omw. Team too. Hang tight.

Then Ramon:

> OMW.

Brine:

> En route.

David:

> Omw.

As I'm skimming them, a text from Naved pops up:

> No sign of shooter aptmnt. Bad scene. 1 dead lobby, 1 dead here. G hangin by thread.

I text back:

> Sirens, 1 minute out.

> G not gonna make it.

I don't know what to say to that. I imagine Naved typing with one hand while he applies pressure on Grygorian's bullet wounds. The apartment streaked with blood, the smell of cordite in the air, the hackle-raising air of sudden violence.

A figure in a dark hoodie comes out of the building lobby and walks toward the gate. The person moves at a casual pace, neither rushing nor dawdling. They have their head down, the cowl of the hoodie pulled low, as if they're trying to avoid being caught on the overhead security cameras.

I grasp the Glock tighter and slide down as low in my seat as possible. My side door is still open. I opened it when we stopped while I tried to make a decision and left it that way in case I had to exit in a hurry. I push it open now and lower myself to the street, crouching low to keep the car between me and the gate.

I rest my back against the cold metal of the rear passenger door. Natalie is only inches behind me, on the other side of this door. From the slow, steady sound of her breathing, I can tell that she's fallen asleep.

The soft sound of sneakered footsteps approaches the gate. The beep of the gate code being punched into the keyboard, then the click and whirr of the gate sliding open.

I bend my head and peek under the Camry.

Black sneakers below black jeans. They stop outside the gate, standing still. My throat catches. From the glimpse I had of her earlier as she exited the lobby, the curve of her lower body and the rise of her chest in that hoodie, I know it's definitely a she.

I know she's looking at the Camry, wondering what it's doing there, where the driver is, whether they're around. The position of the car and the open doors give it away as a law enforcement vehicle. Only cops park this way. In the distance, the sirens draw closer. They're only a few blocks away now, twenty seconds or less.

The shooter makes a decision, and does the very thing I expected them to do. She starts to get in the Camry's driver's seat.

It makes sense.

She can see that the keys are in the ignition. The car's ready to go. It'll be faster than walking to her own vehicle, wherever it's parked. Or maybe she left her vehicle inside because it's been caught on camera and is already burned. The license plate and description would be out on a BOLO within minutes of the shooter driving away in it. With cops converging on the area, she could run straight into their arms. This way, she'll have a clean car, even better, a cop car, and will be several minutes away from the scene before the owner realizes and calls it in. Maybe longer if the owner is upstairs in the apartment and stays with the wounded till the EMTs arrive. The shooter probably thinks the Camry is a gift from the god of serial killers.

Except that this car happens to have my daughter in the back seat.

I snap up like a jack in the box, my gun aimed at the hoodie, and bark, "Hands on the wheel."

The black hoodie freezes.

There's a fraction of a second when I think the shooter's going to go for her gun. I can see it inside the front pocket of her hoodie, ruining the line of the fabric, her fist already on the grip. I'm ready. If that hand moves, I shoot. No hesitation. Not with Natalie's life in the balance. I won't even try for a body shot, just one clean head shot, easy peasy from four feet away. She won't even know she's dead until her face hits the steering wheel.

But hoodie does the unexpected.

She throws herself out of the open driver's door into the street, and out of my line of fire. The car door blocks my shot now. I don't want to risk taking a wild shot and risk a ricochet coming back to Natalie. My spur-of-the-moment plan depended on waiting for her to sit in the car when she would be most vulnerable, and then disarm her without firing a shot. So much for that plan.

I move in a crouch around the car, conscious that I could be running into *her* line of fire now. I pause, still in a crouch, using the engine block to shield me, and try to look around. No sign of her on the street.

Flashing lights are entering the street now, bearing down on me fast.

I come around the Camry and scan the pavement, still aiming my gun. I glimpse a dark shadow on the outer wall of the building, walking away from me. The approaching 911 vehicles can't see it because parked cars block their view of that pavement.

"Shooter!" I yell, waving my free hand at the vehicles screeching to a halt before me. "Stop her, she's getting away!"

Blue uniforms pour out of the patrol cars, guns in hand. "Drop the gun! Put up your hands!"

I want desperately to run after the shooter, chase her down. But it would be suicide to even attempt it now. And I can't leave Natalie alone in the car.

"FBI Special Agent in Charge Susan Parker," I say, holding my gun up sideways, finger off the trigger. "The shooter's a woman in a dark hoodie and black jeans, running that way!"

"Drop the gun," another voice shouts. "Keep your hands up."

I sigh and reluctantly let my weapon drop with a clatter to the street. I know from experience that it's no use arguing with them, they're just doing their job and following protocol.

It's gonna be a long night.

THIRTY-TWO

This time when I enter the FBI Building at 11000 Wilshire Boulevard in downtown Los Angeles, it no longer feels strange. It feels painfully familiar. I feel a sense of déjà vu, flashing back to a year ago. There were Christmas decorations in the offices and hallways then, too, and that sense of bitter-sweet holidays on the horizon that somehow feels both sentimental and depressing. It feels oddly fitting then that I'm facing another committee hearing once again around the same time a year later. *You never learn, Susan Parker. You just don't learn.*

I'm early so take a few minutes in the bathroom to gather my thoughts—and my courage. The last few days haven't been easy. Natalie slept through that horrible night and wasn't aware of anything after she said bye to her grandpa at the hotel, but I had hell to pay from Lata. She didn't even need to say a lot. It was obvious. Some of it had been commented on, indirectly, in the form of the questions asked by the SCVPD officers who first arrived on the scene of the Grygorian shooting: Do you usually bring your seven-year-old daughter to a shootout, Special Agent in Charge Parker? Are you saying you drew your weapon on a suspect seated in a car only four feet from your daughter? Some civilian in the area somehow managed to get a grainy long shot showing me being handcuffed by the first responders and posted it on social media with a snarky comment that I won't even dignify by repeating. But it stung. All of it stung. That was the thing. I know Lata and I will get through this, as we have gotten through so much before, and she understands how it all went down and how I had no choice at the time, but it's the effect on me that's the worst part. I feel like such a heel. Lata will forgive me as she always does. I don't know if I'll forgive myself.

I leave the restroom feeling not much better than when I went in.

There are only a handful of faces seated behind the long table in the conference room this time around. The only new face is one I've only seen once before in the LA field office before. She introduces herself as Deputy Director Zimal Bukhari and explains she's mainly here to observe and report. Bukhari, as I recall, is the Bureau's main liaison with the US attorney as well as the Senate and Congress Oversight and Accountability Committees. For some reason, she seems to be running the show today, not Gantry, who doesn't say much. I don't know if that's a good or a bad thing.

After the usual pleasantries, we get straight to it. It's Christmas Eve and everyone's eager to wind up for the day and get home to their families. Even if said families might only be an adorable corgi or Siamese.

"Thank you for coming in, SAC Parker," Bukhari says. "I know you must be eager to get home to your family for the holidays, I'm sure we all are. Now if we can jump right in. Let's start by retracing the last month's timeline on the Splinter case."

"Sure," I say. My mouth feels unusually dry. I unscrew the cap of a bottle of water and take a small sip.

I start with the night before Thanksgiving, the call from Naved, my trip to the ranch, what we found there, and continue through all the main events of the case. From time to time, one of them asks a question and I answer it to the point. Things go fairly smoothly until we get to the Grygorian part, especially the second interview.

"And I see here from the file that you and your team investigated the link to Henrik Deutermann thoroughly, am I right?" Bukhari asks.

"It's all there," I say, indicating the file. "We were able to find county records and legal documents confirming that Magnusson had changed his name from Deutermann, and that he had a half-sister who had done the same."

"This sister," Bukhari says, looking at her tablet. "She was never a person of interest in the case?"

I think of the nights I spent in my car outside the school-teacher's house, watching her and her family. I remember the taste of sugared pumpkin and the clink of a metal spoon on a porcelain plate on Thanksgiving night. "She was briefly questioned in connection with another case but no, there was nothing connecting her with Splinter or any of the victims."

"That other case would be your husband's death?" Bukhari asks.

"Yes."

"And your team questioned her when you were looking into the Deutermann family?"

"As a routine follow-up, yes. That was our last contact."

"Coming to Aram Grygorian. SAC Parker, could you retrace the events of Friday, November 24th?"

I go through it yet again, as I had to do so many times in the days immediately after Gyrgorian's killing. The call from Bohjalian. The meeting with Grygorian at Bohjalian's Newhall condo. Then the odd texts and voice mail from Daria later that night. My call to Bohjalian. Naved and I rushing to Newhall. Daria's last words on the call to me. The dead private security guards. Naved going into the building while I waited outside in the car. His texts to me. The texts from the team. The shooter trying to take my car. My drawing on her. Her escape. SCVPD's arrival on scene.

"Thank you, SAC Parker," Bukhari says. "So, when SCVPD went in, they found Daria Petrosyan shot to death in the lobby, her associate Aslan also shot to death in the condominium upstairs, and Aram Grygorian dead in the bedroom."

I purse my lips tightly, waiting for a question.

She takes off her reading glasses and looks at me. "And SCVPD found no sign of the shooter. An APB was put out on the description you gave them but no one matching that description was picked up in Santa Carina Valley or in the general vicinity."

I've gone over this before, too: repeating what little I saw of the shooter in the hoodie. She disappeared into the night like a ghost, but it's not true that she disappeared. They could have found her easily if they'd listened to me. If they'd believed me. But of course they didn't. As they don't believe me now.

"You claimed"—here, she holds up her spectacles to glance at the tablet again briefly—"that the shooter was a woman named Gennifer Mason, a UK citizen, who was one of the victims rescued from the Splinter farmhouse. Yet when SCVPD checked, they found that Ms Mason was present at the Keller Wellness Recovery Center in Westwood, over twenty miles away, recovering from her ordeal as an abductee of Splinter. Due to the lack of evidence and legal strictures, they were unable to obtain CCTV footage to confirm whether or not Ms Mason had possibly left the facility that night or to question her directly or to run GSR tests on her to determine if she had operated a firearm. Dr. Keller, the head of the institute, insists that he runs a secure facility and that none of the patients in his care could simply, and I'm quoting here, 'waltz in and out anytime they please'. You even applied for a search warrant but were denied by Judge Tanner due to insufficient grounds."

Bukhari interlaces her fingers on the table and looks at me. "SAC Parker, could you explain why you were convinced that the shooter was Gennifer Mason?"

"As I've explained before, Magnusson and his brother were operating a kind of therapy center on the ranch. They enticed foreign nationals who had a grudge against therapists to check in for intense, grueling treatment based on certain methods developed originally by Dr. Henrik Deutermann in the late 1930s to motivate American GIs heading off to World War II. During this treatment, the Deutermann brothers turned relatively ordinary individuals into killers capable of committing brutal murders without compunction. Gennifer Mason was one of these patients who had undergone this extreme form of 'therapy'. When Aram Grygorian rejected the treatment and was able to successfully resist the expected outcome, it made the younger Deutermann brother angry."

"That's this person you call 'The Therapist' in your notes, is that right? The person born Hans Deutermann, whose new identity has as yet not been confirmed," Bukhari asks.

"That's right. The Therapist was apparently the fanatical one following in his father's footsteps. From what Grygorian told us, Magnusson, the older Deutermann brother, went along for his brother's sake up to a point. But once Magnusson realized he was close to death, once the cancer had metastasized throughout his body, he seemed to experience a period of regret for his actions. From what we could piece together, it seems that Magnusson parted ways with his brother. As a result, either Magnusson himself, or the brother, provided Grygorian with the means to kill Magnusson. As Grygorian saw it, killing Magnusson was an act of mercy as well as his absolution from having to go through with the original plan of killing a therapist and their entire family in the manner of the earlier Splinter killings."

Bukhari frowns, looking around at her colleagues.

"I'm lost, SAC Parker," she says. "I know the rest of you here have gone over this same ground several times already but I'm coming in cold, to provide a pair of fresh eyes on the case, so forgive me if I seem confused. All these people, the twelve patients, the two brothers, the Therapist. Which one was actually Splinter?"

"That's just the thing. Apparently, Splinter wasn't a single person. Splinter was just what the name suggests. A number of splinters, all from the same wood. Like the concept of splinter cells in terrorism. Individuals unconnected to one another, who were brainwashed through extreme, torturous therapeutic methods including starvation, deprivation, incarceration, sensory deprivation, chemical shock treatment, in a systematic and carefully calibrated program designed to dehumanize and transform subjects... at the end, they were turned into killers with the sole purpose of torturing and murdering specific targets."

"Therapists," Bukhari says. Her tone is neutral but the reaction, or the lack of reaction from the rest of the committee, lends a tone of skepticism to the word.

"Yes, therapists," I say.

"So these individuals then went out and committed the Splinter killings? Is that what you're saying?" Bukhari says.

"It's more complicated than that," I say. "Just as in foreign wars, where American soldiers are recruited and trained to go to other countries and engage foreign enemies, the Deutermann brothers trained these Splinters to do the same. So, for instance, a British citizen such as Gennifer Mason who deeply resented the Chicago-based therapist who had misdiagnosed her sister and caused her death, would be sent to kill a therapist in, say, Brussels, Belgium. While another Splinter, whose life had been permanently damaged by a therapist in Hamburg, Germany, would be sent to kill a therapist in say, Osaka, Japan. And so on. A series of international crisscross murders where killers went to different countries, killed specific targets, then returned home."

"A very unusual, and elaborate conspiracy. Quite a complex scheme, wouldn't you say?" Bukhari asks.

"It's not really that different from the way terrorist splinter cells operate. In fact, my team and I believe that's where the younger Deutermann brother got the original idea. He simply adapted the concept of splinter cells to his own purposes," I say.

"Killing therapists?" Bukhari asks.

"Yes."

"But you believe he himself, this younger Deutermann brother, was also a therapist?" Bukhari asks.

"I'm sure of it," I say. "Probably a disgraced, delicensed therapist like his brother, shunned and ostracized by their colleagues for their extreme methods."

"I see," Bukhari says. "And have you been able to find evidence confirming any part of this theory, SAC Parker?"

"That's what I've been trying to explain to my superiors," I say, not looking directly at Gantry but keenly aware of him. "If I could have the resources and backing to create an international task force roping in other major law enforcement agencies like Interpol, Scotland Yard, the Metropolitan Police, the Bundespolizei, the Gendarmerie Nationale, etc, we would be able to prove the similar modus operandi used in all the killings and create a global database. For all we know, Splinter could have been responsible for dozens of such home invasions and family slaughters, apart from the four confirmed cases here in the United States. As you know, Deputy Director Bukhari, serial killers don't just stop. They keep killing until they're caught."

"But these aren't serial killers, are they?" Bukhari says. "They're individuals who've been brainwashed. Like soldiers sent out to commit assassinations during wartime."

"True, but the Therapist, that's the younger brother, Hans Deutermann or whatever his name is now, he's a serial killer.

He's operating vicariously through these 'patients' or soldiers or assassins. Through the Splinters. He's directly responsible for all these killings. And he won't stop until and unless we stop him."

Bukhari stares at me.

I feel flushed. Did I overplay my hand—again? Did I show too much passion for my case? Am I coming on too strong? Giving the impression that I've let the case become an obsession —again? I sit back, sip water again, and try to look calm.

"Let's go back to Grygorian's death, SAC. He wasn't a therapist, was he? Neither were the two lawyers, associates of Andrew Bohjalian. Yet according to you, they were targeted and assassinated by one of these Splinters, the person named Gennifer Mason. Isn't that what you believe?"

"Yes," I say. "Grygorian had to be silenced because he was giving away too much information. He was talking about the therapy, about the Therapist, about the Deutermann family. He was a rogue Splinter. His continued survival threatened the whole network. Grygorian's testimony was the biggest break we've had on this case in years. The Therapist had to eliminate him."

"So he sent Gennifer Mason to kill him that night? And the two lawyers were what, collateral damage?" Bukhari asks.

"Exactly!"

"And yet, SAC Parker, cellphone records show that the text messages to Bohjalian and later his associates all came from your mobile number that evening. You texted Bohjalian asking for another interview with Grygorian."

I shake my head. "I've explained this before. Obviously, my phone was cloned somehow. At some point, I must have come into contact with the Therapist or one of the Splinters, and they cloned my phone. So those texts came from the cloned phone. When Bohjalian and Daria texted back, then both the cloned phone and my phone received their replies, naturally."

"That's what you've claimed before as well," Bukhari says. "But the records only show your number for both the outgoing messages and the incoming ones. So you can see how that looks, SAC Parker."

"I know, but it's the truth. SCVPD as well as the FBI took my phone and ran tests. They didn't find the outgoing texts, did they? How do you explain that?" I say.

"We can't. They weren't in the deleted items folder or the trash either. That's why you got the benefit of the doubt, SAC. But it's thin evidence compared to the evidence stacked against you."

I spread my hands. "So... what do you think happened? That I texted Bohjalian and set up the meet? So I could go in and kill Grygorian? What about my partner, Detective Seth? What about my daughter in the back seat? What about my father-in-law who confirmed that I was picking up Natalie only minutes before the time of the shootings? Do you seriously think they're all part of some conspiracy? That I assassinated three people while my family and partner just went along for the ride?"

Bukhari sighs. "No, we don't. That's why you were cleared. But there are still a lot of unanswered questions, SAC Parker."

"Aren't there always, Deputy Director Bukhari?" I say. "Isn't that always the case with investigations? The deeper you dig, the longer you keep digging, the more questions you have and fewer answers. It's in the nature of the human condition, isn't it?"

She lets a tiny smile escape her lips. "Perhaps." She looks around at the others, then at me. "SAC Parker, as I said, you've been cleared of any suspicion. Nobody questions your motives, your loyalty, or your diligence as a federal agent. You were responsible for discovering the Splinter farm and rescuing twelve abductees, along with Detective Seth of SCVPD. You located the murder weapon which nearly four dozen SCVPD volunteers were unable to find. You identified and apprehended Magnusson's killer, Aram Grygorian. You were able to trace back Magnusson's true identity as Deutermann and provide a credible motive and background for his methodology. In sum, you tracked down and closed the file on one of the most notorious serial killers in this country's history. There's no question that you did some outstanding work on this case, and the Bureau acknowledges your valuable contributions."

I'm more than a little taken aback by this outpouring of praise. I came here half-expecting to be fired, and at the very least anticipating a censure on my record.

"But it's time to let this go," Bukhari says. "The case is officially closed. We will be issuing a public statement today to that effect. Your job here is done for now. Go home to your family. Celebrate. It's time to move on, SAC Parker."

She rises, the rest of the committee members rising with her.

I get to my feet, too, feeling a little dazed.

And just like that, the meeting is over.

THIRTY-THREE

I wander out of Gantry's office and down to my work level in a daze, trying to make sense of the world.

The team is gathered and waiting.

Kayla sees my face and goes, "They fired your ass, didn't they?"

I look at them. "No, they were actually quite nice."

I run down the gist, focusing on Bukhari. "I think if Gantry had been in charge, it might have gone differently, at least in tone. But she was very efficient, and fair. I think that's why she was there."

"That makes sense," David says. "Word is, she's responsible for ethics and answerability in the Bureau. In other words, corporate governance. It's part of the larger federal DEI initiative. The buzz on the street is she's going places."

"Better her than Gantry," I say, exhaling.

Ramon looks up something on his trusty tablet and says, "The main media room is booked for thirty minutes, starting on the hour. It just says 'Press Con'."

"Yeah," I say, "they're closing the file on Splinter. It's the official announcement."

"So that's it?" Brine says. "They're sticking with the story that Magnusson was Splinter and he somehow committed those family invasions and murders, then took twelve random foreign nationals hostage and held them prisoner in his basement? All while being barely functional physically *and* dying of advanced, fourth-stage terminal cancer?"

I shrug. "If the shoe fits."

Naved sighs. "It's about closure. Everyone wants to declare a happy ending and claim the win. It's the same in SCVPD. McDougall's talking about running for Congress because of all the good press he got from the case. All thanks to you, Susan."

"Tell me about it," I say. "He can have it. It's not like I'm planning to run for Congress!"

We talk about it for a few minutes until the press conference starts, then switch on the TV and watch the live feed, along with almost everyone else on the floor.

The press conference is a roaring success.

Everybody who's somebody in the media is there, jostling shoulders to get the story of the year.

Gantry holds court admirably. He's born for this: the smooth, publication-ready soundbite, saying just what's necessary in the simplest, most neatly packaged phrases and words, giving them the perfect readymade quotes and captions they all want. That we all want. Because at heart, we all want to believe that the good guys always win, that the system works, that law and order will always triumph over the forces of chaos, and that even the most fiendish, devilishly clever serial killers *will be* hunted down and brought to justice.

That's what he gives the world: justice accomplished. Bukhari and the others are there to back him up, but it's Gantry's show all the way.

Magnusson makes the perfect patsy. With him dead, with the victims in the basement, with his profile match and his inclusion on our shortlist—*my* shortlist—from the year before, it all fits logically together. The way Gantry spins it, it looks like we ran Magnusson down ourselves, rescued those twelve victims, and that Magnusson got what was coming to him courtesy of one of his own victims. Poetic justice, biblical retribution, take your pick. Works for everyone.

Grygorian's death, Gantry dismisses as an unfortunate event, hinting without actually saying so, that it was likely the work of a drug-addled burglar and had nothing to do with the case itself. He doesn't even take the LAPD and his good friend Chief Applebee to task for it; he smartly blames the fentanyl epidemic and liberal government, laying the seeds for a future run at the big office. Daria and Aslan's deaths don't even come up in the Q&A. They're already forgotten and dismissed, given not even a footnote in the larger story—except to their grieving families for whom their deaths are the *only* thing that matters, which is something I know about personally.

Everyone buys it wholesale.

Gantry knows how to sell a story and more importantly, he knows which stories can be sold.

The media platforms lap it up.

It's a win win all around.

Magnusson is dead and can't dispute it.

The inconsistencies—his physical condition, the terminal cancer—aren't even brought up. They would spoil the line of the perfectly cut fabric Gantry is spinning from whole cloth. A couple of outlets who've done their homework do ask the question, but they're dismissed as being irrelevant.

Who cares how or why the monster carried out his awful acts? He's gone, isn't he? Good riddance. Ding dong, the wicked witch is dead. It's time to celebrate.

I'm given my fifteen minutes—more like fifty seconds, it feels like—and play my part as scripted. I answer the questions asked of me with the usual cliches. Just doing our job. It was a team effort. It takes a village. What choice do I have? Without hard evidence, I can't contradict Gantry's perfect narrative.

As for the twelve.

Gantry continues to refuse to identify or expose them publicly, as is their right under law, and as their own lawyers have asserted.

He tells the court of owls that they're just relieved to have survived and only want to go home to their families. He plays down the foreign nationals part, doesn't even mention that they're all from different countries or the other inconsistent details we've dug up. Anything that doesn't confirm or enhance his narrative is out. Even when speaking of Grygorian, he neither confirms nor denies that he was one of the twelve.

Gantry avoids the numbers thing entirely, just calling them "the intended victims". As in "The intended victims are just happy to be alive and want only to return home to their families."

That's pretty much it, the whole shebang.

Thirty minutes and it's done and dusted. The Q&A drags on a bit, but at thirty-five minutes, Gantry shuts it down, wishes everyone a pleasant, safe day ahead and prepares to make his exit to resounding applause and a standing ovation from the entire press corp. He looks at me as if to say, *See, this is your bow-and-courtesy moment, doesn't it feel great? Remember who gave you a place on the podium so you could enjoy it. That's right. I did!*

Afterward, we call it a day. It's Christmas Eve and everyone has plans.

"I'll see you guys when I see you," I say, waving as I get into my Prius.

Naved comes up beside my window as I start my car. He leans over.

"Hey, you okay?" he asks.

"Copacetic," I say. "Why?"

"I just wanted to fill you in on that property records thing."

"Let me guess, nothing?"

"Pretty much. SK Global owns SK Realty, which owned the last murder house, the one that Dr. Rao leased. But there's absolutely nothing irregular or out-of-line that I could find. Everything checks out clean."

I nod. "Thought as much. Thanks for checking it out anyway."

"I know you were hoping for more. That connection really rattled you when it came up, didn't it?"

"It did," I admit.

"Well, it was just one of those things. Just a coincidence, that's all."

"I know," I say.

"I wish I had more for you. I've tried, Susan. But there's nothing there. I mean, I know it's strange, Amit going to talk to the Deutermann sister and asking her about her father. I couldn't figure out how he found out about the Deutermanns or her connection. But I really don't think it had anything to do with the Splinter case or with his death. If there was, we would have found it."

"I know," I say again. "But thanks for looking into it, Naved."

"Hey, I'm not giving up. I'm going to keep looking. But you know how it goes. Maybe we'll find something, maybe we won't. Always more questions than answers, right?"

"Right," I say.

"Anyway, I just wanted to let you know. You have a great Christmas and if I don't see you before then, a Happy New Year, too. My best wishes to Lata and Natalie as well."

"Thanks. And the same to you. Have a great trip and give my best to Alia and the boys! You're flying out to New York this afternoon, aren't you?"

He looks at his watch. "Already running late. I'd better go."

I wave bye and drive away.

I watch him in the rearview, getting into the Camry. It's strange how you can spend all day and all night with someone working on a case, and then, you suddenly say goodbye and go home to your family. In a way, it feels like I have two families, my home family and work family. It's a reminder of how lucky I am. I'm a widow, yes, and not a day goes by that I don't miss Amit, but I have wonderful, caring people in my life, and I'm thankful for them every day.

My phone pings. It's a text from Lata:

Everyone's here. Where r u?

Speaking of wonderful, caring people and family, this is going to be the first time since Thanksgiving that I'm going to have to spend the whole evening with my mother-in-law Aishwarya again. I am not looking forward to that! I sigh. Every rose has its thorn.

THIRTY-FOUR

I park outside my house.

The decorations are up. Lata and I worked an entire day and the next morning to put them all up.

The front lawn and house look wonderfully festive. Our little suburban side street is a riot of blinking lights and inflatable figures. Reindeer pulling Santa's sled, snowmen, nativity scenes, Santa with a red cowboy stocking hat on a horse, Santa on a helicopter (honest, I have video proof), Santa in a pickup truck with GOD SAVE AMERICA in tricolor neon lights, every possible permutation, combination you can think of and some you would never think of.

Inside, the house is cozy, colorful, and bright.

The Christmas tree in the front window is laden with decorations, its artificial limbs groaning under all that weight. Natalie insisted on helping and wanted to put everything on. The gift-wrapped presents under the tree make an enticing pile that causes her to start elbow-dancing every time she sees them. She can't wait for Christmas morning.

The house smells of eggnog, gingerbread cookies, plum cake

with rum-soaked raisins, roast turkey with cranberry sauce, and a variety of Goan coconut sweets which Lata found at a local bakery and insisted on getting me because of my Goan parentage, even though I told her I hadn't even liked coconut sweets as a kid. Natalie loves them though so that worked out okay.

Our little kopcha—the Mumbai slang word for a private, cozy corner—is packed again for the first time since Thanksgiving. All the usual suspects are present: Lata, Natalie et moi, mais oui. Also the Kapoor family: Aishwarya, Kundan, Kajal, and Sujit.

Neither Lata nor I have forgiven Aishwarya for her treatment of Natalie that night, but Natalie has gotten over it, in the easy-going way kids have. She loves her grandpa, and Kundan is so great with her, it does seem a shame to punish them for Aishwarya's failings. We've come to a compromise: when they're with Natalie, Kundan will be the main carer. Aishwarya doesn't even have to be present if she doesn't want to; in any case, even when she's present physically, she's rarely present. She walks on a higher plane than us mere mortals. She can stay there forever for all I care. Lata concurs.

But tonight, all hostilities are suspended. A ceasefire has been declared. The first one to start an argument gets a glass of eggnog poured over their head, Lata promised, and I swear she means it. Aishwarya seems content with glaring her baleful, disapproving glare at our humble abode, while waxing eloquent about the lavish Christmas parties her family used to host in Delhi. I'm sure they did. When Aishwarya and Kundan were married, thirty-four years ago, Aishwarya's father apparently splurged something resembling twelve million dollars on the wedding. I have no doubt if and when either of her daughters do get married, Aishwarya will easily top that spend. But if she thinks we're grateful she's slumming it tonight to spend Christmas with us humble paisan, she's delusional. Lata and I keep reminding each other to stay cool. The word *iceberg* gets signed a lot!

The music is festive, gaily colored streamers festoon my living room and shiny balloons bump up against our ceiling. I've made my peace with work, for now at least. Not because I've accepted the way things worked out but because I've been in the Bureau long enough to know that you take your wins when they come as they are and accept the rest.

I've been spending more quality time with Natalie, and I think I might even be finally coming to terms with Amit's death. Well, not really, but I'm getting there. At least I now can conceive of the idea that someday, I will be over it. Not over him. That's impossible. I'll love him forever. But at least I will be over that horrible shock of his passing the way he did. I can't say when it will happen, but I now think it's possible that it will.

Kundan is holding center stage for once. He's just finished telling a kid-safe Christmas joke he heard as a boy and Natalie is squealing with delight as she gets it. Everyone else is laughing because she's laughing. Children are like laughter: infectious and heartwarming. Natalie is the best laughing fit anyone could ever have.

When the doorbell rings, Lata says, "That must be the pizza! Could you see, Suse? I need to check on the turkey before it burns."

"Why are we ordering pizza?" I ask. "We have too much food already!"

"For Kajal, remember?" she says softly, elbowing me.

"Oh yeah," I say. "I'll get it."

Kajal suddenly announced, just a little while earlier after she'd arrived, that she's gone vegan and gluten-free. The day was saved by Lata remembering a hip new pizza place which does vegan cheese and toppings and gluten-free bread.

"Or it might be Ariana," Lata says suddenly, remembering.

"I didn't really expect her to turn up, she hates crowds, but you never know."

Ariana is Lata's new girlfriend, the same one she went out with on their third date that fateful black Friday. I've not met her yet, so this comes as a surprise, a good one for a change.

As I open the door, I'm hoping now that it is Ariana and not vegan pizza.

The woman in the parka has her back to me when I open the door. Loud laughter, music, and warm heated air spill out behind me, frosting my breath. It's cold out there. There's even a forecast of a light snowfall this weekend. Snow isn't normal in southern California, but it does happen every decade or so. Natalie is very excited about it, so I hope for her sake that it does fall.

"Oh, hi," I say gaily. "You must be Ariana. It's so good to meet you at last! Lata's told me so much about you, I feel like I know you already."

The woman mumbles something, still turned away from me. She's hunched over something, her elbows up by her chest. I presume it's a phone. She's not on the porch itself, but a couple of steps before it, so I pull the door shut to avoid letting the heat out and take two steps toward her.

"Ariana?" I say.

She turns cobra-quick, the gun a silver gleam in her fist, and my heart stops still.

"Do exactly as I say if you want your family to live," she says in a low voice.

Even though I only caught a brief look at her that night, and never heard her speak, there's not the slightest doubt in my mind that it's her. The shooter who killed Grygorian, Daria and Sukesh. Gennifer Mason. An icy glove clenches my insides, freezing my core.

I know the damage that guns can do even when they miss. If she fires at me, if she doesn't hit me, and possibly even if she does, there's a damn good chance that the bullet could find its way into the house. Even the slimmest chance in hell that it could hit Natalie is too big a chance for me to risk. I'm frozen to the spot, unable to move a muscle. I even stop breathing.

Christmas carolers are making their way down the street, part of a local high school church group. They finish at our neighbor's and come toward our house.

"Okay," I say. "Okay, I'll cooperate. Don't shoot."

The carolers call out to us, assuming that we're both residents, asking if we'd like some carols.

Without looking back at them, Gennifer grimaces at me and says in a tone too low for them to hear, "Get fucking rid of them. And no funny business."

I smile and wave at the carolers, calling out, "Thanks, but you know what? I'll pass. Thanks anyway and happy holidays to you all!"

"Happy holidays!" they chant in chorus, moving on to my neighbor's.

Gennifer's eyes shift sideways, tracking them in her peripheral vision without taking her eyes off me.

"Okay," she says. "Now let's take a ride. Get in your car. And don't fuck around. I'm not alone. You screw with me, and your daughter and sister-in-law get it in the head. You copy?"

"I copy," I say.

Her accent is unmistakably British. She obviously knows what she's doing and has had special training in this kind of thing. She knows enough to make me get in first, keeping the gun trained on me, making me strap myself in tight, then tossing a pair of white plastic ties at my face and ordering me to use them to lash both my wrists to the steering wheel. When I've done that, she goes around to the passenger side door and gets in.

I'm praying all this while that Lata doesn't come to the front door to check what's taking me so long. Hopefully, she's busy checking on the turkey. It's probably done by now, and she's sliding it out of the oven and placing it carefully on the island counter, then finishing preparing it before she serves dinner.

Please, stay busy till we're gone, I pray. *Don't come out.*

The marine in Lata might make her react before she can think. She might try to act to save me and put down the shooter. No matter how fast she moves, Gennifer would easily get off a shot or two. Not to mention the other shooter she just hinted was watching the house. One of the other eleven? It doesn't matter. I can't risk calling her bluff—if it's a bluff at all. In seconds, this could turn into a bloodbath. The very thought of my house being riddled with gunfire and Natalie in harm's way, this time with bullets flying around her, chills my blood. I force myself to breathe to stay focused and calm.

"Drive," she says, moving the shift into reverse with her left hand while keeping the gun in her right hand aimed at my chest. Apparently, she'll be working the gear shift while I drive. With my hands zip-tied to the steering wheel, there's not much I can do except maybe try crashing the car. And what would that achieve? I would end up getting shot, likely killed, and she might still be able to walk away with little or no injuries. I'm not getting out of this one that easily.

She gives me directions but within minutes I know exactly where we're headed.

The Splinter ranch.

For the last few weeks, the place has been overrun with tourists, rubberneckers, serial killer fans (believe it or not, they exist), true crime aficionados, and every other kind of person fascinated by the notorious place. There's even been talk that Universal Studios is planning to recreate the farmhouse and basement for their annual Halloween Horror Nights next year, to coincide with the movie adaptation of one of the several quickie nonfiction true crime books that have already started hitting the stands.

But tonight is Christmas Eve. Even the most diehard of fans is probably taking a break. There'll likely be only a skeleton crew of maybe a single patrol car with two officers, or two patrol cars at most, to make sure high school students don't sneak inside to get some nookie in one of the therapy rooms or even— believe it or not, it's a whole thing—in the kitchen dining area where Magnusson was found. I'm wondering how Gennifer plans to get us past the SCVPD cops. Carolers, it's easy to fool, but not cops, especially not with me zip-tied to the steering wheel and a gun in her hand. Will she risk cutting me loose and keeping the gun out of sight till we're past them? Should I risk an attempt then?

Now that I'm away from the house and Natalie is free of the immediate threat, I'm starting to question whether Gennifer's claim that someone else is watching the house was a bluff. From what I saw that night at Grygorian's, she's a lone wolf. If there was another shooter at my place, they would be taking a much bigger risk than Mason is right now. For one thing, the houses on my lane have modest lots and are situated up close to one another. Anyone might notice a person with a gun lurking in someone's back yard. Also: the downstairs has windows looking out on all four sides. Sooner or later, someone from my family itself would probably spot the lurker.

Now that I'm thinking more clearly, I'm betting that the talk of another shooter was a bluff.

Still, I had no choice. I couldn't afford to gamble and lose.

Putting my life at risk is part of my job.

Risking Natalie's is unthinkable.

To my surprise, Gennifer tells me to turn left before we reach the road to the ranch.

I do as she says without question.

My mind races.

Is she taking me somewhere else?

The answer becomes clear soon enough: she makes me turn

off onto a dirt road that is less road than a walking path. If the dirt road to the ranch is a bumpy rollercoaster, then this one is an off-road adventure. The Prius bounces and grinds until I'm convinced it'll break down at any minute.

"Stop," she says suddenly.

She takes the keys with her as she gets out, coming around to the driver's side.

Smart girl.

She takes out a slim blade and without letting the gun waver from my face, she cuts the zip-ties off.

"Get out," she says.

She makes me walk up the slope, past the boulder that blocked our way. I picture the layout of the property and the copies of the land deed that I studied weeks earlier. I picture a large Y-shaped formation with the farm on the upper right hand. We're somewhere on the upper left. That puts us about seven or eight miles from the rear perimeter of the farm.

Another smart move.

Any SCVPD cops on duty would be posted at the turnoff, or by the main ranch house at the most. There's no reason to expect anyone, even eager fans, to make a three-mile trek in this weather, tonight of all nights. High school kids looking to spice up their night probably resent leaving the comfort of their car heaters for even a minute. And there's always tomorrow.

"What's the plan?" I ask without turning around. "You taking me to Magnusson's farm to do what? Talk about old times? Share a cup of hot cocoa? Eggnog, maybe? Sing carols under a Christmas tree?"

"Shut up," she says.

I wait for her to poke me in the back, giving me an opportunity to spin around and grab the gun.

But like the pro she's already shown herself to be, she keeps her distance, staying at least a meter behind me at all times, close enough not to miss, but too far for me to risk making a move.

The night is cold, and I don't have a jacket on. I'm dressed in a new dress, my one concession to Natalie's insistence that we dress up for the family get-together. I have nothing on underneath except underwear. This is an unusually cold winter, one of several in the past few years that have seemed set to become a permanent fixture. The temperature must be barely above freezing if not actually zero degrees centigrade. The grass brushing against my bare ankles feels like tiny icicles cutting into my skin. I wrap my arms around my chest to try to hold in some warmth. The walking helps but I can see my breath misting with every breath and I'm starting to get a headache from the cold.

Still, those are minor discomforts.

I'm trying to figure out what the endgame is here.

If Gennifer Mason wanted me dead, she would have shot me on my front porch. Or in the car before we got out a few minutes ago. This area is pretty desolate. Not much out here except the coyotes.

Maybe she wants to shoot me in the farmhouse? That makes a sick kind of sense, I suppose.

The cold makes it hard to think. My teeth are starting to chatter. I blow on my hands to warm them up and rub them briskly together as I walk. How far have we come? Three miles? Four? It's hard to tell in the moonlight. If not for the full moon on the horizon, I wouldn't be able to see at all.

The house appears seemingly out of nowhere. One minute I can only see empty fields and the occasional tree, the next minute, I reach the top of a small rise and pause before a dip in the ground. In a hollow surrounded by trees on three sides and this rise on the fourth, is a small cottage with a chimney.

The caretaker's residence.

It was on the property plans. We checked it out back then,

but it showed no signs of having been used in decades. And it's a good four miles or so from the main farmhouse, with no road access. I was so focused on the main farmhouse that I forgot about it. The cold hasn't been much help either, but it seems crystal clear now.

This is where I'm supposed to die.

THIRTY-FIVE

I'm in pitch darkness. I've been here for an indeterminate period of time but based on my bladder and stomach and my thirst, I'd guess it's somewhere between three and five hours. We left the house at around five in the evening, at dusk. It's night now. What must Lata and Natalie be thinking? I picture Natalie crying, out of her mind with worry for me and push it away. Not now. That won't help me here. I have to focus on my surroundings, try to prepare myself for whatever's coming next.

If Gennifer wanted a remote place to get rid of me without witnesses, where I would be unlikely to be found for at least a day or two, possibly longer, she's got it.

She could have put a bullet in the back of my head, walked back to the car, driven as far as she needed, then gone on her way. No one's looking for her. She could leave the country on a flight tonight itself and be home in time for Christmas lunch.

Clearly, she has other plans for me.

My entire body hurts from the intense cold and from being restricted at my wrists, ankles, waist, neck, and head, forced to sit upright in the same position for hours upon hours.

I try to search for the familiar bodily needs to help guide me but they're not much help. After a certain amount of time, suffering for five hours or ten hours is indistinguishable. It's just more of the same agony.

It's tough to keep my mind off Natalie and Lata. Off my body's need to purge waste and imbibe nourishment and fluids. Off the biting cold that seems several degrees more intense in this dark, musty basement than in the open air above, unlikely as that is.

I hear the sound of someone coming.

Moments later, a bright light is switched on, pointed directly at my face.

"SAC Parker," says a voice so familiar that recognition comes not as a shock but as a revelation.

The light is harsh, blinding, sending needles of pain into my dark-adapted pupils.

I try to raise my hands to shield them, but they're fastened securely to the arms of the chair I'm strapped into. A metal band around my forehead and neck force my head to stay upright. I couldn't go anywhere even if I wanted to.

The voice speaks again from the darkness behind the blinding light. It's a lamp, shaped to direct the light in one direction only. The dark walls—either blackened by filth over time or deliberately painted black, it's hard to tell—don't reflect the glow of ambient light that would usually enable me to see beyond the lamp itself.

All I have to go on is that voice.

That authoritarian, no-nonsense voice.

"It was time we had this chat," he says. "Don't you think?"

I haven't tried screaming since Gennifer Mason brought me down here and made me zip-tie my ankles and wrists at gunpoint before bringing out this chair from an alcove and securing me more effectively. After she cut off the ties and went upstairs, I've seen or heard no sign of her. I could have tried screaming but there seemed little point. There would be nobody around to hear me even on a sunny summer day, and definitely not on a cold wintry Christmas Eve.

Besides, by that time, I wanted to wait and see what happened next.

I had a strong inkling that she hadn't been acting alone.

Someone else had to be pulling her strings.

I wanted to meet the puppet master.

And here he is.

"Dr. Keller," I say hoarsely. Even though I haven't so much as spoken in hours, my throat feels parched and painful, as if I've been screaming my head off all this while.

It's the restraints and the hard wooden chair.

Five minutes in, it would be torture. Several hours later, every muscle, tendon and nerve in my being is aflame with misery.

"Or should I say Splinter?" I manage.

He laughs softly, the sound echoing somewhere behind him.

A closet perhaps? Or an adjoining room in the basement? It must be larger than this one, to produce such a resounding echo.

"Oh no, SAC Parker," he says. "You're way off the mark there. Most assuredly, I am not Splinter."

That makes me blink.

My eyes are tearing up from the cold and the brutally harsh light, and I imagine I can feel the tears freezing to ice on my cheeks.

Could it be that cold? It is one of the coldest winters in southern California, I recall reading somewhere. If it really is that cold, then hypothermia is a given, assuming it hasn't set in already. I try to wriggle my toes. They're numb but that could just be the lack of circulation.

"You're not?" I say, pretending to sound astonished.

"SAC Parker, have you forgotten our past interactions? Don't you recall you considered me as a suspect last year, along with Magnusson and several other of our colleagues. In the end, you found that the Splinter murders overlapped with my travel itinerary and several hundred witnesses at each of my touring locations as well as video recordings and live media interviews provided unassailable alibis for each and every one. You told me that yourself or have you forgotten?"

I try to work some saliva into my mouth, but my tongue keeps sticking to my teeth and the roof of my mouth. It's a struggle just to be able to free it long enough to form a whole sentence.

"You know what I meant, doctor," I say, trying to put some bite and authority into my tone. "I also told you at a later date, just about a year ago now, that I had figured out how you could have done it. By using an accomplice to carry out the actual killings. A serial killer pair. Perhaps you've forgotten that part? It's okay, I don't blame you for your poor memory. I was busy beating the shit out of you at the time after all. That might have hampered your ability to think clearly."

Keller laughs again, this time with a bitter undertone. "Oh, I remember quite well. But your alternate theory was fatally flawed. Serial killer pairs have existed, but in every case, both partners partake in the kills. They are serial killers, remember? Not serial thrill-seekers! In almost all known cases, each of the partners also killed independently of each other, as well as collaborated. For me to be off pursuing my career while someone else had all the fun would contradict the very definition of serial killer."

"So you say," I reply, not yielding an inch. "Call them whatever you like. A pair of psychos working together. The point is, I always suspected you were Splinter. Or part of Splinter."

"Ah," he says. "But there's your biggest mistake, Parker. You've failed to consider the essential nature of Splinter. The word as well as the concept."

"Why don't you enlighten me then?" I say.

"That would be too boring," he says. "Come now. Take a shot. Didn't the scarecrow provide a clue?"

I flash back to that first night. My very first glimpse of the scarecrow as I drove up the dirt road. The sharp needle-pointed lengths of wood bulging out from the sides of the dungarees.

The twelve prisoners in the basement.

Each in their own therapy rooms.

Therapy.

The common link between all the victims and their killer.

The twelve foreign nationals, all with a reason to hate therapists.

Yet all ended up in the same place, undergoing their own torturous, twisted therapy.

Grygorian's half-crazed ramblings.

Splinter kills a therapist in the USA, then goes back to his home country.

Then, months later, Splinter kills another US therapist, then returns to his home country.

Repeat.

And repeat again.

And again.

Splinter.

Chips.

Parts of a whole.

Like splinter cells.

Some as small as a single individual.

Individual terrorists who carry out missions with the same common purpose.

Splinter serial killers.

Each working alone.

Attacking and killing the remote therapist who treated their loved one and instead of helping them, drove them to destruction.

An act of revenge.

Individual acts of retribution.

Planned to a tee, honed to perfection, prepped and trained for under a common master.

The puppet master.

Pulling the strings of each individual killer.

Training, instructing, guiding, preparing, each one of his splinters.

Before sending them out to accomplish their individual missions.

"They're all Splinter," I say with wonderment. "That's what Grygorian meant. The Splinter that killed Dr. Rao and his family wasn't the one who killed the earlier victims. They were all individual Splinters, each killing just one family, avenging themselves, then going back home."

Dr. Keller laughs, sounding pleased. "Finally! I was beginning to worry about you, Parker!"

"But why you? You're a therapist yourself. Why would you aid and abet these people in killing your own colleagues?"

"I don't. I have no part in their acts of violence. I merely provide therapy. I treat them as patients."

"The therapy rooms in Magnusson's basement. You were the Therapist. Magnusson was only their jailor. And in the end, your front."

"Indeed. Therapy rooms. Like this one, SAC Parker. You'd be amazed at what you can achieve through concentrated sustained methods. By the time we complete your therapy, you will be well prepared to go forth and achieve your own mission as well."

I laugh, the sound hurting my throat and surprising me almost as much as it surprises Keller. "You think you're going to turn me into a Splinter, too? Make me a killer? To kill whom? Not you, of course. You don't have a family. You're too much of an asshole for any woman to love you and want to have your children."

He sounds irritated. "I choose to stay single. It's a valid choice. But yes, your target wouldn't be me. It would be the person whom you blame the most in your life. The person who caused you the most pain and suffering."

"You've lost me now, Keller. The only person who caused me that much pain and suffering, apart from you, of course, is my husband Amit. And it was his death that brought me all that pain, not Amit himself."

"Yes, but the person who killed him caused it all, didn't he?" Keller says softly.

I'm speechless for a moment.

"Ah, I see I've touched a tender spot," he says. "But then, I thought Grygorian had already told you that Amit Kapoor didn't kill himself. He was murdered."

I remain silent.

"Perhaps he didn't tell you who killed him? Because Grygorian didn't know that. He couldn't have. He only knew what little he knew because I intended for him to kill Magnusson. You see, I knew by then that Grygorian wasn't like the other eleven. He didn't take to the Splinter therapy the way the others did. He had too much conscience or morality or whatever term you wish to use for foolish human scruples. He blamed himself for his sister's death. I worked hard to direct his rage and grief at the therapist who had remotely treated the boy, but Grygorian was too firmly locked into his own guilt. In the end, I used him to end my brother and trigger the events that led us here."

"Because you knew that sooner or later the FBI would catch up with you and your little merry band of serial killers?"

He laughs. "Of course not! I've been doing this for far too long, Parker. If they were going to catch me, they would have done so a decade ago, or two decades ago."

My skin crawls with horror at the implications. "You've been running this Splinter therapy for that long? Turning ordinary people into mass murderers? Using them to slaughter therapists and their families? That can't be true. We went back as far as there were records. The Splinter killings only started three years ago."

"In the US, yes. But it's a big world. And there are therapists everywhere, Parker. Germany, France, Russia, Japan, South Korea, Vietnam, Adelaide, Brisbane, even Reykjavik. Need I go on? You didn't think to expand your search to the entire globe, did you?"

"Well," I lie, "the FBI only serves the American people, whether in country or abroad. We don't have jurisdiction over non-Americans unless they're residents here."

"And because most of the earlier killings were spread across multiple countries and regions, neither Interpol or Scotland Yard or the Mumbai Police or any of the other local law enforcement agencies were aware of the killings in other countries. Even when they might have found out about, say, three or four killings across European countries, once the killings stopped, they had no further leads to go on."

"And in every case, the Splinter killers had already done their dirty work and left that country, right?"

"It varied. Initially, I trained my Splinters to kill therapists in their own country. But I soon saw the potential risk in that and changed my approach. You have to understand that I have come a long way in my methodologies. The first therapy rooms I devised and used were much less refined. More, how shall I say it...?"

"Torture chambers?" I suggest. "Mind control deprivation tanks? Brainwashing laundromats? That is what you're doing, isn't it, Keller? Using a person's own psychology against them, urging them to act out their most violent fantasies, act on their worst impulses, unleash their deepest drives."

"Over-simplification can be so tiresome," he says. "I didn't even invent this methodology, Parker. The therapy rooms were not my creation, originally. You see, our father was a pioneer in the field. He devised this treatment process to help prepare American GIs for the challenges of combat in WWII. After the war ended, he tried to adapt the methods to civilian life. That was when he found that it was too effective. He had literally empowered the patients to go out and do whatever it was they had been wanting to do, except that now they were able to live with those deeds and resume a normal, productive life afterwards. Think of it as a kind of psychological purge, an expunging of one's worst desires, leaving one feeling refreshed and rejuvenated."

"The psychiatric equivalent of Jim Jones and Charles Manson," I say.

"You're mocking me now," he says. "That's only understandable. My father was mocked, too, when he tried to convince the American Psychiatric Association of the effectiveness of his methods. They threw him out, discredited him, ruined his career and life. He ended up a broken man, shunned and reviled by his own colleagues. The very therapists who should have been able to see the genius of his vision. He revolutionized therapy! He showed a way to make it actually work scientifically. A methodology that could be replicated time and again and achieve an extremely high rate of success every time. He should be in the history books. Instead, they made him a pariah."

"And you expect to be known as, what? A hero? A visionary? You need to check yourself for delusions of grandeur, Keller," I say.

He sighs the weary sigh of the intellectually superior when confronted by a mere mortal. "I hardly expect you to understand, Parker. You have multiple issues overlaying your congenital neurodivergence. It will take a great deal of time and work in this therapy room before you can begin to glimpse the whole picture. But just to be clear, I am not foolish enough to simply continue my father's methods. What worked for American GIs eighty or ninety years ago is hardly likely to work on today's far more sophisticated populace. Human psychology is constantly evolving as is the human brain. Did you know, for instance, that each new generation is more intelligent than the one before? A measurable growth of almost three percent per decade. Your daughter Natalie, for instance, is substantially more self-aware and conscious of things that your grandmother or her mother would hardly have thought of during their lifetimes."

The very mention of Natalie in this monster's mouth throws me off for a moment. It scares me to even think of him being aware of her, because it reminds me of how vulnerable she would be if Gennifer had been dispatched to abduct her instead of me. The thought sends a shudder through me. "Spare me the lecture, doctor, I'm not one of your patients," I say with more bravado than I feel.

He continues as if I hadn't spoken. "The Deutermann Therapy that I developed, with the occasional assist from my brother Wolfgang, is designed to work on twenty-first-century neurology, you see. It's quite revolutionary."

"Really?" I ask, injecting as much sarcasm into my tone as I can. "I thought torture chambers and dungeons have been around for a hell of a long time."

"Precisely," he says, surprising me. "What else were they if not behavioral modification units? Therapy rooms, in other words!"

The man really is crazy. "Are you fucking serious?"

"Isn't the CIA serious? What do you think waterboarding was meant to achieve? Or Guantanamo? Or the black sites which, as we all know, still exist unofficially. Without the use of these methods to extract vital information, the intelligence community would be completely useless. What I did was adapt my father's methods into a twenty-first-century therapy process. One that I hope to sell to buyers such as the CIA, or if the US proves too morally upright to embrace such cutting-edge methods, then there are any number of international buyers who are happy to pay handsomely."

"You're talking about a new form of torture?" I say. "Selling it to foreign states. Even our enemies. Terrorist organizations. You can't be serious."

"Behavioral modification, Parker. That's what therapy really is, isn't it? A year ago, you attacked me like a wild animal. Did your year of therapy with Dr. Sharif change you? If I were to release you now, would you simply try to arrest me or would you regress instantly to the same wild Susan Parker again? What do you think?" He chuckles softly.

"Why don't you let me out of this chair and see for yourself?" I snarl.

"You see?" he says triumphantly. "That's why conventional therapy methods are largely placebos. They don't bring about permanent behavioral change. The Deutermann Therapy does. And there are people out there willing to pay handsomely for such a method. In fact, I'm already in talks with several parties via the dark net. You're not the only one who has cottoned on to my Splinter killings, Parker. In certain circles, I'm quite highly regarded and talked about."

"Sure," I say, "fascist regimes and deep states must love you. But you'll still be reviled and ignored by your colleagues and the establishment, Keller. Just like your father was."

"Ah, but that's where you're wrong," he says. "You are thinking only of what you have seen. Like all scientific methods, the Deutermann Therapy required extreme experiments to explore its limits and boundaries. That variation is what I propose to market to those foreign states you speak of. All those transactions, very lucrative ones I can assure you, will be in cryptocurrency via the dark net. Totally off the books and off the record. But those funds will enable me to expand my practice here in the US, and build a legitimate empire based on the more universally applicable variant of the same methods! Why, Agent Parker, in a few years, your daughter could be undergoing a milder but no less effective form of Deutermann Therapy in her own school! Books, TV shows, movies, Deutermann Therapy Institutes across the country. There's no limit to the practical applications of this process!"

"Keep my daughter's name out of your mouth, you monster!" I shout hoarsely. Then I am racked by a bout of coughing. "You're delusional, Keller," I say. "You'll never achieve the respectability you dream of. You're psychotic. You torture people and turn them into mass murderers who slaughter innocent people and their families. Women and children. You can pretend all you want, but you're as culpable for those crimes as the Splinters who carry out those executions. And when you're brought to trial, I'll make it my life's mission to make sure that you're given the maximum sentence for every single one of those crimes, to be run consecutively not simultaneously. You'll get, oh, I don't know, several hundred years, I think. Unfortunately, you won't live long enough to enjoy your incarceration fully. But I think you'll find that prison is its own kind of therapy room. One in which you're no longer the person in control, you're just one of a thousand others. I don't think you'll like that very much, Dr. Keller, and that is exactly what you deserve."

He's silent for a moment. Then he says, "I believe you are another write-off, Parker. Much like Grygorian. You're too locked into your own outdated morality to see the larger picture. That's why you couldn't stop your husband's murder even though it practically happened under your nose. You even came close to finding the connection. The woman Amit Kapoor stopped off to speak to before he went to the house Rao was killed in."

The unexpected mention of the schoolteacher rocks me back, mentally. "What about her?"

"She was my half-sister. But you know that already, don't you?"

"I do?"

"Oh yes. I know you've been pretending that this is all news to you, Parker. But I know Grygorian told you enough to enable you and your team to forage out the rest. And you're no simpleton, so stop acting like one. I know you figured out Splinter weeks ago."

"All right," I say, giving up the pretense. "So I did. But what were you saying about your half-sister? What does she have to do with anything?"

"Ah, there's the rub. That's the nature of your work, isn't it, Parker? Always questions, and more questions. It's much the same as what I do, in a way. You probe into people's motivations so you can lock them up and punish them. I probe so I can help them take back control of their own lives. Those therapists my Splinters killed deserved what they got. This new-fangled psychiatry relies on medicating people till they're barely functional. It takes away their most basic, most essential human impulses. Subverts and denies them satisfaction. My method, the Deutermann Therapy, encourages them to use those impulses and drives. Give in to them. Unleash them. It's enormously liberating. Cathartic. It's how humans have always survived and thrived, by giving in to their needs and desires, not by suppressing them!"

I ignore the pain as I say calmly, "Thanks for the lecture, but I'm still not hearing the answer to my question."

He's silent for a moment. I have a sense that he's offended, but then he chuckles. "Ah, so you see? That's your motivation. Your husband's death. It's your obsession. That's why the Deutermann Therapy would work wonderfully on you, Parker. I can show you how to free that wild beast of rage bottled up inside you. Unleash you to avenge your husband's death by slaying his killer. When you finish, you will feel more alive, more fulfilled than ever before in your life!"

"Do you ever get to the point?" I say with deliberate coolness. "Or do you just enjoy hearing the sound of your own voice? If you want to yak, start a podcast!"

Keller chuckles. "Feeling frustrated, Parker? By this point, that chair must be excruciating. The pain and numbness has passed all human capacity to endure. I'm actually impressed that you're still conscious and coherent. Kudos for that. But don't fret. Your suffering will end very soon. I'll be calling Gennifer back down here in a minute and asking her to put a bullet through your head after I'm gone. I would have loved to stay and spend some more time with you. I still have a few extreme methods I reserve for the more obdurate cases like yours. But alas, I have to be on a plane in a few hours. Off to Stockholm to deliver a talk to the—"

"Oh, shut the fuck up," I say, sounding bored. In a way, I am. I'm barely able to stay conscious from the pain and discomfort. The last thing I want is to hear Keller droning on. "I know you're just bluffing. You don't know any more about Amit's death than Grygorian did. He didn't know jack and neither do you."

"Oh, but I do, Parker. I very definitely do. Grygorian only knew what my brother did, but my brother didn't know the whole story. He only ranted as much as he did toward the end because the cancer was eating his brain. That's why he had to die. Grygorian did him a service by ending his life."

I think back to the night Naved and I found Magnusson's body in the kitchen, stabbed fifty-three times. Some service.

"So tell me then," I say. "Prove that you know who actually killed my husband."

Keller chuckles again. "It's infuriating, isn't it? Being so close to the answer and still not knowing? But I'm not the one causing that frustration, Parker. That's your husband's killer.

He's the one responsible. You need to go after him, end his life. That's the only way your rage and frustration will have an outlet. It will free you to be able to go on with your own life, be a better mother, a better person, even a better agent."

"Is that what you believe about your Splinters? That they all go on to become productive, happy people? Lead wonderful lives? Get real, Keller. Once you take another life, a human life, there's no coming back from that. It changes you forever. It corrupts your soul."

"Soul. Corruption. Human life. All these terms, these concepts, they're outdated, unrealistic. The truth is flesh and desire, blood and lust. We are animals, bathed in original sin, we are doomed to repeat the same cycles over and over eternally. Why not accept that truth and revel in our earthly impulses? Enjoy!"

"I'm going to take a nap now, if you don't mind. Since you don't seem to be willing to tell me who killed my husband, why don't you go off to a corner and treat yourself for a while. Use the Deutermann Method on yourself for a change."

"Oh, but that's already been done. That's what our father did. He perfected the Deutermann Method on my brother and me. He did the same to my mother, but the problem with her was that she was too religious, god-fearing, a noble Christian. She resisted and that destroyed her mind. Our sister, on the other hand, would have been a perfect subject. But her mother didn't recognize our father's genius, she took her away, found another man, married him, changed their names. By then, our father was too old and ailing to go after her. That's how Wolfgang and I were able to overcome him and do what we had to do."

"You killed your own father?" I ask. That's one I never saw coming.

"That was the end game. It was the ultimate test, to prove that his method worked."

"I bet you passed with flying colors."

"You joke about it, but it was a profound moment for us. Or at least it was for me. I always felt that Wolfgang balked at the last minute. He was the weak one. He went through with it. He had to, because he knew I would kill him if he didn't, but he balked. I saw it in his eyes when the moment came to push the butcher's knife into our father's chest."

I fall silent. I don't even know how to respond to that. It's the ultimate perversion of everything I know and feel about family. To be killed by your own children? Nobody deserves a death that horrible.

"You're a monster," I say at last.

"We're all monsters, Parker, you're just not ready to admit it to yourself. We all know the darkness that lurks inside us. I'm honest enough to acknowledge it, to set it free, but we all have it. If I told you who killed your husband, you'd go after him in an instant. And you would see your own monster unleashed. Don't deny it."

"Face it, you haven't the faintest idea who it was. You're just toying with me."

"Oh, but I do, Susan. And so do you, if you only let yourself admit it to yourself. You already know who it is. Who killed your husband and made it look like suicide."

"Sorry to disappoint you, Keller. But I don't."

"Denial is a powerful tool. But when you're ready, you'll find the truth inside your heart. Closer to home than you could ever imagine."

Suddenly, the light is switched off, plunging me into a blackness so absolute, it physically hurts my senses. The dark rushes in, smothering me from all sides, even as my eyes flash and explode with echoes of light, like sense-memories of the visual agony.

"Time to leave you now, Susan," Keller says, his voice

already fading away. "I'm glad we had this talk though. I look forward to our next."

"Wait," I call out, unable to help myself. "What do you intend to do with me?"

"Why, isn't that obvious? I intend to treat you, Susan. That's why I brought you here. To the therapy room."

THIRTY-SIX

I've lost track of time.

I've been down here in the dark and cold so long, in such agony, that every second feels like an hour, and every hour like days. The pain center of my brain is so overwhelmed, I keep slipping in and out of consciousness. In a sense, I'm unable to achieve full consciousness anymore. My body itself is so wracked with misery that it occupies every bit of my brain. Even trying to think past the suffering seems like a herculean task.

Besides, what's the point?

My restraints are too strong, too binding, impossible to break out of. I have no magic wand that I can wave to free myself. Keller is smart enough to know that if he releases me for even a moment, I won't hesitate to attack him. Or so he assumes. In my present state, I doubt I would be able to do more than just fall forward and face-plant on the ground. Every nerve ending, every fiber of muscle, tendon and sinew is on fire. The cold only stokes the fire, making every cell feel as if it's inflamed, swollen to bursting. My brain screams for release.

How long have I been down here?

Two days? Three? Ten?

It's impossible to say for sure.

I'm dehydrated, starving, depleted.

I'll spare you the description of my inability to control my bodily functions. I wish I could pretend that I was stoic and resolute enough to hold fast, but the truth is, I lost control of my body within the first few hours of being strapped into this torture seat. I understand now why such devices were so popular in medieval torture chambers. Why go to all the bother of pulling out fingernails and heating hot pokers, when all you had to do was strap in someone and leave them to rot? If this were an interrogation, I'd probably have screamed out every last bit of information I possessed by now. Or soon enough.

Keller has been to see me... five or six times, I think? It could be many more than that. It's hard to be sure. I can't tell day from night down here and I don't know if he comes to see me once a day or several times. So it could be half a dozen times over a few days or once a day for a week, I have no idea.

He still hasn't told me about Amit's murderer. He insists that I already know the person's name, I just need to look at the facts head on and be willing to accept the unacceptable. It doesn't seem to matter much. At the rate things are going, I'll be joining Amit soon enough. I can ask him myself then.

The thought of Amit makes me cry.

Not because I miss Amit—though of course I do—but because I can't think of Amit without thinking of Natalie.

The thought of the light of my life living through these past days, not knowing where I am or what happened to me, is unbearable.

Ever since she understood what it is that her mommy does for a living, Natalie's greatest fear has been that 'the bad men' would get me.

That fear has come true.

How horrible must her nightmares be now?

The thought of her lying in her bed night after night, crying herself to sleep, crying for me, breaks my heart.

Shatters it to a million tiny shards.

Shards.

Splinters.

Splinters piercing me, every inch of my body, racking my being with impossible, excruciating pain.

"...ready to proceed?"

I blink, opening my eyes, only to realize they're already open.

I've been staring at the light so long that it's blinded me.

My optic nerve is washed out.

Still, if I struggle through the waterfall of agony, I can make out a silhouette.

Keller.

How long has he been here?

Has he been talking?

I think he has, but I blanked out. Time and consciousness have been fragmented, too.

Splintered.

"Can you hear me, Susan?"

I hate that he calls me by my first name.

I hate the sound of those syllables in his evil mouth.

He has no right!

The anger stokes my pain, sending adrenalin coursing through my body, bringing alive nerve endings numbed by the cold and lack of movement but also sending spider-tinglings of reawakened feeling to the already-suffering parts.

"I said, are you ready to proceed to the next stage? Or do you want to continue suffering in misery this way? The choice is yours."

I try to speak but no words come out.

My throat is beyond dry.

This part of southern California is basically a desert climate.

Reclaimed by the artificial piping in of water from distant sources, it's been turned green and lush enough to support human habitation, but the sudden temperature fluctuations and dry air are a constant reminder that before the settling of the Wild West, this was all just a desert wasteland.

I feel like the insides of my mouth and throat are parchment, crackling and splintering.

"Would you like some water? Are you having trouble forming words?" he asks with amusement, mocking my misery.

"Wa..." I struggle to form saliva and try again. "Water. Please."

"Sure," he says cheerfully, "all you had to do was ask. Gennifer, if you will."

So she's here too?

Has she been here all along?

Does she only come when he visits?

She holds up a bottle with a sipper, the kind that Natalie used when she was a toddler, touching the sipper to my lips.

It takes me a few seconds just to summon the strength to suckle on it.

I feel like I've barely imbibed a sip or two when Keller says, "That's enough."

Still, there's the smallest pause before Gennifer takes the bottle away, during which time I manage to suck in a few more drops.

In my addled state, even that micro-second of delay feels like an immense kindness.

She feels sorry for me, I think. *That's why she let me drink that one last sip.*

I'm probably delusional, suffering from the onset of Stockholm Syndrome, but it's all I have, so I hold on to it.

The two or three sips are sorely needed, but rather than

nourish me, they feel like a punishment, a reminder of how much more I need to hydrate myself, and how pathetic that little gesture was.

Still, I try to make the most of it, licking my chapped lips.

I wince as my tongue rubs against the cracks in the skin, the cuts stinging.

It feels as if my mouth was lashed with a tiny cat o' nine tails.

The cold did that.

It's probably already given me pneumonia, too.

And it's going to get a lot worse if I stay here a few more days.

"It won't work," I manage to say.

The silhouette moves to a standing position.

"What was that?" Keller asks.

"Deutermann Method. Won't work. On. Me." Each word feels like a struggle, each sentence a victory.

"Oh, you've hardly begun," he says casually. "Give it a few more weeks. About twelve and a half more to be exact. Thirteen weeks in all. In thirteen weeks, either you turn completely. Or you break. There is no middle path."

Thirteen minus twelve and a half equals...

Half a week?

Three days?

Four?

Is that how long I've been down here in the therapy room?

It feels like forever.

"Then. I'll. Break," I say through gritted teeth.

He laughs.

"So. Be. It," he says, imitating and mocking my tone. "You see," he goes on, settling into the tone I know so well by now, the one he uses when he's off on one of his pet rants, his lectures.

He calls it 'conditioning', this droning litany of psychological mumbo-jumbo claptrap that he believes constitutes actual psychotherapeutic treatment.

I call it mind vomit.

The expulsion of a sick, twisted mind.

I start to tell him that then realize I've already used that one before.

It got a laugh out of him yesterday.

Or was it the day before?

But it also irritated him, I think, because like most psychopaths, he genuinely believes that he's a genius.

"Fuck you and your Deutermann Method, Hans," I say.

The anger has lubricated my throat, making it easier to speak. Hoarsely but clearly enough.

Keller laughs but I hear the irritation in his voice.

That's his weak spot.

His precious Deutermann Method.

He really believes that it's the universal panacea for all that ails the human mind.

I try to think of another way to denigrate it, to pierce his ego, get a rise out of him.

If I can only make him mad enough to commit the smallest mistake, for even a minute...

Then what?

What will I do?

I don't know yet.

But something.

I'll do *something*.

Anything.

Because.

Natalie.

I have to try.

For her sake.

Keller has got a good rhythm going, spouting his usual tripe, when I feel it. He's too self-absorbed to pay attention, but I sense a shadow moving at the periphery of my vision.

Gennifer.

She feels it, too.

She's going upstairs to check.

"So, you see, Susan, all you have to do is surrender to the flow. Let yourself succumb to the impulses that are already overwhelming you. Let them take over. They will do the rest. All you need to do—"

Keller breaks off abruptly as he feels what I've been feeling for the past several minutes.

A vibration in the ground, more sustained and regular than an earthquake.

I can't hear the helicopter just yet but I know it's somewhere up there, hovering over us.

It's about time, too. I'm way past my limit here.

"That sound—" he starts to say.

"Police chopper," I say. "They're homing in on the cellphone signal. Tracking the GPS to find us."

"Impossible," he says. "Gennifer made sure you didn't have a cellphone on you and that your vehicle's GPS was turned off, too."

"Not my cellphone, Keller," I say, "yours."

Silence.

I go on, struggling to raise my voice as the sound of the rotors grows louder. "You see, Keller, I thought something like this might happen sooner or later. The mistake you made was when you cloned my phone that day when I came to meet you at your office. That's what you were doing on your phone, weren't you? You had an app that uses Bluetooth to force a connection, didn't you? You used that to steal my phone and clone it."

Keller chuckles. "The great FBI agent finally figures it out."

"Well, for starters, I had a lot on my mind at the time.

289

Otherwise, I'd have figured it out a lot sooner. But after Gennifer used the cloned phone to text Bohjalian and set up the Grygorian killing, I was dead certain. But there was no way to prove it, not so that a judge would issue a warrant, or to convince the Bureau."

"How annoying for you!" He sounds distracted.

I can see his silhouette moving around, as he listens to the growing rumble of the approaching chopper.

"Well, there's a catch to it. You see, I have a member of my team, Ramon Diaz, who's a whiz with such things. He figured out a way for me to backtrack that same link, using VPNs over the internet this time, to find your phone's IP address, and install spyware. Once your little Splinter abducted me at gunpoint from my home, you set into motion a chain of events that ended with my partner Naved Seth, the rest of the team, and the entire police department tracing your cellphone's GPS to find me."

"Impossible," Keller says. "I tracked your little team. Detective Seth flew to New York on Christmas Eve to spend Christmas with his family. He was already gone by the time Gennifer picked you up from your house."

"Yes," I say. "Unfortunately for me. That's why it took this long. He had to fly back here and get SCVPD moving on this. He probably hit a hitch or two because you're obviously not camping out here in the middle of nowhere, you probably go back to your center, your house, the hospital, other places, so they had to be sure they were following you to the right location. What is it today? Boxing Day? December 26th, right? Less than thirty-six hours isn't bad, all things considered."

"You're lying," Keller says, sounding angry now.

"You wish! They'll be here any minute, and there's no escape for you or Gennifer. They'll have secured and surrounded the whole area by now. Cops tend to come out in force when you mess with one of their own, especially a high-ranking FBI agent. And Christmas time happens to be one of the busiest nights for law enforcement. Something about the holidays brings out all the crazies. Or maybe it's the full moon. What do you think?"

He steps into the beam of the light, partially blocking it. Even that much relief from the blinding glare is a relief.

"I think you'll be dead before they get here," he says. "Even if I have to kill you with my own bare hands."

"You don't have the balls!" I say as loudly as I can.

He makes an animal sound in his throat and lunges at me. His hands go straight to my throat, finding the gap above the metal band to the soft flesh. He comes closer, forgetting himself in the heat of his bloodlust, as he starts to squeeze.

My vision starts to blacken. Stars pop in the darkness.

Mustering strength and will I didn't think I had, I force myself against the restraints, twisting a tendon in my neck and shoulder, and clamp down on Keller's throat as hard as I can bite. His grip loosens and then a scream, high-pitched and agonized, escapes from his lips. Hot blood spurts, fever-hot against my frozen skin, drenching me.

Keller staggers back, backing into the lamp and knocking it over. It spins on the floor, casting crazy monstrous shadows as the good doctor flails about, clutching his ruined throat. Blood jets in an arc from the wound, spraying the walls, the floor, showering me. I keep my lips tightly pressed, nauseated already by the ferrous taste of skin, flesh and tissue. I try to spit out as much as I can manage.

Shots break out above.

The sound of a body hitting the floor above, audible through the ceiling of the basement.

The steady thudding of helicopter rotors outside.

Feet coming down the basement stairs, cautiously at first.

Flashlight beams crisscross.

Finding Keller, now sitting with his back against the wall,

choking on his own blood, both hands clamped to his throat.

"Here she is!" Naved's voice shouts.

When the last restraint is off, I tumble forward like a bag of bones.

He catches me, holds me, bears my weight, and lowers me gently to the ground, sitting on the filthy floor and using his arms to keep me from falling. "Stretcher!"

My limbs feel absent.

I feel like a spirit unmoored, a balloon drifting up into the sky.

Slowly, by degrees, feeling returns to my body in stages.

With it comes excruciating agony.

I scream, I think.

It's hard to tell if it's aloud or only in my head.

"I'm giving you a sedative to calm your nerves. It will help with the pain, too," says an unfamiliar voice. The EMT.

An indeterminate amount of time later, I feel myself being lifted up and carried up the basement stairs.

Out of the therapy room.

THIRTY-SEVEN

"You sure you're up for this?" Lata asks as she pulls into the parking lot.

It's been over three months since Christmas.

In fact, it's Easter Monday.

I've been out a few times in the past few weeks. Up and about and getting around, but this is the first major outing since my time in the therapy room. That's why Lata's concerned.

I smile at her. "Hell yeah," I say. "I need this."

Lata smiles. "Good!"

We get out of the car.

I tap Natalie on the shoulder and point to the big sign that says: *LA COUNTY ZOO*.

Natalie whoops and pumps her fist in excitement.

She and I lock elbows and do our silly little zoo dance together. That is, I sing, while she signs the lyrics and dances with me. Lata joins in, too.

"*I went to the animals' fair. The birds and the bees were there. The monkey sat on the elephant's trunk. The elephant sneezed and fell to his knees, and what became of the monkey, monkey, monkey...*"

A family getting out of a van nearby smile at us. The kids wave at Natalie who waves back. They come over to her and say something. Natalie signs to tell them about her condition. They get it instantly, and tug at their grandmother's elbow. Apparently, she knows some ASL and helps translate while Natalie and the kids chat.

I watch her with pride and a sense of deep, abiding contentment.

"This is good," Lata says beside me, "for her and for you."

"And you?" I ask, elbowing her in the ribs. "How're things with you and Ariana going?"

"Good, good," she says, laughing and dodging my elbow.

"When are you bringing her over for dinner?" I ask.

"Soon, I promise."

"Promises, promises!" I say, pretending to kick her backside.

The slight tenderness in my muscles when I extend them is the only lingering sign of the time I spent in that torture chair. The body heals, as they say, and so does the mind, but some scars remain.

The zoo visit turns out to be awesome therapy.

Much needed salve for the weary soul, energy reviver for the jaded young federal agent and single mom.

As usual, Lata refuses to join us in the reptile house. Snakes creep her out. A marine gunnery sergeant, two foreign tours, a bunch of citations, two bullet wounds, one shrapnel injury, survivor of an IED attack which totaled her Humvee and wiped out most of her unit, but she draws the line at reptiles. Go figure.

Natalie and I love them.

Well, not *love* love.

But there's something about those creepy creatures that fascinates both of us.

Afterwards, we grab lunch on the go.

Hot dogs from our favorite hot dog vendor, Javier's Pooches. Funny name, seriously good food.

Amit and I discovered it back when we were dating and too broke to afford a sit-down meal. Once Natalie was old enough to appreciate fine outdoor dining, she joined the fan club.

Our favorite is Javier's legendary chili dog. *"It'll knock you out of the park!"* promises the legend on the side of his cart. Indeed, it does pack a pretty big wallop.

Natalie always hops from foot to foot while eating hers, which she claims helps relieve her screaming taste buds.

Lata, being a vegetarian (at least this year she is), joins us grudgingly, complaining about not getting a real meal.

Javier makes a gourmet vegan chili dog that I'm told is pretty tasty, but Lata doesn't consider sitting on a park bench and eating bread and wieners to be fine dining. Go figure.

She does seem to appreciate the spice level, which she agrees is on a par with "Indian spicy".

It's how we desis roll!

The kids from the van come around just as we're finishing up lunch. They're excited to see Natalie again and with Lata's help this time, they decide to go for churros. Lata offers to take Natalie, but I tag along, too. More than ever now, I know how precious every minute I get with my daughter can be, and I don't intend to waste even a single one.

Natalie comes running back to me with a paper bag filled with little hook-shaped churros.

"Mom," she signs. "You have to try these! They're so yummy! But be careful, they're hot!"

I take one and thank her. She runs back to join her friends as they lean on the railings, munching their churros and watching the hippos soak in the mud.

As I bite into the crunchy sweetness, my cellphone buzzes.

Naved calling.

"Hey, what's up?" I say.

"You out?"

"I'm with a bunch of fat mud-slathered animals, actually," I say.

A moment of silence.

I laugh. "I'm at the zoo. With Lata and Natalie."

"Oh," he laughs briefly but his tone sounds serious.

My heart pounds. Is this about Amit? Did Naved finally find something?

"What's up?" I ask, trying to keep my tone casual. "Everything okay?"

"Something came up," he says. "I have to fly to New York."

"Oh," I say, "Okay."

"I know you were hoping I'd have news about Amit."

"Not really," I lie. "I know it's a very long shot that you'll find anything."

Or that there's anything to find, I think but don't say.

"Anyway," he goes on, "I might be in the Big Apple a while, so I just thought I'd keep you posted."

"That's thoughtful," I say. "What's up in NYC? Everything okay?"

He hesitates. "I'll tell you about it when I'm back. It's a long story."

"Sure," I say.

We chat for another minute then hang up.

I feel a sense of disappointment.

Lata notices and signs a question: *Everything okay?*

Copacetic, I sign back one-handed, with a smile for reassurance.

She doesn't look convinced but lets it go. She knows me too well.

Everything isn't okay. I was hoping that Naved would be able to pull a Hail Mary and break open Amit's case. But that isn't how crime investigation works.

"It's about Amit, isn't it?" Lata asks.

I shrug.

She glances over at Natalie who's still busy laughing and chattering in sign with her friend and isn't paying attention to what we're doing.

Lata puts a hand on my arm. "Maybe it's time to let it go, Suse."

I nod.

She gestures at Natalie.

"She needs you. We both need you. All of you."

"I get it," I sign back. "And I'm here. All of me."

"Good," she says. "You've gotta try these churros. They're so good!"

I bite into one of the churros and agree. They are good.

It's a wonderful day.

I'm alive.

I'm with the two people I love most in the world.

My fam.

I should be happy.

And I am.

Sorta.

But there's a part of me that feels as if, by letting go of Amit's memory, I'm betraying him. Betraying *us*.

And even though I'm disappointed that Naved hasn't been able to find a break in Amit's case, I promise myself once again, that I won't rest until I do crack it open.

No matter how hard it proves.

No matter how long it takes.

I will not rest until I find out the truth about my husband's murder and bring his murderer to justice.

So help me God.

A LETTER FROM THE AUTHOR

Hi!

I hope you enjoyed *The Therapy Room*, the first in my Susan Parker FBI series, as much as I enjoyed writing it. As a lifelong thriller fan myself, I love reading twisty thrillers in which interesting detectives chase monstrous killers down labyrinthine rabbit holes, juggling personal conflicts with the demands of their job. When Susan Parker, Natalie and their family first took shape on the page, it was an incredible feeling. I knew I had something special. I love writing these characters and have a lifetime's worth of stories stored up, just waiting to be told. I do hope you've liked them enough to want to continue the journey with them.

If you want to stay in touch with Susan and the others, why not sign up for my newsletter here! That way, you can be the first to know about my upcoming releases.

www.stormpublishing.co/sam-baron

The only thing more wonderful than a great read is sharing it with another avid reader. I would really appreciate it if you could spare a few moments to leave a review. Even a short review of just a couple of lines and that all-important five-star rating can make a huge difference to an author and book. Sharing is caring, after all! Thank you so much!

Susan and family and friends have just started out on

what's going to be a long, eventful, action-packed journey through some terrible but cathartic twists and turns. I want you to know that before I wrote this first book, I had a clear vision of their entire life history from start to finish. It's truly an epic journey and the best part is, you'll get to enjoy each book on its own. Because as a voracious reader, I want the mystery and villain to be strong and daunting every time out. But as you read along, book by book, you will also have the added pleasure of discovering, layer by layer, one of the most shocking family mysteries in thriller fiction. I won't spoil it by saying more, but you can expect the larger, continuing storyline of Susan and her family to play out over several books in this series, with some very big payoffs. Be prepared to be shocked, stunned and surprised more than once along the way. Just when you think you've got it all figured out, there will be one more shocking revelation around the corner! And on the way, you get to watch over Susan's shoulder as she hunts down—and is hunted by—some of the most formidable killers you've never encountered.

Be prepared to be amazed, over and over again!

Wishing you plenty of love, family, friendship, great food—and loads of good books!

Sam Baron

 facebook.com/samkbaron

 x.com/samkbaron

instagram.com/samkbaron

 tiktok.com/@samkbaron